He's alive?"

Zorena nodded.

"And you knew? You knew the whole time?" Sonya turned to face Zorena who stood above her facing the window.

The light of day behind magnified Zorena's presence. But anger surged through Sonya with every breath.

"Well, where the hell is he?" she demanded.

Zorena shook her head. "In a very dark place." She went to the table and sat.

Sonya watched in disbelief. How could anyone be so unfair? After all she'd done to help, didn't she deserve honesty at the very least?

"You knew and you didn't tell me!"

Sonya went to Zorena, grabbed her by the shoulders and pulled her around so violently that the chair moved with her. Zorena's face showed only weariness. At first, Sonya wanted to curse Zorena with whatever horrible names came to mind. But words could not express her rage. Sonya lifted her hand to strike, but pulled back in shame and confusion. She smashed her fist on the mantel, whirled around, and shouted.

"Why didn't you tell me? Who do you think you are? Damn it! And damn you! I want to know why you didn't tell me. I demand to know!"

Zorena's eyes flashed at the commanding tone. But her bearing remained unchanged. She simply didn't have the energy to act otherwise.

"I could not tell you, Sonya. You will realize that yourself if you think for a moment."

"But I left him there," Sonya waved vaguely at the window, her voice cracking faintly.

"I would've stayed if I knew. I could've gone back and found him." Her voice cracked again, and she inhaled deeply, refusing to cry. She straightened and leaned against the stone of the fireplace.

Zorena stood slowly, wearily, one hand on the back of the chair.

"That is precisely why I could not tell you. You had the Medallion, not he."

Sonya rested her head on the mantel. No, she wouldn't cry, she was much too angry. Zorena placed a hand on Sonya's shoulder but she pushed it away and ran out the door.

Acknowledgements

There are many people and circumstances to thank for the possibility of this little tale. There are dozens of people who have influenced me (one way or the other) and have, therefore, made a difference. There is the nun who taught me to read a year early, the various authors whose books line my shelves; there are the White Mountains of New Hampshire, where inspiration abounds. And there are those I need to name for their help.

To my mother, who bought me my first book of fairy tales and still waits up for Santa Claus every Christmas Eve. To my father who did not live to see the result of all my tapping away at that old manual typewriter. To my siblings for their vast and varied support. To Victoria, Samuel, and David, for helping me rediscover the child within. To Rita Good, who helped me find the courage. To my Aunt Mary Ann, whose grammatical expertise is invaluable. (If anything is still incorrect, blame it on my stubbornness.)

I would also like to thank my old high school friend Annie Kennedy, the first person to read this book in one of its early drafts more than 25 years ago. To Carol Duphily and my cousin Rachael Thomas, who read the new manuscript and made some helpful suggestions. For Rachael's help choosing the photos. To my brother for letting me use some shots from his great adventures. And last, but certainly not least, to Mary Davin, my high school English teacher and the person who introduced me to the works of J.R.R. Tolkien.

I hope you all enjoy this little trip to the Vastness called Loraden.

Dedicated to
The Child Within

To Pat Perry,
Good luck with your
Books. Writing them
Is fun, huh? But
Having written them
Is even more fun!,

See ya,

Butch

12/6/10

Zorena
And the Medallion of Corandu

Published by
Elizabeth A. David
PO Box 766
Fairhaven, Massachusetts 02719-0700 USA
www.zorena.com

Cover photo (horizontally reversed):
From the top of Mount Washington in the
White Mountain National Forest, New Hampshire,
on an exceptionally clear day in August 1983.
Photo © 2003 Elizabeth A. David.

Visit us at www.zorena.com
to buy reprints of photos contained
in this book.

Photos on pages 67, 108, & 123
Copyright 2003 Anthony David
All other photos © 2003 Elizabeth A. David

ISBN 0-9740170-0-0

4/03

Zorena

And the Medallion of Corandu
by Beth David

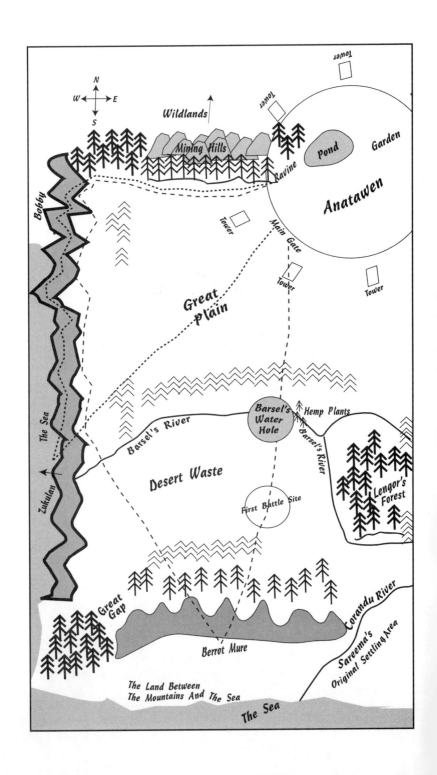

Chapter One

Rule Number One Is For The Faint of Heart

Sonya dropped the match with a curse and sucked at her burned finger. The cave went black as ink, but she kept moving, feeling the wall with her left hand.

She was sure she had heard footsteps behind her, or were they in front?

Why had she taken off in the middle of the night like that? Rule Number One echoed in her mind: no one goes farther than shouting distance alone. That's why she'd waited until everyone in her campsite had fallen asleep.

The moon shone brightly, lighting the path. All day long the mountains had beckoned to her. She just couldn't resist them any longer.

Better do something about that willpower . . . or lack

thereof, she thought derisively.

Her breath came in gasps as she moved along the wall, wondering where the path would take her and wondering how her life had gotten so mixed up so fast. Something about nature, hiking, camping, even fishing . . . it all pulled at her so stubbornly. She just couldn't ignore it anymore.

She dreamed of riding her little pinto pony as fast as he could run, up the highest mountain she could find. But around home, it was so impractical.

And probably illegal, she thought. *I wonder what Thoreau would think about Rule Number One.*

Just then, she heard the footstep again. She turned towards the sound, but saw only blackness. Suddenly the wall ended, then the ground. She slid, reaching behind her frantically as she fell.

Sonya's face screwed up with anger, fear, and a feeble attempt at courage. She braced herself, expecting to be stopped abruptly by stone at any second.

But the fall seemed everlasting and she cursed aloud at her stupidity. First, she snuck away from the campsite, climbing so high that her toes froze painfully. Then, she found this cave and let her imagination run away with tales of fortunes just because the walls sparkled. *A cave, with a "Keep Out" sign, and I get excited over sparkling walls, as if it could be gold or something.*

Her thoughts and her descent stopped abruptly in a splash of icy water swirling around her. Sonya's heart raced as she kicked and flailed her arms, trying to rise to the top. But something pulled her down, and soon she could hold her breath no longer.

ZZZZZ

Sonya woke abruptly, her stomach tight. She lay in bed. She sighed. It was only a dream.

"Thank God," she whispered.

"Who is god, and for what reason does tey merit your thanks?"

Sonya sat up and looked for the owner of the deep, soft voice. The down-filled tick gave way under her elbows, and the thick bedclothes creaked from her movements.

They were in a large, sunny room; a warm but refreshing breeze came through the open window. Hot embers crackled in the fireplace.

Sonya stared in disbelief at the man who spoke. He could have come out of an old book or movie.

He had a long, black beard; he wore a white outfit of baggy pants and a wrap top resembling a martial artist's gi that was tied with a belt encrusted with sparkling stones. His feet were wrapped in a moccasin-like fabric and tied on with twine. A headband that matched the belt completed the outfit and held his flowing black hair in check.

The fire glowed behind him.

"Who are *you?* Where am I? Where did I get these clothes? And what on earth is 'tey?'"

"One so young who knows not the meaning of "tey?" Interesting. If you do not know where your clothes are, there is no way for me to know. I am Tagor, and this is my home." He watched her.

She waited for him to continue, but he only stared back at her.

"Can I at least have my shoes? Then I can get out of here, anyway."

He smiled and nodded, but made no attempt to move.

Sonya got scared. "Listen, mister, I'm not as helpless as I look. I'm perfectly capable of defending myself if I have to. And I don't intend to stay here. So get my stuff, and you'd better *move it!*"

He laughed, raising an eyebrow at her overemphasis of "move it."

At that moment a woman walked into the room.

Sonya watched as the woman moved towards the bed with a natural, flowing energy.

Her hair hung near her waist, thick and shiny-black with just the slightest wave at the shoulders. Her features were sharp and pronounced. When she smiled, every inch of her face responded. Her skin was dark and almost brown, with a vivacious sheen. She wore an outfit similar to Tagor's, but tailored to fit and show the curve and shape of her body. Instead of a headband, she wore a colorful bandanna, keeping her hair out of the way but flowing freely behind. The only jewelry she wore was a medallion that seemed to change shape and size and color whenever it moved.

Sonya couldn't keep her eyes off of it, except to stare at the woman's eyes. They were wide and dark and deep and trying to laugh from far beneath the tiny glimmer the world could see. The gleam jumped out at Sonya and leapt into her mind. She suddenly found herself thinking of the various lies and dishonesties of her life, including that she had snuck away from camp, leading her right into this predicament. Sonya couldn't look at those eyes for long.

The woman put a bundle at the foot of the bed and stood smiling for a moment.

"I am Zorena. I trust my brother has been kind enough to answer your many questions? Though it is unlikely. He is not one for long or involved discourses."

She nodded to Tagor who bowed and left the room.

Sonya almost laughed. He actually bowed! But she held her tongue. Better to be quiet and watch. She didn't want to offend anyone, at least not until she knew more about her situation, which she felt must be only a dream.

Zorena closed the door after Tagor and handed the bundle to Sonya.

"Would you care to tell me your name?" asked Zorena.

Sonya detected no sarcasm in her tone.

"Sonya."

"Sonya. I hope you have rested well. You must be hungry. It has been some time since you ate last."

Curiously, Sonya felt comfortable with Zorena; as though an old friendship had resumed the moment she walked into the room. Sonya felt she could ask all of the questions that had popped into her mind. She didn't ask any of them.

"What's 'tey'?"

"One so young who knows not the meaning of tey? Interesting."

"That's what Tagor said. Why is it so interesting?"

Zorena laughed, a clear, light sound that made Sonya smile.

"Oh. My brother. Now I understand why he so thoughtfully studied you. 'Tey' is a somewhat new word — more of a concept. Maybe 100 years old. It means 'she' or 'he' when one is not sure of the gender of the person. It took quite some time for its acceptance to be complete. Just as it took quite some time for men to gain the equality they so effectively misuse these days. They fought hard to eliminate discriminatory customs, laws, and finally words. Many women helped them. I suppose it is all for the better — I am sure of it.

"You see, in the past, when one did not know the gender of a creature, one said 'she.' That was fine when decent beings were involved, but it was discomfiting at times. About 50 years or so after Vowed men received the right to keep their own names, things changed. And they changed rapidly at times. Hence 'tey' was invented.

"Of course, the Ruling Family always practiced equality within itself."

This time Sonya laughed out loud.

Zorena smiled politely and said, "I am delighted to have amused you, but what is amusing?"

Sonya tried to explain. "Well, it's just that, where I'm from, we have the opposite problem — women are still fighting for equality. And we still have no such word as 'tey.' We have to use 'he.'"

"How fascinating!" Zorena's sincerity surprised Sonya. "I now understand why you escaped from it."

"Escaped? I didn't escape from it. I still don't know for sure how I got here. I fell here, I think. And I don't know where here is, or where my clothes are, or how long I've been here, and a million other things."

"They will all be explained in time. But first, you must dress, and I will take you to the best laid table this side of the Corandu River."

Sonya looked for a mirror. Her hair smelled fresh and clean, and she wished she could see it. It felt like it shone. Her outfit was like Zorena's, though unfancy, and was made of a thick, but not unyielding material. She didn't try to guess the fabric, she just felt comfortable in it, but afraid it would be too hot for the summer-like weather.

Didn't she remember coldness while climbing the mountain? It already seemed like a long time ago.

She felt a sudden and fierce desire to get back. But she couldn't wake up — and suddenly it didn't feel like a dream anymore.

Before they reached the door, Sonya stopped and tried again.

"When and how did I get here and where is here?"

Zorena sighed and motioned for Sonya to sit.

"You are very impatient, Sonya. But youth gives way to such luxuries. You were brought here two days ago by my uncle Rubad, and my brother Tagor. They found you while hunting in the mountains. Your precious clothes were not on or near you. They warmed you by a fire and brought you here. You were near death from the cold. Homak has tended to your needs; he has a touch of the healer in him.

"You understand, then, that we do not know where your clothes are, unless it is the custom of your people to go naked when it is near the snowing point. And we do not know *how* you got there. As for here —this is Anatawen, of the land of Ruberken on the Vastness of Loraden. Homak is Anatawen's Ruler and my father.

"Anatawen is the central city for about ten thousand families. There is room within its walls for all of the inhabitants, if there should arise the need for protection. It is an old, but effective system, and one of the main factors in the success and strength of Anatawen. And I am very thirsty and hungry. Come, we will finish your lesson at table."

Sonya followed, trying to digest the answer piece by piece.

I guess I asked for it, she thought.

They walked down a long staircase overlooking a large hall. People were still arriving. Small groups sat drinking and laughing.

"This is the main hall. We have arrived in time for the feasting. Most of the people you see are from the outer fortresses. The others are friends, neighbors, and anyone else who wishes to be here. Although we are not at war, we keep the outer defenses garrisoned to capacity at all times. The people in full dress have been relieved for the next three months. They have been on duty for the same.

"All of the outposts changed garrisons this week. So we are celebrating with those off duty. Of course, in a crisis we are all on duty."

Sonya followed and Zorena sat her at a table near the fireplace. She supposed it was the head table. It was larger than the others and covered with a thick, sea-green tablecloth.

Sonya waited, and soon Zorena appeared through the crowd carrying two large glasses filled with a clear liquid.

She sat across from Sonya and turned her chair to face the other tables. Sonya sipped her drink. It tasted like a licorice lemonade — both sweet and tart.

"Is there any alcohol in this?"

"Alcohol? Explain."

Sonya hesitated. How does one explain alcohol?

"Well, if I drink a lot of this, will it affect me strangely? Will it make me feel light-headed . . . laugh too much? Y'understand?"

Zorena laughed and shook her head.

"You are describing the effects of too much wine on the inexperienced. No, you need not worry about this. It is only zul. It contains no spirits. You may drink as much as you like without fear of unexpected side effects."

Sonya drank gratefully. She forgot the dryness in her throat and the cold zul helped to wake her. As she gulped down the last of it, a servant came by and refilled her cup.

Then the general din quieted down. Sonya focused her attention where the quiet had started.

A large, dark-haired man entered the hall, followed by a long line of men and women. She presumed the man was Homak. Tagor followed, then two other men who looked like his brothers. She turned to Zorena.

"Is that your father? And brothers?"

"Yes," Zorena answered as she studied them.

Sonya watched with her and tried to match the names Zorena gave her to the correct faces. But when she got to Cowis, Sonya stopped.

Cowis stood less tall than the others, but he had an indefinable quality that made Sonya stare. Zorena laughed, and Sonya realized her sigh was audible.

"Many women react that way to Cowis. BEWARE," Zorena said in mock warning, "he, too, is aware of this."

Sonya managed a smile and forced a shrug. Did Zorena understand shrugs?

Sonya turned her attention to the rest of the family. Homak was a tall heavyset man with thick, powerful arms. His eyes, black and bright, took in the scene slowly and fully. Last, he looked at Sonya and smiled.

A simple smile had never so thoroughly unbalanced Sonya. And his eyes looked through her with a sharpness that made her shiver. Sonya didn't know how to react and felt an urgent need to. Simply returning the smile didn't occur to her until he sat, and as soon as he did, the crowd resumed its merrymaking. She felt her face get hot and turned her attention to Tagor.

Tagor's resemblance to his father went beyond appearance. He governed his every movement with the same, slow study, and bore the same expression of instant understanding.

Barska was different. He pulled his sight through the hall quickly, his eyes darting haphazardly all around. A slight smile twitched on his face, and Sonya laughed quietly. He seemed familiar somehow, in a comfortable, sitcom kind of way.

She realized then that Cowis watched her watching them. She found herself studying him — in a typically sexist manner — and it infuriated her. She blushed again and turned to her zul.

Zorena moved to Sonya's side of the table. Cowis immediately offered her his seat — closer to Homak he said.

He then took the seat next to Sonya. She laughed at his exaggerated politeness, but could think of absolutely nothing to say to him.

"You are Sonya? The one my father tended these past days?"

She nodded and wondered how he knew her name since Zorena had only just asked.

"Yes, I am. And you're Cowis, right?"

"I am."

Now what? she thought.

She stared dumbly and tried to smile. It felt like a sour smile. He didn't seem to notice.

"You have not eaten solid food since your ... arrival. But do not fill yourself. Afterwards, we will take a walk in the garden, before it is dark. You will enjoy the beauty of it, I think. And there you will have a meal befitting an honored guest of the Ruler of Anatawen."

Sonya smiled in answer and wondered what was wrong with the food being served. It smelled good enough and she suddenly felt very hungry. She wondered how many days she'd been 'tended.'

Her food tasted fine, though not fancy, and she stuffed herself despite Cowis's advice.

As if by some prearranged signal, Cowis stood up and quickly escorted her from the hall. Her awareness of the eyes following them was almost painful.

Zorena caught up with them at the door and whispered, "Not too far, Cowis. It is only her first day out of bed," and slipped away again.

Cowis nodded and hailed a servant.

"Tell Sorano we will have two of my favorite — in the garden."

Sonya followed him out the door and breathed deeply. It was her first step outside since waking and it seemed like weeks since she'd been out. She walked slowly, and away from the building to catch the fading sunlight. Cowis followed her example.

The garden lay behind the house enclosed by a stone wall about four feet high and thick enough to sit on.

Sonya walked through each path and corner, gawking and raving about the colors of the odd-sized plants and trees.

"Strawberries!" Sonya picked one and popped it into her mouth anticipating the luscious sweetness its size and color promised. But the bitterness tore at her taste buds and she spat, coughing through tears.

Cowis came to her rescue, amazed at her innocence.

"Watch," he said, and picked two large ones, cupping his hands to shield them from the sun.

Sonya watched his hands anxiously and he opened them just enough for her to peek at the berries. She couldn't believe her eyes.

"The strawberries are turning purple!" She picked one herself and shaded it from the light, watching the color slowly grow from within.

"We call them Scandra's Berries," Cowis explained, "because Scandra was the first one to discover that they were not only edible, but quite good if we would only be patient enough to wait for them. Now taste."

The sourness in Sonya's mouth quickly turned into the sweetest strawberry taste she ever knew, with just the faintest tang to add a touch of variety. She grabbed a handful and watched as they turned.

"The longer you wait, the sweeter they become," instructed Cowis. "The larger and redder when you start, the better."

"They could be addictive," Sonya added with her mouth full. She picked another batch, and they sat at the table under the grapevine.

The vines stretched to seven or eight feet high, supported by narrow logs crisscrossing and allowing the grapes to hang below. The only sound came from some small birds resting on the vines above them and pecking at the grapes between trills.

Servants soon brought two trays of food and a large carafe of wine. Sonya wondered how she'd eat another bite, but she was curious about his "favorite." And she found the aroma irresistible. A colorful array of vegetables surrounded a large slab of meat topped very lightly with a sweet smelling sauce. It didn't look too special to her.

They toasted with wine, and she tasted the meat. Cowis laughed at her reaction.

It tasted like a pleasant cross between the juiciest steak and ham, with a faint hint of something sweet. She frowned in confusion, looked pleased and took another bite. Then she frowned again as she tried to dissect the tastes.

"What is it?"

"It does not yet have a special name all to itself, though it should. It is from an animal in my father's special herd. The animal is a crossbreed that also has no proper name." Cowis whispered now, "I call it Homak's Delight."

Sonya could understand the Delight. She ate the whole thing even though she wasn't hungry at all when she'd started.

The wine, too, tasted exquisite, and she had just started to wonder how much she'd drunk when Cowis refilled her glass.

And Cowis talked so easily. She didn't even know what he rambled on about. She just watched him talk and drank her wine. And spilled it when the horns started.

Horns, bells, and people suddenly cried out from all around her.

"Back to the house!" Cowis grabbed her arm and pulled her back along the path.

Sonya looked around frantically as Cowis pushed her through the side door. People ran to and from every direction, shouting orders and following them.

Cowis led her to a relatively quiet corner and told her to stay there. Then he left, making apologies and giving explanations.

Sonya leaned against the wall and tried to hear him. The noise around her, the beating of her heart, and her suddenly limited vision prevented her from comprehending his words. Why did everything blur so stubbornly? Like something got stuck on her eyelashes and she couldn't rub it off. All she heard for sure was "Stay here, I will return."

Thank God, thought Sonya, *because I don't have the strength to go anywhere.*

She closed her eyes and tried to control her breathing. Her heart still beat wildly, a static noise filled her head, and she was unbearably hot. She felt weak and tried to find something to hold onto.

When she opened her eyes a searing pain flashed through her forehead. Then she spotted the stairs and somehow thought it would be safe there, though she didn't really feel *unsafe* where she stood.

She followed the wall, trying to reach the stairs. When the wall ended she lost her balance, teetered, and reached out blindly for something to hold her up.

Zorena found her there, and Sonya leaned heavily on the arm that Zorena offered. When Zorena picked her up and started climbing the stairs, Sonya felt more embarrassed than surprised.

"Zorena, put me down! I can walk. I just need a little fresh air, that's all. Help me a little, and I'll be fine." She had to listen for her voice; it sounded far away.

Zorena shook her head and kept walking. Sonya relinquished control and tried to figure out where the walls were — in relation to the ceiling. Homak reached them halfway up.

"I will take her now, Zorena. Go to where you are needed."

He picked up Sonya, amid her protests, and carried her to her room.

Calais, Maine, Waterfront Walkway. June, 2002
Copyright 2003 Beth David

Chapter Two

Lessons of Life, Love, and Longings

Bright sunshine lit the room when Sonya woke. Cowis sat in the chair by the window.

"Well, I see MacArthur has finally returned."

Cowis jumped up and leaned over her.

"Are you all right? You scared me nearly to death when I went back and you were gone. I feared it was my fault."

He stopped abruptly and asked, "Who is MacArthur?"

Sonya laughed. He was like a child; his eyes shone and she suddenly wanted to kiss him.

"He was a famous general who said 'I will return!' And he did; and now the statement is famous." She smiled foolishly, enjoying her private joke.

Cowis smiled politely.

"It seems like all I do is sleep around here. What happened? I never felt like that before — I almost fainted."

"You did faint. But do not be concerned. You were up only one day. Two or three days of quiet and you will be completely recovered."

Sonya's whole body ached. Two or three days of quiet sounded great; maybe she could even figure out where, and what, this place really was.

"Cowis, what was all that about? The horns and everything."

"A minor clash with the Mountain Dwellers."

"And who are they?"

"They are a race of — people. They are a squat, pale-skinned sickly-hued and ugly race — or at least most of them. I am sure, though, that they feel we are quite ugly also." He whispered the last sentence and smiled brightly, moving around to display himself.

Sonya smiled and shook her head. He was, if nothing else, nice to look at.

"Does it happen often, that they attack?"

"No! Not, at least, as often as it would were I a Mountain Dweller." He moved to the window and spoke forcefully, as though pleading his case to a judge.

"They have been taunted, hunted, and pushed into the mountains. They are not mountain dwellers by choice. There are not enough of them, you see, they were never as disciplined as we. These are the only reasons they have been beaten.

"Admittedly, things are not as bad now as they once were. Generally, they are ignored, and they ignore us. Each living in our own parts of the world. But recently they have taken to sneaking down to attack. Something is happening . . . I would love to know what.

"You see, it is my belief, though I believe almost alone, that we could live peacefully together. The Mountain Dwellers are not an evil people by nature. They never were. They are simply different from us and have been treated cruelly for it. We could change the thinking of our peoples. It would take time, but it is possible. And we *must* start. But they are impossible to talk to. We do not know who rules them. And if we did, how could it help? They strike us down as soon as they see us.

"I fear I do not blame them. But we must talk to each other. There is no need to continue this fruitless fighting. Historians alone know why we fight at all."

He bolted around the room, pointing, punching, and waving at the air. Her presence made no difference to his discourse — the lecture aimed at convincing the world.

Almost, she jumped up to go with him to the mountains, to right all the wrongs of this world.

But the door swung open and Zorena motioned for Cowis to leave. He collected himself quickly and walked calmly out the door.

"Well, what's up?"

Zorena sat in a chair near the bed.

"I trust you feel better?"

Sonya nodded.

"Cowis, I presume, was more helpful than troublesome?

"It is time to answer as many of your questions as I can."

Sonya didn't hesitate for a moment.

"How did I get here? And how do I get back?"

"I do not know the exact manner of your transfer to this place, because I do not know where you came from. Therefore, I cannot tell you how to get back. But do not look so despondent. I, at least, know more about *here* than do you. And this I can say for certain: you should not feel so helpless in this journey. The powers of your own mind have done more to bring you here than any other force. Now, tell me everything you remember."

Sonya tried to hide her fear and think of one thing at a time. She felt homesick, right in her stomach. The last thing she needed was to tell a story. But she recounted all she could remember, even the details of her fears and excitement over leaving the campground and exploring things on her own.

Zorena listened patiently, without expression — or

interruption. When Sonya finished, a long moment of silence followed. Zorena leaned against the back of the chair and looked up at the ceiling with a slight, sideward tilt of her head.

"The only thing I can suggest, if you truly wish only to return, is that you go to the mountains — where you entered this world. Tagor and Rubad found you, they alone know the exact spot.

"But, after what happened yesterday, there will be no travel to that area for some time."

Sonya's brief hope died in the silence. Zorena smiled.

"But it may not matter in any case. We have an old wisdom in Anatawen: 'You cannot go back the same way you came.'"

Sonya tried to return the smile. But every part of her wanted to cry. What would she tell people when she finally did get back? They'd never believe the truth: 'Hi, mom, just fell into another world, that's all.'

She sighed. There had to be *some* way to get there. But getting killed wasn't the answer. She'd have to ask Cowis. He'd know. He might even be willing to take her there.

Zorena must have read her mind.

"Be careful with Cowis, Sonya. Some of his ideas are — not reliable. Some of them are very good. But many of them are ill-conceived, misguided notions that could cause much difficulty if heeded. He is young, he will learn. Meanwhile, do not let him convince you that we all agree with him. He is very persuasive — a family trait."

Sonya stuffed the impulse to argue right back down her throat. It was just a typical big-sister attitude and not worth a reaction. A pang of annoyance leapt to the surface, but she said nothing.

Zorena sighed and started towards the door.

"I will send up some food. It is nearly dusk already."

Sonya soon felt a little regret at wanting to ignore Zorena's advice. Who was this woman who could make her feel this way after such a short acquaintance? What was this place? It was so strange, yet she didn't necessarily want to go back as much as she let on.

She decided to look at this adventure from a new perspective. What would be so terrible about being here for a little while? Why not jump right in and learn all about the place? Become part of its happenings?

I'm part of it already, she thought, *even though it wasn't my idea — whatever she says. If I tried to get home, some Mountain Dweller would shoot me down anyway. So, since I'm trapped, maybe I can even help. It sure would be better than just complaining about it.*

The food came quickly and Sonya ate all of it. The zul tasted as refreshing as before, and she drank nearly a pitcher of it.

She stood by the window, looking at the stars, and wondering if she could get a cup of coffee, when she heard a quiet knock.

"Come in," she called.

She turned towards the door and smiled when Cowis walked in. To her surprise and complete contentment, he greeted her with a kiss.

"Shall we take a walk? The night is not cold and there are no distractions. Homak has given his full permission and approval," he almost pleaded.

Sonya nodded and followed him.

The moon enhanced the garden's beauty, lighting the way softly, reflecting off a branch or a fruit. The night birds sang.

Soon a servant brought a tray of a hot drink called zukha. It tasted more like hot chocolate than coffee, but it satisfied her craving admirably.

They sat for a short while, then Cowis led her to the other side of the garden and through the gate, where two of the finest looking horses she'd ever seen stood tethered to the post. Cowis laughed at her reaction.

"You do ride, then? I know things are different wherever you come from. I can get a wagon if you prefer."

"Don't you dare," answered Sonya. "I ride, and pretty well, too."

"Good," Cowis looked almost proud. "I prefer the saddle to the wagon anytime."

Sonya hopped on without the help Cowis offered. The saddle was odd and fancy and took a little getting used to. But Sonya quickly settled in and asked Cowis for a short race.

"The moon is almost full," she argued. "It *is* light enough, Cowis, and I haven't ridden in so long . . ."

"To that tree?" he needed little convincing.

Sonya agreed and took off with a shout. The wind in her face was cool, but not cold. She became so entranced with her own ride, she passed the tree without a glance.

Suddenly a pond appeared before her and the horse stopped abruptly. She jumped off and waited for Cowis.

"Thank you, Cowis. That was the best ride I've ever had." She embraced him with an energy she'd never felt before and didn't understand.

She could feel every inch of her body and grew aware of his gentlest touch. He held her close, and she pulled back, confused and a little scared.

"What is wrong?" Confusion was in his voice.

"Nothing. Let's go back." Sonya grabbed the reins and jumped into the saddle.

"Why? Now?" He looked more surprised than anything else.

Sonya looked at him blankly and said nothing.

Crushed his ego, thought Sonya. *But damn! I hardly know the guy. How can I know how to act here on the 'Vastness of Loraden' when I hardly know how to act anywhere? What's what in this crazy place anyway? And why all the complications? This adventure promises enough excitement already.*

She laughed despite herself. If there was to be any lovemaking, she'd say when — was this not a woman's world?

Zorena

Z Z Z Z Z

Sonya found the house through a deep trance of adolescent depression and confusion. Maybe she could find some way to ask Zorena. Sonya felt so stupid.

She stumbled through the hall and into the kitchen without noticing Zorena at the table.

"Did you enjoy your ride?"

"How appropriate to find you here, Zorena. Do you know everything that goes on around here, or do you just guess to keep us guessing?" The harshness of her tone surprised Sonya as much as Zorena.

"Something to drink?" asked Zorena casually.

Sonya nodded and tried to look apologetic. Zorena tried to look understanding.

"I am sorry that it did not go well. I did not intend to upset you with my question. Word for word, it is harmless enough, is it not?"

Sonya had to laugh. "I'm sorry, Zorena. It's just that . . . well, right now I feel pretty lousy. I'm a little embarrassed, and have to find answers to some questions that aren't easy to ask. And after what you said about Cowis, I'm not exactly sure I can trust *him* at all. And I'm very bad at being on this end of a conversation like this."

Zorena nodded with a knowing look.

Sonya hid her skepticism. What did *she* know? Sonya doubted that Zorena ever felt helpless or embarrassed or stupid. But who else *was* there? Sonya quickly turned her thoughts back to herself.

"We will go to my rooms," offered Zorena. "And I will have some zukha brought up. It is private there."

Sonya followed Zorena to her rooms. And rooms they were: six of them, large and comfortable. If Zorena was only second in command, what were Homak's rooms like?

They sat at a small table by the window sipping zukha. Now that it came to it, Sonya didn't know how to start.

"What do you need to know?"

Sonya turned from the stars and looked at Zorena,

right into that steady, unyielding gaze. Sonya didn't know how to react to it. She was used to eyes that darted away from meeting other eyes on busy streets. She looked at her cup and took another sip. What was she supposed to say? 'Hey, is it proper for me to seduce your little brother?'

"Cowis and I went for a ride, as you know. We ended up by the pond." Sonya hesitated, but Zorena took up the story.

"And the next thing you knew you were in his arms?" Sonya nodded.

"And now you would like to know how you *should* have acted, in compliance with our customs and laws? Am I nearing the truth?"

Sonya sighed relief, "Nearing it? You hit it! You're making this a lot easier."

"It must be difficult coming from a world that cannot grasp the concept of equality. I have, of course, learned of our old world and its ways, but I was not born until after these problems were over. I have, though, given the matter much thought — to try and understand it.

"I think it is easy for you to believe the answer is simply to reverse everything here. But you cannot do that. You must understand that your feelings and opinions are of equal value to those of Cowis — not more or less. You must try to imagine true equality.

"I know it is a difficult thing for you." She added with a secret smile.

Sonya watched her closely. "Those presumptions are a little close for comfort. How did you know?"

"I will caution you with a simple rule: Never ask Rulers, or the heirs of Rulers, *how* they know anything. It is a matter of birth . . . Cowis may wish to try and explain."

"If he'll talk to me, I'll ask him."

"He will, I assure you. He recovers quickly. He always has."

A servant brought a steaming pot of zukha. A long silence followed his departure. Sonya fidgeted but tried not to say anything.

"Tell me what it is like where you come from," Zorena suggested.

"It's kind of confusing — depends on your own particular schooling, I guess."

Zorena looked puzzled. Sonya re-worded her answer.

"There are many different ideas and opinions. I guess I never thought about it much because I never got into a serious relationship with anyone. And one thing's for sure — it is serious."

"It is not something we take lightly, either, Sonya. Making love to someone surely means a commitment of some kind. The people are bound to each other until the consent and approval of both clearly changes that. Some people may know each other for a short time, and others for many years before they think about love-making. It does not matter, as long as the terms of the relationship are clear to those involved.

"But if two people decide to pledge themselves to each other in a formal ceremony, publicly, then it is a bond for life, and cannot be broken — ever. There is no way out. We are unyielding on this.

"A person is only worth the worth of tey's word, therefore, we do not give it lightly. So do not worry about offending anyone by feeling what you feel openly. There is no penalty for loving someone; there is harsh penalty for deceit.

"When making love with a man of course, a woman must consider the possibility of childbirth. It is usually wise to decide who will be responsible for the child beforehand. When the relationship is between two women or between two men, this complication is eliminated.

"We have many ways to control fertility, but they do not work by magic. One must pay attention. And we have yet to devise a way that a woman can have a child without the use of a man for at least a little while. Someday we will control birth with more accuracy and our freedoms will be greater. But not yet.

"Have I made it clear and simple enough?"

Sonya searched for a hint of sarcasm, but Zorena, in her naturally on-the-edge-of-intimidation manner, was being sincere. Sonya nodded — still a little nervous about Zorena's uncanny perception. But she felt too grateful and too exhausted to think further about it.

Sonya stood up to excuse herself when Zorena asked, "What is schooling?"

"Oh, it's . . . learning . . . a school is a place where people go to learn."

"A special place? I do not understand."

"It's sort of a . . . formal training program."

"Like the soldiers have?"

"Yes, and no. Instead of learning to fight, we learn about history, languages, sciences, and even, on occasion, basket weaving."

"Basket weaving? A formal training program for basket weaving?"

Sonya laughed; she'd have to keep the humor in check.

"We have schools for just about everything, including self-defense. Some are more valuable than others. But all of them serve a purpose for someone."

Zorena thought for a moment and then asked quickly, "Can you read?"

"Yes, it's one of the first things taught."

"And you are not from a Ruling Family?"

"No, everyone goes to school, or almost everyone."

"The majority reads? Tell me — who decided it was necessary for everyone to be so knowledgeable?"

"I don't know. But I'd guess it was probably the people who weren't, and they wanted to be. And reading is the first step.

"I guess it became more and more difficult for people to make it through their lives without being able to read. Eventually, even the simplest tasks required some reading ability — like putting together a toy."

Sonya looked at Zorena's troubled expression.

"I suppose it's a pretty complicated place. But when

you're familiar with it, it doesn't seem so bad. It *is* difficult to explain, though."

"Yes, I understand. It is also difficult for me to explain our customs to you. Is this not enough for learning? Why must you have schools? Why do the parents and leaders not teach what must be taught? And if one wants to learn to weave baskets, why does tey not go to the basket shop and ask?"

Sonya realized it would be much more difficult than she'd thought, and she didn't want to continue. But she sat down again, anyway.

"I suppose it was an attempt to keep certain basic knowledge and skills constant, or at least alive," Sonya said. "There are basics that everyone seemed to need. Once the basics are learned, you can go to almost anything that interests you. But without some measure of consistency there could be lost knowledge, and that's just a waste."

She paused and wondered at how strictly ordered it all sounded. Not at all the mishmash of degrees, diplomas and fancy-worded claims to knowledge that she knew.

"Y'see, if you have no way of learning what was already known, without actually experiencing it, then you'd waste time making the same mistakes. And in order to learn, one must read: you can't go to a person who's been dead for 100 years and ask why the idea didn't work. Scientists can take a failed experiment and pick up where others left off. Historians look for trends to warn of what can happen.

"But don't get the idea that it's all so great;" she'd noticed Zorena's wide-eyed look. "We still have conflicts. Our experts are wrong at least as many times as they're right."

Poor Zorena, she wore the face of perfect perplexity.

"But we have managed, somehow or other, to progress.

"Look at it this way. There are a million facts and ideas that millions of people know. Reading and schools are the ways we keep that knowledge in circulation, although there must be other ways. But, if only a handful of people know something, and then something happens to them, that knowledge would be lost, maybe forever, but at least until evolution took a similar course. It could take thousands of years. But with *everyone* learning this stuff, anyone who wants to can relearn it."

"Do the people not feel uncomfortable with such control over their knowledge? Surely you realize that those who control the schools are then able to control the kind of knowledge you all have."

"Well," Sonya hesitated. "We do seem to have ongoing debates about that. There are . . . variations. But," and here she stressed her point, "most people are able to find out pretty much anything if they try hard enough. How they use this knowledge is, of course, subject to human whims."

Zorena smiled gently. "I see now why you and Cowis were instantly attracted to each other.

"With all this knowledge available to everyone, there must be many interesting things you can tell me."

Sonya decided she'd said more than enough, or she'd end up trying to explain electricity, or some other impossible thing. And when it didn't work, she'd probably be burned as a witch or something.

She left Zorena in a state of serious concentration.

Mt. Desert Island, Maine, February, 1984. Copyright 2003 Beth David

Chapter Three

More Lessons...

The next day Sonya woke early and felt normal again. Zorena found her in the kitchen.

"Sonya, I would like you to come with me this morning. There are some places I must inspect. It might interest you. You will learn about us, and I could ask you more questions. Do you mind?"

"No, I'd love to. I haven't seen the city yet. And I was wondering how I'd spend the day."

She wanted to ask about Cowis but controlled the impulse.

"You may go wherever you wish. Any of the servants about the house will help you with anything you need. Surriya is the one to ask if you want one of them to accompany you."

She waved down Surriya and introduced them.

She was a big woman, about 50 years old and perfect for the part. She was in charge of keeping the house running according to plan. Sonya smiled and wondered if they had a custom similar to shaking hands; bowing hardly qualified.

Surriya went about her duties without giving Sonya a chance for a handshake anyway.

Sonya immediately gave her a new title: Manager of Household Operations. She smiled at her private joke as Zorena led her out the door. Outside, two horses waited.

"I usually make my inspections on horseback — as undignified as it may seem to some. I know you also prefer the saddle to the carriage, so I had one made ready for you. His name is Appy. You may use him when you wish — he is reserved for you during your time in Anatawen."

Zorena mounted a large, chestnut mare.

Sonya admired the horse for a moment, but couldn't help feeling that a palomino would serve as a better contrast for that long black hair.

Sonya mounted and followed. She could come to enjoy this. She always wanted to use horseback riding as a primary means of transportation. Maybe she really was dreaming.

"Where has Tagor been? I haven't seen him since the night of the party — or the attack, whichever you prefer to remember."

"Since the attack, Tagor has moved to the outer defenses. We had become lax in our watch. The attackers never should have made it to the first tower. Tagor has gone to coordinate the new vigilance.

"It has been more than five years since Mountain Dwellers left their caves to attack. Something is happening."

Sonya wondered if Zorena suspected anything about Sonya's untimely arrival. *She* would have. Sonya sighed. If you're going to go to a place that you hadn't planned on going to, you might as well go at the worst possible time.

They stopped first at the metal-working shop. Here,

everything from swords to wagon parts were forged. Salock was in charge. He never loosened the hammer from his blackened hand as he croaked a 'hello' and honored Zorena with an almost bow.

"Salock, this is Sonya."

He grunted with a nod and managed what Sonya guessed *could* be considered a smile.

Zorena slid gracefully past him and walked from table to table looking over each worker's shoulder, nodding her approval or shaking her head otherwise. She wore a puzzling smirk on her face.

Sonya leaned against a relatively clean post and watched with amusement as a disgruntled Salock followed behind Zorena.

Through this soot-covered barn Zorena moved with the ease and confidence of a Ruler. She wore riding clothes, but over all hung a black cape that made her *look* like royalty. The medallion gleamed in bright contrast to it.

At the end of her round, Zorena swung towards the door and motioned for Salock to follow.

He squinted at the sun and waited for the verdict.

"All seems to be going well, Salock. The work goes quickly. Do you need additional people?"

He shook his head and mumbled something about too many to handle.

The moment they rode out of hearing, Zorena laughed aloud, and long. Sonya's confused expression demanded an explanation. Zorena complied.

"He hates being watched, especially by me. And I hate watching him. He has absolutely no idea how he should act in my presence. Therefore, I usually avoid going there. I sometimes wonder if it is I whom he hates, or the position I hold in the Ruling Family. The only reason I went at all was to appease Homak. Salock can handle it himself, but my father insists we keep a close eye on his progress. Anyone could check, but Homak insists that I do it.

"Salock's position is of utmost importance at this

critical time. I, personally, feel he is aware of that. He may even think he is indispensable. I am not certain why Homak is obsessed with watching him so closely, or that I be the one to do the watching."

"But I bet you have a theory or two."

"Yes, I do. But we will not discuss them." She shot Sonya a sideward glance and returned to her explanation.

"It is Salock's responsibility to see that the arms and other metal supplies are sufficient for normal *and* unexpected needs. After what happened two days ago, we checked the stores thoroughly. We found them not only insufficient in quantity but also in quality. Many of the swords were rusted and most of them were made of the old, heavy metal no longer used in battle. There were practically no spears, the bows were stacked poorly and were therefore unbalanced. Salock has much to do these days."

They rode for awhile in silence. The streets, wide enough to fit ten or more horses across, were paved with smooth, white cobblestone. Each was painstakingly placed to avoid the usual, wide gaps.

Small cottages lined the sides of the streets and it all looked normal to Sonya — even cozy. Some lawns had real, bona fide laundry hanging on a line; people even gossiped by the well, or over fences. Only the absence of cars and a few other luxuries reminded Sonya that this wasn't a tourist spot.

And the wall.

Fifteen feet it rose, and stretched around the city. Wherever she looked, the wall popped up in the distance. It was actually two walls placed back to back. They built the inner wall thick enough to walk two abreast, and a few feet lower than the other. Holes dotted the outer wall at regular intervals for, Sonya guessed, shooting.

The gate stood open. Wide wheels with thick cables opened and closed it. Sonya wanted to see how they worked, but Zorena moved on.

Kurtch, the Builderkhan, received them with the ease

and dignity expected of a master in the Ruling Family's employ. He wore the same kind of wrap top almost everyone wore, with less baggy jeans and a leather apron much like a blacksmith's. His group worked to repair a section of the wall being eaten away by time.

"Zorena, I expected you on such a cool day. It is the perfect time for a ride."

Zorena shed her regal stand-offishness and put her hand on his shoulder, giving a friendly squeeze.

Sonya jumped down from her horse to be introduced. She stood dumbly, nodded and smiled. Kurtch only laughed and led them to a ladder leading to a large pitcher of zul on the parapet.

"I wanted to see you anyway," he began. "I will need Barska for an hour or two before we are ready to finish this section. To repair this wall properly I must rely heavily on the old archives. I did not realize how much we needed them until now.

"I am the first to work on the wall since the beginning. It is a masterpiece of construction. There are crossings of metals and substances I could not begin to describe, let alone duplicate. The old masters were, indeed, masters."

He shook his head, fascinated, staring at the wall. Sonya looked closely. *Normal old cement?* she thought, *holding boulders together, but smooth to the touch. No big deal.*

Zorena glanced at Sonya, then looked long at Kurtch.

"I think, Kurtch, that it would be better if you could read the old scripts yourself. Do you agree? The translations of one who knows nothing of the simplest procedures take time. Time that could be better spent elsewhere. It may be time for others, besides the Ruling Family, to learn to understand things of the past."

Kurtch nodded his head, and then looked up quickly, surprised, but anxious to learn how the city was built. To be able to read the documents himself would give him insight into the minds of the early masters.

Zorena did little inspecting of the progress on the wall. She and Kurtch said little as they sat above the city, drinking zul and enjoying the day. Their conversation dealt mostly with nothing that had to do with anything, as far as Sonya could tell. So she walked along the wall, looking at a clear, blue, hot sky.

From there they rode to the outer defenses — a series of towers about a mile out from the wall. They spread all around the city at the edge of sight from each other.

Zorena and Sonya found Tagor inside a stuffy room at the base of one of these towers. He wore the brown garb of the soldiers and made his report tediously precise and complete.

Sonya's mind drifted to the sun-filled plain where she should've been riding toward the mountains. She wondered if Zorena had a real reason for asking her along. Should she be listening to such things? She sipped at her zul and ate some dry cake.

Two hours later she walked through the Drilling Ground where soldiers practiced hand-to-hand combat and combat with crude weapons.

"This exercise is to prepare them for the time in battle when their swords and shields are gone. They must then fight with whatever they can get their hands on — or with nothing but their hands and feet," explained Tagor.

What else would it be for? thought Sonya derisively. She thought of her own Karate lessons and wondered if she'd ever really need what she'd learned, or be any good in a real-life situation.

She watched the soldiers. It didn't look like a drill to her. Except for the lack of blood, for which she was grateful, it looked and sounded like real combat, or at least what she imagined real combat would look and sound like.

"Are you capable of such feats, Sonya?" Tagor pointed to a large man fighting with three smaller men. He made an easy target: unbalanced, ungraceful, but winning easily.

Sonya laughed.

"No! Maybe I could handle one of them — a small one — but not three."

Tagor's brow lifted arrogantly.

"You could handle one of them? Would you mind giving us a demonstration?"

Why did they take everything so literally? At any other time Sonya would have refused. But Tagor stood with his arms folded, his face with the same expression as when they first met. He expected her to decline. *Smug creep!*

"A small demonstration then," she returned Tagor's smug grin.

His eyes widened.

"Bodani, come here!"

Sonya did her best to remember everything she could. She controlled her breathing and tried not to look like she knew what she was doing — no need to make the guy over-cautious and give herself more trouble than absolutely necessary. Her legs felt funny.

Bodani circle around, crouched, ready to dive. Good, that would make it easy. She waited for his move. Quick as she'd ever seen he lunged. More quickly than she'd ever moved she deflected a well aimed fist. So, when it came to it, she *could* defend herself!

Bodani's foot snapped in front of her face before she could move. She slammed her V-shaped arms upward, stepped forward and to the side. He fell backwards, dropped into a roll and faced her unharmed.

She attacked. With a series of round kicks and sidekicks, she drove him back. A poorly performed flying sidekick knocked him down. She fell, too. But before he could recover, she followed through with two well placed — but not full force — punches. Sonya bowed to her opponent as she'd been taught. He imitated her.

An exhilaration surged through her. Something that she'd never felt before, but wished she had.

She composed herself quickly and returned to Zorena and Tagor, slowly. Somewhere in the scuffle, she caught a nasty knock in her side. Her stomach felt pushed into her back. She took a deep breath and coughed. But Tagor's expression had changed.

"Very impressive, Sonya. I apologize for my lack of faith."

"That's okay," she answered. She would've said more, but it hurt to talk.

Tagor excused himself, and they watched him walk towards the next group.

Zorena laughed. "Tagor prides himself on being able to judge people's character and ability almost instantly. You surprised him; he is unaccustomed to that." She paused a moment.

"I thought you said your schools did not teach fighting."

"They don't. But I also said there are schools for just about everything. We call it Karate."

"Karate. Could you teach it?"

Sonya looked up, both astonished and flattered.

"No, I don't think so. Y'see, Karate's not just fighting. It's an art and should only be taught by a Master, or at least under his direction. The idea is that a Master can't be beaten by anyone, except another Master — that's what makes him (or her) a Master. I, on the other hand, could be beaten by just about anyone. In this instance, it could be very harmful for the student to surpass the teacher — for the teacher. And that's me.

"No, I don't think I'll be teaching anyone anything."

Sonya had taught children before, but that was different. The thought of teaching powerful soldiers to fight terrified her.

"I think you would be a good teacher."

Did Zorena know her thoughts?

"It would be an insult to Masters of the art — to the art itself." Sonya may have believed what she said, but fear prompted her words, not belief.

"I thought you were committed to sharing knowledge and skills."

Sonya did not have to search for the sarcastic tones this time.

"Zorena, you don't understand. Karate is an *art!*" She stressed the last word fiercely. "It's not just a bunch of kicking and punching. It's a lesson in . . . in self control, perfection, patience, and . . . it's a way of life. It's wrong for me to presume that I know enough to teach these people correctly, because I haven't even come close to mastering it."

Sonya's tone left no room for doubt. She would stand firm. She would not teach!

Z Z Z Z Z

The next morning, saddlesore and cursing horseback riding as a primary means of transportation, Sonya was on the Drilling Ground with Zorena, Tagor, Barska and Cowis as her first karate students. She knew each of them could easily defeat her. But she did her best to act the teacher, and they the students.

She taught them exercises and learned similar ones from them. She took them through the drills mercilessly, and they never flinched.

They took a break, more for herself than her students, and she started to explain the concentration process.

"Close your eyes. Think about nothing. You must do that to become totally relaxed. Forget everything on your mind. Feel nothing. You must relax totally to locate your inner strength. Your mind will travel through you to find it — the strength that will make you capable of doing incredible things. Eventually, you will be able to call upon this strength in an instant. Don't worry about doing it now, just relax. Keep your eyes closed. Follow your consciousness through every inch of your body."

Sonya fell silent, unfortunately unable to follow her own advice. She wondered if they just humored her. She wondered what would happen when she sparred with each of them. She decided to let them spar with each other first;

she'd watch to form an opinion of each.

She taught them the basic kicks and punches. They learned too quickly for her to relax for even a moment. She would have precious little much time to get herself in shape.

Tagor was swift, fluid and precise. She wouldn't want to meet up with him in a dark alley. Barska was powerful, but stiff and unbalanced. Zorena was graceful; each move smooth and effortless. She was confident and in complete control — as usual. It was difficult to judge Cowis. He was apparently serious and attentive, but just going through the motions.

She paired them off: Zorena and Tagor; Barska and Cowis. Then she asked them to sit. It was her duty — however painful it might turn out — to spar with each one herself. She had to experience, first hand, how they handled themselves. But who first? Since everything else seemed to be done by age, she chose Zorena.

It was a challenge. Zorena was made for the martial arts. She could attack with fierceness but had the patience to wait. She could read her opponent's body, anticipate each move, and defend more than adequately.

Tagor was next. He was methodical and logical; but quick enough to be good. He followed each move with another equally good — but predictable — one. As Sonya thought about this, he caught her off guard. A simple succession of round kicks almost knocked her down. One caught her rather painfully in the side. She winced, and counter-attacked. She hopped around, hissing and looking foolish, totally immersed in her new character. Tagor smiled. She threw him to the ground and ended the sparring. Tagor never lost his composure; he bowed and sat.

Barska was next. Surely, he was the odd one of the family. She spoke to him as they sparred, telling him to relax and use what he knew, not what he wished he knew. "Become an animal, Barska, one you know and respect. Fight as it would fight." She hung back. Suddenly, he tossed his head. A perfectly executed double front kick almost got her.

Double front kick?

He went into a stance similar to the horse stance she'd learned and had *not* taught them. She smiled slyly and became the cat. She confused him with a series of feints with her 'claws.' A quick fake-kick to his stomach went unblocked.

Cowis rose slowly and offhandedly. Sonya kept her expression blank. He managed fairly well, but he looked bored. Sonya played the attacker and forced him to defend himself. He blocked or dodged each blow adequately, uncreatively.

One studies an art; one does not copy the motions of another. Cowis obviously needed to learn that. A quick sidekick to his unprotected side, just hard enough to make him keel over, ended the match. It was so simple that she had to deliberately control a grin.

She stood still for a second. No one left. Sonya tried not to let her relief show, and led them through the first steps of a kata, ending the lesson. She'd made it through alive and with her dignity intact.

The sun beat down from directly above them and she wished she had a watch. Zorena announced lunch and walked ahead with Tagor and Barska. Sonya breathed deeply and consciously relaxed her muscles. Cowis moved slowly to her side.

"Well, I suppose you felt I deserved that teacher. You do take this all rather seriously."

Sonya smiled. "It happens to be a serious thing."

Z Z Z Z Z

Back at the house, Cowis and Sonya sat under the grapevine drinking wine and trying to stay cool. Who said dry heat wasn't uncomfortable? They watched the sun turn the mountain range red and every shade of orange. The harmless clouds looked dark and made the colors swirl. The edges of the white-tipped peaks looked on fire.

Sonya stood up and felt her heart skip — she wanted to be there. Cowis must have felt it.

"If you were there, you would not be able to see it. You can only see it when you are not near it. I know, because I have been there." He paused a moment and smiled. "You have not seen a sun set, until you have seen an Anatawen sunset.

"Shall we go now, to the main hall? Dinner is ready by now."

Sonya nodded and grabbed her wine goblet.

The empty hall felt cool compared to outside. A fire burned brightly, as always, and crackled its warm invitation. So they sat on the floor after dinner, sipping wine and watching the flames. To her unending embarrassment, Sonya fell asleep.

A field in Mentone, Alabama, November, 1984. © 2003 Beth David

Chapter Four

History Rears Its Ugly Head

It was dawn when Sonya woke in her room. The clanging and shouting must have awakened her. *Clanging?* She jumped up and fell backward with a groan. Her stomach twisted and gurgled — she never felt anything worse or more violent, with the possible exception of her head.

She got to the window and squinted outside, but it didn't face the street and the sun shone painfully bright. She took a step toward the bed and stopped abruptly. Aspirin in Anatawen? She laughed despite her head and went down the stairs. The family was preparing a great exit. A mob filled the hall to follow them. Sonya tried to make it to the front. Zorena turned and waited for her.

"Thanks, I never could've caught up."

Zorena answered softly, "Just do not say anything and there will be no problem. Tagor's people are bringing something from the tower."

They stood waiting on the wall near the gate. About halfway between the tower and the wall, a group of 30 or more soldiers dragged a large structure.

Sonya leaned against the outer wall laughing, "The Trojan Horse, no doubt."

Zorena smiled slightly at the joke she did not understand. A few minutes later Sonya could see it clearly. It *was* a horse! She gasped, then laughed again — louder. Homak turned a searing gaze in her direction. Zorena's eyes flamed.

"Sonya, please be silent!"

Sonya's laughter gave way to fear.

"You can't be serious, Zorena. That there's a bona fide Trojan Horse. You can't bring *that* into the city. At least not without checking it out." She added the last as an afterthought. How could she expect these people to instantly accept her fear of a wooden horse?

"It was sent by Lengor, as a gift to Homak — to seal a pact against the Mountain Dwellers."

"How can you be sure?"

"How? Tagor is seldom fooled," Zorena retorted.

"Seldom does not mean never."

Her bitter tone surprised them both. Why did she shake so much? The crowd below cheered, and soldiers talked about a new link, one that would crush the Mountain Dwellers forever. A noble gesture this wooden horse — a symbol for all the world to see. Sonya thought it was an ugly horse.

"Zorena, you're not taking me seriously. I know what that is, or could be. You don't. I may be hung over, but I'm not blind. All I'm asking is that you look at it before they bring it into the city."

"And you, therefore, presume that Tagor did not?"

"Don't try that my-brother's-perfect routine with me. He's only human . . . I think. What can it hurt if I'm wrong? It'll only take a few minutes. Besides, where are the guys who brought it? I only see Tagor's people."

"Go back to bed, Sonya. Your mind is fogged from the wine. Your thinking is not sound. Be silent, now; you are annoying Homak."

"Good! He should be annoyed. Maybe he'll listen to me."

Zorena slowly turned her gaze from the field.

"Sonya, I have been very patient with you simply because you are an outsider. But you have now stretched my tolerance to its limit. You will leave the wall now and go back to the house where you cannot further interfere."

Sonya fought with her temper and lost in a few seconds. She grabbed Zorena's arm and swung her around.

"Damn you, Zorena! You're making the biggest mistake of your damned stubborn life! That is no gift. It's a weapon."

Zorena's stare grew cold; her big eyes shrunk to two little dots surrounded by pure white. But she said nothing, hesitating with sudden doubt. Sonya trembled all over. She put her hands on Zorena's shoulders and spoke quietly, quickly.

"Zorena, please listen. For just one minute. It's one of the oldest, most famous tricks in my world. They probably found it with one person guarding it, right? Or, okay . . . it looks like a battle was fought near it and the horse was the only thing left, right?"

Zorena's uncertainty grew as Sonya's guesses came nearer the truth.

"And there's some kind of writing or symbols carved into it. And it will take days to verify it with Lengor — right?" She took a deep breath before continuing.

"You've got to keep it outside the wall. Let me show you. If I don't find anything, I'll leave, or whatever you say. Just *look* at the size of it. Look! How many men do you think that could hold? You don't think it's solid wood, do you? And how many would it have to hold? Only enough to get the gate open in the confusion of battle."

Zorena's gaze softened and Sonya's trembling lessened, but she didn't let go. Zorena looked thoughtfully at Sonya, and she had to turn away. Why couldn't she look Zorena in the eye? Damn!

Zorena put her hand on Homak's shoulder but said nothing. He nodded towards Barska who climbed down and rode out at full speed.

Zorena motioned for Sonya to follow and they left, with less speed, more dignity.

Sonya's fear grew with every moment. Suppose she was wrong? Suppose she was right? She had to be right. It was the oldest trick in the book. And it almost worked. It didn't make her feel very good.

Someone else is here, she thought, *and on the other side.*

Maybe her timing wasn't so bad, or accidental. A shudder crawled up her spine. She turned her thoughts back to where they belonged.

Sonya stood a few feet from the horse and studied it with her eyes. There had to be lines in the wood that could hide a door. She supposed that if she'd been a better student, she'd know exactly where to find the door. She felt along with her hand. It couldn't be too high, could it? The surface was smooth, the wood light and plain. She crawled underneath and found the slightest crack that was the door.

Now they had to get in, and Tagor took over. They tied two strong ropes to the wooden beast, one around its neck, the other around its tail. They tied the other end of the ropes to saddles. The two riders urged their horses until the huge wooden thing crashed on its side. They heard exclamations of surprise and pain from within and the latch popped open. A bleary-eyed Mountain Dweller, looking half asleep — or drugged — stuck his head out into the sunlight.

Zorena looked long and hard at Sonya, who squirmed in her saddle and rode back to the city alone. She should've felt proud of herself, but instead she felt hung over and more homesick than ever.

Fear crept into her every thought. Who built Lengor's Trojan Horse? Someone else was there — fighting for the other guys. She couldn't deal with such a complicated notion in her present state of mind and body.

She curled up on a sunlit cushion in the garden and fell asleep. The ocean seeped into her dreams. She floated, looking at a blue sky. Waves lapped about her pulling her out to sea. She did not fight them.

A servant woke her, as gently as urgency allowed.

"Zorena wants you, in her rooms. Please hurry; she sent me searching for you some time ago."

"Go away! If she wants me she can come here."

The servant stood at a loss.

"Go tell her that!"

"There is no need. I could have heard you from the gate!"

"Ah, yes, I forgot. The great Zorena knows all, sees all, hears all. Why did you bother the servant to use such a conventional method of search?"

Zorena motioned for the servant to leave. Sonya broke off a bunch of grapes and sat at the table. She popped one into her mouth and knew her stomach didn't like it. Zorena watched her and Sonya found she had no difficulty meeting that gaze now.

Must be losing her touch, she thought.

Sonya felt strange, as though she wanted to say something but didn't know what. It shocked her to feel the tears fill her eyes and her throat tighten, but she couldn't stop it. Zorena laid a hand on her shoulder and said nothing. Sonya appreciated the silence as she sobbed, trying frantically to stop. It seemed like a long time before she did. She just wanted to curl up into a little ball and roll home.

When she looked up she saw a steaming pot of zukha on the table. She didn't know how it got there, or when — she didn't care. She sipped the drink and swallowed hard. Zorena kept silent, but Sonya no longer felt angry or uncomfortable with her. She smiled weakly.

"I don't know what happened. It's the first time I've ever done that."

Zorena smiled. "You have suddenly been forced into a difficult situation. You have been thrown into a whole series of surprises. I am sorry."

Sonya tried to identify the odd tone in Zorena's voice. "You sound like you're responsible."

"I believe that I am, to a small extent or to a great. I have not yet decided."

Sonya's smirk went unnoticed. Zorena probably wouldn't explain if she did know. How could she explain if she hadn't decided yet? Sonya changed the subject.

"You realize what that," Sonya pointed towards the gate, "means, don't you?"

Zorena looked up quickly, her thoughts interrupted.

"I will after I ask you some questions. Tell me the story of this Trojan Horse."

Sonya remembered her words at the wall and tried to stammer an apology.

"Do not apologize. You spoke the truth as you felt it. Did I not tell you there is no penalty for honest emotion? It is I who should have listened sooner, before you were forced to be fierce; but I did not know you. I will be more careful in the future. Go on, tell me your story."

Sonya told the story as well as she could. Zorena listened without interruption, thought for a while, then looked up with a sideward tilt of her head.

"There is a natural order of things, Sonya. A balance of sorts. I knew something was happening in the mountains. I could feel it in the soil itself. Tagor and Rubad were not hunting for sport when they found you. They were searching for something else — the cause of the uneasiness around me. I knew something was up there — now I know it is a someone. You must have been sent as a counterbalance to that someone, an answer to my need. I wish I had seen it sooner. But that is the way of such things."

"How could you play a part in something you knew nothing about?"

Zorena smiled a cunning smile, as an old man about to explain something that cannot be explained; and so decides not to.

"It is a matter of birth," was all she said.

Sonya said nothing.

Hurray for birth, she thought. *But where does that leave me?*

"I should not say, however, that I knew nothing about it. Let us simply say that I knew no details. For the hills in which you were found are heavy with power of a mysterious sort. Often from that direction the cool breeze of reason seems to come. Members of the Ruling Family have for centuries traveled there to find answers to unknown questions.

"Is there anything you can guess about the person we speak of?"

"How can I guess? I don't know anything about him."

"How do you know it is a man?" Zorena asked anxiously.

"I don't," Sonya shrugged. "Reverting to my old ways, I guess."

Zorena nodded in disappointment and understanding.

"Think carefully, Sonya. Any small guess may help."

"Well, I suppose it's safe to assume that he's no genius or scientist, or anything close. If he was, he would've thought of something more original, and deadly. And especially if I was sent as a counterbalance. I couldn't even make a windmill work."

Sonya still wanted to meet him, or her. How did he get there, and did he know how to get back?

"I have an idea, Sonya. It may not be a good idea, but it might be our only chance." She paused, as though preparing herself for the next sentence.

"Would you be willing to go, secretly, to the mountains to find this person?"

Sonya nodded eagerly.

"Do not answer in such haste. You cannot realize what I am asking you to do. You will not go alone, but you cannot have many traveling with you. Two, maybe three. Cowis, of course. He will go with or without you now. The others can be chosen at another time, carefully."

"Where would I be heading?"

"That is what demands you to think carefully. You will be close to where we found you. It is dangerous for two reasons. One, you will be out of our protective range. Two, you will be the closest to home you have been since your arrival — that is dangerous for us, not you."

Sonya forced her mind to slow down. This was her chance to go home, and her chance to — to do what? Was there really a balance of things? The idea spooked her. She didn't want to make a decision.

"What exactly would be my purpose?"

"There is a reason for the hostility between the Mountain Dwellers and us. Some ancient history is in order here. Please listen carefully. Much of what I am about to tell you is known only to the Ruling Family of Anatawen, and possibly only the Ruling Families of the Mountain Dwellers. To breathe a word of it will cause your undoing. I do not speak idle threats — it is not our way. Are you prepared to vow to secrecy under these conditions?"

Sonya nodded.

"Once, we did not fight the Mountain Dwellers — when they did not dwell in the mountains. A woman called Sareema led those who would follow her out of the darkness of the land that was theirs. No one knows where that land is, or was. I am Sareema's direct descendant.

"The Mountain Dwellers befriended Sareema's people and showed them how to survive the heat and weather the sandbursts. They taught us to defend ourselves from the snakes and other dangerous creatures of this place that was so strange to us. They taught us to eat fish from the sea. Together we lived, sharing our knowledge. We accepted each other as equals and bonds of love between individuals of both races were not even noticed — a natural result of acceptance. Then we discovered Anatawen.

"Sareema was long dead. Her grandson, Barsel, Ruled. He saw the beauty and richness of Anatawen and claimed it for his own. You see, no other had ever ventured more than five days from the sea and its frequent rain. But Barsel had a talent for finding water and using it wisely. He passed through the drylands and headed for the mountains. He had planned to settle much closer to them. But the sunset from Anatawen, and especially from this garden, swayed him.

"Dissent sprang from the two peoples. Centuries old national pride and national independence cannot be wiped out in a few generations. The Zukulan, that is what the Mountain Dwellers called themselves, claimed the rich plain as theirs, for they lived in this land first. Barsel claimed it as his, for he discovered it. A battle followed: Barsel and his followers against the Zukulan and some of his own people, of whom Lengor is a descendant. During this battle the Image of Corandu disappeared."

"Didn't you mention that before?"

"I named the river, called so after the woman. The woman the Zukulan call the mother of their race. I do not know anything else about her.

"The Zukulan became a race driven by insanity. They turned on the ancestors of Lengor, who fled, leaderless, into the forest. There they have remained, an independent city, bound neither to us, nor the Mountain Dwellers. Barsel's eldest child was killed in the battle. Barsel was wounded and died but a few days later. During his sickness, the people turned to Joneen — the mother of his children — for leadership. That was a logical thing to do in any other family, but not the Ruling Family.

That was their grave mistake. She was not trained to Rule. His second child, and youngest, Charmeen, should have taken over. He had the . . . right. But he was only twelve summers alive and not considered wise enough. They were foolish. He had more wisdom than his mother would ever have. Maybe if he had been a girl child they would have considered it. But that is the way of such prejudices.

"Joneen's heart, broken by the death of her son and the injury to Barsel, took over the logic of her mind. She swore revenge, and the people listened. They hunted the Zukulan, killed them and drove them into the safety of the mountains; and they did not come down.

"Barsel's death fed into her rage and intensified Joneen's drive to kill the Zukulan. She had them pursued beyond the point where they would have been a threat to Anatawen, beyond the point of reconciliation, or even distant communication. Charmeen did not understand his right to use his new power until it was too late. And so it has been.

"The Mountain Dwellers believe we took the Image of Corandu, and so did the ancestors of Lengor. We did not. We had no need for its Power. But since our Power was hidden they could not know that their Image was no threat or any great prize for us.

"It is my belief that the Image was stolen by the Zukulan themselves. Not with the knowledge of the Rulers, or the majority. It was, I think, a group within them, led by a person whose name is forgotten, or maybe was never known. There was dissent among the Zukulan from the first. A frustrated, distant cousin of the Rulers, I would guess. With the Image of Corandu, tey could rally the support necessary to challenge the Ruler.

"Old lore states that the Image of Corandu lends power to the Ruler who wears its Medallion. Exactly what that Power is, or to what extent, we do not know. But only a Mountain Dweller, with some trace of the Ruling blood, can wield that Power.

"The Image of Corandu was stolen; but the Medallion was lost, or so it seemed."

It took a while to sink in. Then Sonya gasped, pointing to the medallion that Zorena wore. But she couldn't speak.

"That is correct. This is the Medallion of the Image of Corandu. It has been the duty of my family to keep it hidden. No one knows the secret history, therefore, it is safe to wear it. The belief in my family was to keep it from the Mountain Dwellers, for fear they would regain too much power and overcome us.

"I believe it is time to give it back. I do not believe we were attacked by the Mountain Dwellers we exiled long ago, but by the Mountain Dwellers who exiled themselves. *They* must not get the Medallion. The true Ruling Family should have it. Then they will be able to deal with this other faction and we might live in peace again."

She fell silent and poured some wine. Sonya took a sip of zukha and grimaced; it was cold. Zorena produced a skin from beneath the table and handed it to Sonya. She took a sip and again appreciated the soothing effect of zul. She let it swish around in her mouth, cooling, before she swallowed. Her stomach accepted it without repercussion. Zorena stood and walked around the garden. Sonya was again aware of her surroundings. Funny how her mind could slip away like that.

She considered the alternative; spending lazy afternoons in the sun, after giving a Karate lesson and taking a long ride. She could have fun in the city — the stories she could tell! Maybe she could teach Kurtch to build a windmill, or something.

No, that would get boring very fast. Getting here was one thing; she didn't make that decision. It was an accident — or at least out of her control, no matter what Zorena said. Now she could decide — must decide. The luxury of royalty, or the excitement of true adventure? In the comfort of a warm chair and in the company of a good book, she would without hesitation have chosen the latter. But now?

"Zorena," Sonya turned to find her.

"Yes."

Sonya started at the sound. Zorena lay on the mat

just a few feet from her. Zorena's eyes were closed, her face turned toward the sinking sun. She looked almost tired, a condition Sonya had trouble associating with Zorena. But she looked beautiful as well. The full light of a clear Anatawen sun shone down upon her face. Sonya felt a strange tenderness towards this woman who so recently and easily had rankled her to tears.

"You still haven't told me exactly what I'm supposed to do up there."

"Your task will be to find the Mountain Dwellers who belong to the Medallion and give it to their Ruler." She stood and faced Sonya with a serious expression, much like Homak.

"Are you prepared to try this?"

Laughter and fear pulled at either side of Sonya, but she did not hesitate.

"I am. If you'll help me prepare for the trip. I'm used to the weather by the mountains and the sea, not this heat. And the only snakes I've ever seen were either harmless or behind glass. I've never walked more than a couple of miles at a stretch; and as far as horseback riding, well, I'm still saddlesore. Do *you* think I'm ready to try this?"

Zorena's eyes glinted.

"You will be, after some training. You will go?"

"Yes, I will."

Zorena raised her glass in triumph.

"Come, we must see Homak. One thing I must warn — he knows nothing of this. We must tell him carefully. Say nothing until Tagor, Cowis and Barska have joined us. It may very well take all of us to convince him."

Sonya nodded, a little confused.

"Zorena, why do you wear the–" she stopped at Zorena's warning glance.

"Later, Sonya. Any questions must wait. You may ask any of us, except Homak. He will not approve, I think."

Then she added in a lighter tone, "Cowis will be willing to answer your questions."

Sonya nodded, relieved. Zorena seemed to know everything about everything. And though she talked enough in answer, she never quite satisfied curiosity. Cowis, on the other hand, would ramble on and on, filling in every detail. She'd have to steal some time with him after the meeting.

Homak's rooms were, by no stretch of the imagination, common. But compared to Zorena's they were not, by any means, special. Sonya studied Zorena. Was Homak just a figurehead, a pawn in the cloak of a king? She must remember to ask Cowis, although she'd certainly have to rephrase the question. Homak acted like no pawn, but Sonya couldn't dismiss the notion that Zorena really controlled things.

And Homak's bearing reflected his position. He walked carefully, yet with confidence. His voice traveled across a room subtly, swiftly, with the eerie firmness of a command. His way was steady, slowly patient, as was Tagor's. But he seemed to have none of the verve and fire she often saw in Zorena, or surprisingly, Cowis. She'd never thought of him as being alike to Zorena, but maybe he was.

Tagor and Barska sat by the window drinking zukha with Homak. Before Sonya and Zorena took three steps, Cowis burst in with a rush, flushed with excitement. Did everyone know except Homak? How could they? There it was again — the 'how' question. Sonya's sigh drew all eyes toward her.

Would she have to say something? She looked at Zorena for help. Zorena laughed out loud.

"Father, we have a proposition for you. For Anatawen."

"I am aware that the sudden presence of all my children at once could not be construed as mere coincidence. Come, Zorena, you have that unmistakable look about you. Tell me your proposition."

He grinned with amusement. So, Zorena had figured out why this young outsider had arrived and was ready to take advantage of the opportunity.

Zorena looked at her father and handled the Medallion. Sonya had never seen her do that. Nervous reaction? *Zorena?*

Zorena explained carefully what she intended. Tagor sat back in his chair, his long legs stretched far under the table. He listened, reading his father's face with slow scrutiny. Barska watched one face, then the other, shifting his gaze swiftly. Cowis watched Sonya, who promptly blushed when she noticed.

Homak listened carefully and silently. When Zorena finished her story, Homak studied Sonya, as though sizing up her ability. Sonya met his gaze steadily, though her innards reeled. Cowis shifted in his chair and smiled foolishly. Tagor shot a stern look at his younger brother, who immediately frowned and cleared his throat. Sonya raised an eyebrow at Cowis. He winked and nodded. Zorena caught the exchange and smiled.

"I think she is capable of the journey and the task. With our help, she will be ready to go in fifteen days. Naturally, we will not send her without your approval."

Homak raised a brow in surprise. "Naturally."

"We need more than that, Zorena. We must all agree to full support in this. There must be a total commitment from all of us," added Tagor. "If anyone is unsure for any reason, in any way, speak now. If your mind will not be changed, we dare not try it."

Tagor spoke softly, with a scary firmness that Sonya didn't understand. Zorena turned quickly to her brother in uncertainty. Cowis spoke next.

"Are we to understand that you, my dear brother, are not in agreement?"

"I, among others, have doubts about the feasibility of such an expedition, and its ramifications. But that is not the question, yet. The travelers must have the full support of every member of this family. If not, they will undoubtedly fail."

He turned gently to Zorena. "Even you, Zorena, cannot

hope to sustain them alone. We can not foresee what trials will beset them. If the Medallion is lost, our chances of regaining it are almost nil. We must take every precaution. Zorena, you do understand my feelings, do you not?"

Zorena nodded, but she didn't look happy. She had hoped to convince Homak to tolerate her decision. But unconditional support?

"Certainly, we must be together on this," she said.

Homak turned to the window and watched the sun sliding toward the peaks. This stage of life was meant for rest, for slowing down. He had little time left and the plan had been to live it out in quiet peace, and then to give Zorena the Rule during that peace.

But the matter could not be decided by him. Zorena had taken control, as she should have, and fate had decided to fill his last days with this instead of calm and quiet ease.

The discussion lasted through three pots of zukha. Sonya learned more than she needed or wanted. As soon as she could learn to survive alone in the wilderness, they'd leave. She fell on the bed, exhausted.

Shelburne Falls, Mass., The Bridge of Flowers, 9/02
Copyright 2003 Beth David

Chapter Five

Of Family Ties, Brotherly Love, and Longings Fulfilled

A cool breeze pushed at the curtain's edge and let the growing light pass through. Sonya rolled over and groaned, but something nagged at her brain until she got out of bed. She dressed quickly and went to Zorena's rooms where Tagor, Zorena, Barska and Cowis were deciding who would go with her. Zorena didn't even pause when Sonya walked in.

"Cowis will lead the group. He has wanted this for a long time. Since you will be leading, have you anyone special in mind?"

Cowis looked at Tagor apprehensively and paused before answering.

"I want Sayeeda to guide us."

Tagor's face showed the slight twists of controlled anger; his teeth clenched onto his pipe.

"No! I will not allow it."

Zorena watched the two; Barska turned away. Cowis faced Tagor.

"And I believe that she is the only logical choice."

Sonya waited for Zorena's opinion, but she voiced none. Sonya suddenly saw Tagor as very powerful and much too much the quiet type. Did a fierce temper lurk closely beneath that steady exterior?

"Have you no conscience, young brother? How can you ask such a thing of her — and of me? What of Todam? Our son is not ready to be without her."

A fleeting expression of pain passed through Cowis's face. Sonya wanted to rush to his side, but felt Zorena's arm hold her to the chair. She turned angrily toward Zorena who only watched the brothers closely. Sonya decided to follow her lead. She, too, watched.

"I do not ask without thinking about it carefully. Who would *you* choose, Tagor? We have no right to decide in this case. It is her decision. Zorena, would you send for her?" he asked without turning from Tagor.

"I already have."

Sonya forgot to contain her surprise.

"No, you didn't. When? How? . . ."

The door opened and Sayeeda stepped in quickly. Her clothes hung loosely and crooked; her light brown hair tousled, and tightly cropped. Her eyes were nearly closed, but her voice sang slightly and carried a carefree note.

"You called?"

Sonya watched Tagor. Could he really be on the verge of tears? Or did she imagine it?

Tagor and Sayeeda greeted each other with a warm embrace, and Cowis turned away.

Zorena stood abruptly and motioned for Sayeeda to sit. Sayeeda sat next to Sonya and nodded a silent 'hello.' Then she grabbed a roll and looked up at the faces around her, waiting, with a guarded innocence, to hear the reason for the summons. Tagor turned from Zorena's gaze and stood near the window, half turned from them. Zorena started.

"Sayeeda, I have asked you here–"

"No. I have asked you here," broke in Cowis. "We are planning a journey to the mountains; a peace mission, of sorts, with the Mountain Dwellers. I would like for you to accompany us, as our guide. Will you accept?"

A strangled cough escaped from Sayeeda and she reached for wine. Her eyes swelled with tears, but she said nothing and looked only at Tagor. He turned around to face her.

"It is your decision, Sayeeda. I have no say in this matter." His tone was rimmed with fear, his eyes forcibly held steady.

Sayeeda's shoulders dropped. She poured more wine and drained her cup in one, quick swallow. She refilled the goblet and turned to Zorena.

"This is, I suspect, a journey of utmost importance?"

Zorena nodded, her face holding no expression. Sayeeda sighed and moved close to Tagor, her hands on the crook of his arms. Zorena motioned for the others to follow her.

"They must be alone. We will move to Cowis's rooms."

She closed the door quietly behind them. Cowis frowned, and Zorena laid a hand on his shoulder.

"Do not worry, you will have your guide."

Cowis smiled brightly and put his arm around Zorena, pulling her toward him as they walked.

"I thank you for the information. I am glad you understand."

She smiled a small smile.

"But what about Tagor. I do not wish to cause him grief," said Cowis.

"I will take care of Tagor as long as you take care of Sayeeda."

Sonya was finally annoyed enough to ask the question

that nagged her.

"Will somebody please tell me what's going on? Who *is* Sayeeda? I'm so confused."

"We will explain. You are much too impatient, Sonya. There are some complications."

She waited until they settled by the window that faced the garden. Zorena spread the drapes apart to let out some of the darkness.

"Cowis, you do have the best windowscene, why is that?"

He smiled and shrugged, about to answer when Sonya interrupted.

"Wait a minute! What about me and my questions? Who is Sayeeda?"

Cowis laughed out loud and poured wine. Zorena turned, sighing.

"I will explain."

She paused and took the goblet from Cowis, tasted the wine. Sonya wanted to burst.

"You should learn patience before you go, Sonya. It is sad that it cannot be given but must be learned.

"Sayeeda is the person who knows the mountain range better than anyone else in Anatawen ever could. She grew to adulthood there and hid there for years before Tagor found her. Her mother was a Mountain Dweller, her father Anatawen. They lived outside the city for a time. Her father died when she was still young, and her mother took her to the mountains where she was treated poorly. She left as soon as she was able to survive alone. And there Tagor found her. They are Vowed to each other.

"Sayeeda seldom speaks of her time in the mountains. She hoped never to return; she has mortal enemies among the Mountain Dwellers. It will not be pleasant for her, to say the least. We are asking much of her — and of Tagor."

"But she would be invaluable to us as a guide," Cowis added. "With her, our chances are better than doubled. Tagor knows that. He simply does not want to let her go. I can understand his feelings."

"I think you do not, Cowis."

It surprised Sonya to hear Barska's voice.

"Have you thought much about it? She is his whole life. And their young son, Todam, needs her as well. You seem to forget the difficulties they encountered when she first arrived. They suffered long before they were truly accepted. It has not been long since they have been able to feel secure. Now, he could very well lose her. For anyone that is difficult, even for Tagor."

"But if Zorena says Sayeeda will be your guide, then she will be your guide. Though it is more likely she will be taking care of you, Cowis, rather than the other way around."

They sat at the table and tried to continue the discussion. Zorena interrupted the silence.

"We must wait for Sayeeda's decision. First, we cannot decide who else will best complement the group until it is final that she will join you. Second, Tagor must take part in the decision."

Sonya took advantage of the break.

"Zorena, why do you wear the Medallion openly? Even if the story is not generally known, isn't it dangerous?" She sipped her wine — to give Zorena time to prepare the involved answer. The brothers laughed and Zorena smiled, slightly embarrassed. Sonya watched her face and waited. Zorena's voice sounded different, almost childlike.

"Because I like it," was all she said.

Sonya laughed hard at her surprise. Why was it so strange that Zorena could display such a weakness as vanity?

"I suppose that's as good a reason as any. Don't know why it didn't occur to me."

"There is no danger, Sonya. No one has ever seen the Medallion on the Image of Corandu, except the Mountain Dwellers. None of those who saw it are alive, and discussing it is sacrilege. Therefore, none of our people would ever have the opportunity to tell them of it."

The sun had already started its long descent when Tagor and Sayeeda came in. They walked to the couch slowly and sat, capitalizing on the tenseness in the room. Sayeeda spoke.

"I need a frothing, near-frozen mug of ale."

Cowis broke down first.

"Well? What have you decided?"

She shot him a stern look.

"We," she stressed the pronoun, "have decided that I will go."

Cowis let out a shout, but she ignored him and turned to Sonya.

"Sonya, we have not properly met. I am Sayeeda; I have been out of the city these past days."

She bowed, and Sonya followed suit — she felt foolish. Sayeeda laughed.

"You learn quickly. We have much in common, you and I. Not least that we were both found by Tagor, and were in need of finding."

Cowis paced, trying to keep quiet.

"Can we complete the courtesies and get to the matter at hand?" He looked at Tagor who nodded seriously.

Sayeeda sat at the table, next to Sonya. Tagor sat on the other side.

"Tagor explained everything to me," Sayeeda giggled. "You are remarkable, Zorena — walking around with the Medallion of Corandu around your neck!"

Sayeeda's hard, square features scrunched in laughter. Her skin looked tough; weathered by hard nights in the mountains. A carefree note lived in her voice, a childlike mischievousness in her eyes. Sonya felt comfortable enough to ask a question.

"There's still something I don't understand. Why do you want me to take the Medallion? Why not Cowis, or Sayeeda, or *anyone?*" She looked at Zorena, but Sayeeda answered her.

"Lots of reasons. We will surely confront this other

person at some point. When we do, you will be more apt to guess tey's mind than anyone else in Anatawen.

"We are rigidly set in our ways. Our reactions are often sadly traditional — predictable. The Mountain Dwellers know how we are. But with your ideas, we can perhaps surprise them, take them off guard, as they have done to us. And as we did to them when the Trojan Horse failed. You cannot do this from the safety of the city. You offer us our best chance for success. Especially since we believe this is the very reason for your arrival. And, of course," she added with a wry smile, "Cowis is going."

Sonya needed no more convincing, and the selection process continued.

Tagor insisted they include someone who understood the ways of animals, not only their horses, but the wild ones they would encounter as well. No one challenged Bilzite as the logical choice. And Zorena insisted that Mishwan go, despite much protest from Cowis. Zorena spoke with authority.

"He is intelligent. His stamina is unrivaled in the city. He is trustworthy. And — he was born Beneath the Fallen Star."

"A lot of people were born at the Time of the Fallen Star — pick one of the others if you must have that on your side."

Zorena reacted angrily.

"You know well that I did not say what you said. He is a true Starborn. You know that, Cowis, though you may wish to forget it at times. I still become amazed at how easily I Reach his mind even though he stands among many, or far away. He nearly Reached Out to me during the attack and he has no trace of the Ruling blood."

"But he is a child. I do not believe he is capable of understanding the importance of this expedition."

"You underrate him. The destiny surrounding him holds a uniqueness that may be calling upon this very task to make him what he must become. Let go of your trivial irritations! Are we of proper mind to deny him his very fate?"

She sounded weary of the debate now. "You simply do not like the boy. And that, simply, is too bad for you. He is perfect. He will go. You will thank me before your journey ends."

No one argued on behalf of Cowis. His voice came out with an angry edge.

"I hope so, Zorena," but his face expressed acceptance. Losing the argument hurt more than actually taking Mishwan along, and he couldn't think of a better choice.

Sayeeda whispered to Sonya amidst a stream of giggles. "Cowis is upset because Mishwan has a habit of plaguing him with practical jokes. He adores Cowis, who in the past not only played games with him but taught him many of the tricks he knows. The boy has an ingenious imagination. And he will be flattered to be asked to join us." She laughed again, and Sonya noticed the others had stopped talking.

"Time to eat," Sayeeda said and jumped up, leading the way. Sonya followed eagerly. Why was she so hungry? She reached the door, but gentle hands held her back. Cowis whispered in her ear.

"Homak's Delight in the garden?"

Sonya turned, put her arm around him and nodded, but she said, "No! Homak's Delight by the pond."

The setting sun colored the sky as it usually did, and the pond mirrored every shade and cloudied orange. No matter where she looked, the Anatawen sunset filled her sight. She wondered for a moment and slid over to where Cowis lay. He rested, eyes closed, on his back.

Sonya watched him for a long moment. She would have to make the first move this time, after her rejection of him.

He lay on a patch of soft grass in the shade of a large maple tree, his hands folded behind his head. Sonya smoothed back his hair, and he smiled, opening his eyes to see her hair glow from the orange of the fading sun. Sonya sat close, and slowly bent down to kiss him. He returned a gentle touch with his lips and Sonya pressed herself to him. It was late when they returned to the house.

Z Z Z Z Z

A servant woke Sonya shortly after dawn. She shivered in the morning chill, and it surprised her. It had to be at least 70 degrees in even the coldest hour. How would she fare in the mountain snows? The thought made her shiver again, and she sipped at her zukha. She stared out the window, unthinking, eyes unfocused, until a shout abruptly focused them. Cowis stood below the window with a small rucksack. She took her zukha and met him.

"I have nourishment for us," he bowed as he spoke, then led the way to the east side of the house, sitting where the sun would reach them. He unslung his wineskin and poured zul into a wine goblet. Then he laid out a spread of pastries, scandra, and a round fruit different than Sonya had ever tasted — sweet, a little tart, and very juicy with a thin, edible skin. But she couldn't identify the tastes.

"It is a crossbreed of several different fruits."

"Which ones?" Sonya bit into another.

"Homak, alone, I think, knows that. If, indeed, he remembers. As a rule, people just eat the fruit. It is called citron."

"Very creative."

Cowis ignored her sarcasm. Soon a soldier interrupted them to go to the field.

Her training began immediately. She practiced killing blocks of wood with strange and primitive weapons: arrows and slingshots — primitive toys to her, deadly and precise weapons to those around her.

For the skilled soldier, an arrow would reach as far as an eagle's sight; and the shot from a sling could fell a bear — at least that's what the tales insisted.

And then there was the hideskiver — a piece of rawhide weighted at the ends with balls of iron. The large hideskiver could be used as a bola; the smaller, when properly thrown, could sever an arm. It could also give the unskilled student a nasty headache and a colorful assortment of bruises.

Sonya also had to listen to Bilzite's uninterrupted discourses on the habits and tricks of various animals — and his ramblings on the edibles and unedibles of the wilderness. Only Mishwan's pranks dared to intrude, on occasion.

It seemed a challenge to him, somehow, to send Bilzite's blood rushing up to his ears, just so he could run off while Bilzite bellowed after him.

Sometimes Sonya's boredom threatened to make her back out on her promise. Then Mishwan would do something, and her depression would at least be diverted. As when he caught 30 or more sparrows, fed them wine, and sent them chirruping through the room.

Bilzite's face turned four or five shades of red within seconds. When it reached the color of a vigorously polished apple in the peak of ripeness, he bellowed so loudly the sparrows spasmed about in their drunken state, trying to escape the noise that pressed in around them. They flew up and down and back and forth, banging into walls and people while Bilzite kicked and cursed. Mishwan watched through the window for a while and ran off before Bilzite's color faded to normal.

That proved to be one of his best, since it gave Sonya and Cowis a chance to escape to the pond for a leisurely swim. Sonya began to enjoy Anatawen then.

Glacier National Park, Montana, looking out towards Canada's Waterton Lakes National Park, 1986. Copyright 2003 Anthony David

Chapter Six

Of Mountains, Snakes, and Dry Biscuits

The day of their departure dawned as brightly as every day in Anatawen. As the sun came into full view, Zorena and Sonya drank zukha by the window. Zorena slipped the chain over her head and handed the Medallion to Sonya.

How it glistened! And then it didn't. Sonya laid it against the palm of her hand and held it up. It felt the same but looked as though it changed constantly, altering shape and hue with every breath. She became so fascinated with it, she forgot what she was supposed to do with it.

Zorena laughed quietly.

"I, too, reacted as you. It seems to respond to the emotions or something within the person holding or wearing it. Keep it hidden. We are not certain who knows about it. But I am sure there are those who would guess."

The others already waited at the garden when Sonya

and Zorena left the house. Sonya's spirits were lower than ever; but the blood coursed through her veins, rushing excitement to every part of her body. She didn't know it was possible to feel such opposing emotions at the same time. Her stomach hurt.

They mounted their horses without speaking and said little as they turned away. All good-byes should've taken place already, privately.

Zorena stood in the morning breeze watching, motionless, as the animals took the travelers slowly along the path that would lead them around the south side of the pond and through the belt of trees to the mountains beyond.

Tagor watched from the window-walk of his room, still and silent.

They crossed through the belt of trees and looked upon a wide expanse of land stretching between them and the mountains. Sonya became confused.

"Cowis, I thought the wall surrounded the city, but where is it?"

"It ends at your left," Cowis answered. "Barsel could not bear to upset the pond, or sully the mountain view. There is a wide, deep pit with but a single narrow bridge. Most of it is natural. Barsel extended it. You will see where it meets the wall to completely enclose the city."

As they rounded the pond, he continued, "It is the weakest point in our defense, but not very weak. Only one person can pass at a time. One stout soldier could defend against an entire garrison with not much difficulty."

Sonya listened and tried to enjoy the ride. Bushes and trees of myriad colors and names patched this first part of the plain. They seemed to shimmer and fade in the bright heat, blurring at one moment and suddenly appearing sharp, clear in the next.

To the right the land rose and fell in green, yellow, and rock-strewn hills. Sonya nearly turned this way. These hills sent forth a call that brought a special warmth to the deepest portions of her heart — to a place she didn't even know needed warming.

Ahead, the mountains reached up, high and far, and deep, deep into the plain, as though thrown to the earth from a distance beyond the sight of the clouds.

The first night they camped nearly at the foot of the mountains, or so Sonya thought. It seemed that for the whole afternoon, she'd expected to reach them. But still they sat just out of reach.

Now the mountains filled all her sight, and the sun began to fall behind them. She turned to face the other way and stared into the fire. Sayeeda sat next to her.

"A rather overwhelming sight, isn't it." She pointed toward the largest peak.

Sonya grunted and nodded. She was stiff and sore. When she'd tried to walk, her legs wobbled and disobeyed her; she'd never ridden so far in one stretch. Still, she had questions to ask.

"Sayeeda, why are we taking horses to the mountains? Shouldn't we have mules, or ponies, or something? Horses are too clumsy for such rocky mountains, aren't they?" She was so tired, her voice was nearly a whisper.

"These horses will be fine. They are a breed of the Ruling Family. Barsel first bred them specifically for the mountains. It is said that he often rode far into the range for days at a time, to be alone. Some say to regain his Power, others say to use his Power to gain knowledge. But he had little time to do either before the war.

"The Ruling Family kept the line intact, though they seldom went to the mountains. There are few like them. Did you not notice their looks?"

Sonya shook her head. Depression, mixed with excitement, caused her to miss much that day. She wanted to sleep.

Cowis sat by the fire and produced a large flute exquisitely carved and painted. He started to play softly, and Sayeeda, Mishwan, and Bilzite joined in a song. Sonya listened, trying to learn the words.

Sayeeda's voice was soft and high; Bilzite's was low and a perfect partner. Poor Mishwan couldn't sing to save his life. They sang the Ballad of Anatawen. *Sort of a national anthem,* thought Sonya. She smiled as Mishwan's voice rang high, then low, out of time and tune with the others. She slowly faded off to sleep.

The horizon held the sun at eye level when Cowis woke them. Sonya dragged herself to her feet and tried to stretch out the pain in her back and neck. She walked a little, taking time to look closely at her horse.

How could she have missed it? He looked so strange in the morning light — depending on what she compared him to anyway. He had huge ears and a short, thick neck; his legs were short and strong, and his shoes didn't look like the standard metal. She remembered that he didn't stumble on the way, not even at the end of the long day.

Before the sun had climbed overhead they reached the foot of the mountains. Sayeeda found the right path and took the lead. Now the way grew more difficult and the ride went slowly.

The horses set their own pace, ignoring any encouragement or discouragement from their riders. Sonya sat back and tried to get comfortable. But the saddle provided as much comfort as riding bareback through an equestrian obstacle course.

They stopped on a wide grassy shelf for the midday meal. Cowis told them to take their jackets out of their packs.

"But it's still 100 degrees. What're you trying to do? Roast us?" Sonya felt hot, dirty and tired. Just thinking about the jacket made her sick.

"If you mean it is very hot, it will not last. You do not have to wear the jacket yet. But there is a storm moving towards us, and when the time comes for it to strike, it will not wait for you to unpack. You remember what you should about the jacket, I trust?"

Sonya nodded. The jacket looked like a parka with at

least 12 pockets. Each had a useful item stored in it: a jacknife for carving; a small hideskiver; a large hideskiver; a slingshot; a wrap to protect from the cold or sandbursts of the desert, that could also be used as a tiny tent; a piece of flint for lighting fires; twine for making a bow; arrowheads; a throwing knife.

More like a superhero's utility belt than a jacket, she thought.

As she pulled it out of her pack she turned to make some searing, sarcastic remark. But she screamed instead, pointing towards Sayeeda.

In one cat-like maneuver, Sayeeda sprang forward and spun around to face the danger behind her — the long hunting knife unsheathed. There, perched on the rock just above where she'd sat, a large snake turned its head from side to side; its tongue darting in and out. Sonya's heart skipped a beat.

"Cowis," she said.

"Silence," Cowis sounded angry.

"Why? Snakes can't hear," she said.

"Oh? Since when?"

"Since forever. Everybody knows that. They only feel vibrations and . . . "

"Silence, Sonya! They not only hear, they comprehend your words."

His eyes were on the snake; Mishwan and Bilzite circled around Sayeeda who held her hideskiver loosely in her hand, ready for the throw.

Suddenly the snake heaved itself at Sayeeda and she let loose the hideskiver at precisely the same moment — or so it seemed to Sonya. The hideskiver caught the snake in the middle and passed through, leaving two lifeless pieces, each almost four feet long. Cowis spoke first.

"We will eat as quickly as we can and leave this place."

Sonya couldn't control herself any longer.

"But they don't even have ears!"

Cowis shot her a stern look, and Mishwan brought

the head of the snake to her.

"Get it away from me!"

"Do you not want to see its ears?" Mishwan's poorly controlled grin stretched widely across his face.

"I'll take your word for it."

Mishwan didn't move, and no one tried to make him. After some delay, Sonya looked at the small slits on the sides of the dead snake's head. She realized, suddenly, how far from home she'd really come.

She looked at Cowis, but he was busy exchanging worried looks with Sayeeda.

Mishwan threw the carcass as far as he could. Sonya calmed herself and got her wits together.

"Well, if they can hear and understand, why did Zorena speak so openly in the garden?"

They all laughed then, Bilzite's voice ringing loud and echoing about them. Cowis answered.

"No snake that values its life would go within a thousand feet of the wall of Anatawen." He paused to chuckle, "Zorena would feel its presence and crush it before it could slither one length of its own body."

Sonya also smiled. It figured. Why did she constantly ask such foolish questions?

The afternoon's ride bounced and jostled them at least as much as the morning's while it took them up the mountain's twisted side.

Sonya looked about her nervously. Snakes with ears? Zorena could *feel* them? The meaning of these things slowly came to her. Sometimes she just wished that she had a less adventurous spirit.

Mishwan rode behind her now and embarked on an uninterrupted, mostly one-sided conversation. Sonya nodded, and only occasionally asked a question.

Mishwan's father, Margon, was a miner in charge of one of the mines in the hills to the north of the city. Mishwan proved to be a poor heir to his father's trade. He preferred the sun and open fields, choosing to run off during the midday meal and not return until the next morning. It took some time for Margon to realize that Mishwan would never make full miner's status. He sent his son to the city to study under Kurtch, the builderkhan.

Mishwan didn't particularly like any kind of work or study, but the art of building appealed to him much more than digging holes in the ground.

Sonya listened patiently, grateful for the excuse to keep her foolish tongue still.

He told her of the things he did to disrupt boring afternoons and lend a spirit of adventure to his sorely incurious life. He told her how he had climbed the bell tower, engaged in one of these schemes, the night of the attack.

While the tower guard chased his friends (a carefully planned diversion) Mishwan climbed the tower — aiming to cut the bell line and then re-tie it, rendering it inoperable. Then the evening hour would never strike, and time would stand still — in a way.

It was a popular fantasy among Anatawen's youth — to silence the great bell at the Hour.

But the task posed a mighty challenge. The tower was never without guard — the bell's prime purpose was to warn of impending danger or attack. And it served as a timepiece.

Moments before the sun inched above the horizon it rang. It rang once to signal midday, and again when dusk turned into night.

Mishwan's planning had started early. He waited for Tresham to be on duty. He knew there would be a better chance for success with Tresham guarding. Poor old Tresham got more ill-tempered by the day; it would be easy to annoy him enough so that he would leave the tower.

He did, cursing and shaking a fist, threatening to draw his sword as he dragged himself after the children.

So Mishwan found himself perched on top of the bell with his knife out and a rope slung around his shoulder. He looked up, paused to admire the sun on the mountains, and thought for a moment that he saw an unnatural reflection. He watched for a few seconds to be certain — there *was* moving metal out there, hiding in the shadow of the mountains, waiting for night to fall.

Terror seized him and he flew off the bell, grasping the rope with a painful grip. As he slid and bounced, the clanging of the bell drowned out all of his senses.

The whole tower shook. Mishwan's heart no longer felt a part of him, but something clinging to his chest, alive and moving wildly of its own volition. But still, he had to open his eyes and look out.

It seemed as though he could see straight to the base of the mountains. It seemed that someone watched with him. But when he looked, old Tresham hadn't even made it to the door. Mishwan held on as long as he could and then slipped to the floor, sucking at his raw hands.

"When I left the tower, old Tresham was waiting to grab me. At first I was afraid everyone would see *me* leaving and think I had contrived some game. But somehow, the city believed the bell. Someone from the wall must have also seen them, and tey, too, must have blown a charge horn." Mishwan paused.

"I still feel frightened when I think of that strange feeling about me when I first rang the bell." He shook his head and spoke softly, as though Sonya weren't even there.

"Almost like someone else was right there and forcing me to hold on just a little longer, and then a little longer still; seeing through my eyes — even more clearly than I could see. I do not understand it . . . so real. I have never experienced such a sensation."

He turned toward Sonya, puzzled, looking for some sign of understanding, hoping for an explanation. Sonya could offer neither.

Z Z Z Z Z

The storm hit before dusk and they rode for more than an hour before finding a shallow cave to settle in.

Sonya didn't trust the place. The smell of wet leather

filled it too quickly. Noise bounced off its walls and fell dead in the middle. It was a dull, dreary place that stifled the breath.

They ate another meal of gren, a tough biscuit strong with the taste of cold egg. Sonya got sick of it the first time she tasted it. They couldn't even chance a fire for zukha.

"Who invented this stuff, anyway? And why? It'd make a great crash diet — you can't swallow it; it just sticks right here." She pressed her finger against the base of her throat and swallowed hard.

Cowis sighed impatiently.

"We do not need a detailed description of the undesirable traits of gren — we are all aware of its imperfections and do not wish to be reminded of them overmuch."

Overmuch? Sonya bit back a laugh.

"Well, what about the other stuff we brought? The salted meat and dried fruit? We didn't lug it all the way up here for nothing, did we?"

"First, let me point out that *you* did not *lug* anything up here. The animals did. Second, trust me, please — we will have greater need of the other food later. But now, be grateful for the gren. It provides strength beyond the promise of its appearance — or taste."

Sayeeda elbowed Sonya and laughed, "Eat the gren now, Sonya, and when we finally do taste the meat and fruit, it will seem a feast beyond the reaches of your remembrances."

Bilzite nodded his agreement with a grunt as he popped another biscuit into his mouth. Mishwan already slept soundly at the far end of the cave. The others got ready to do the same.

Sonya wrapped a blanket around her and sat at the cave opening. She had the first watch, but hesitated to call it that. She couldn't see past the dirt swirling in front of the entrance, and the wind's howling filled her ears. She spent the time squinting to see, not breathing to hear; and thinking to figure out if she shivered from cold, fear, or both.

Sayeeda relieved her, and Sonya slowly faded off to sleep. But her dreams were plagued by visions of short Mountain Dwellers, snakes with ears, and other animals swarming over them, smothering them.

She woke with a start and held her breath for a second. Nothing happened; all was quiet. She looked up and saw Bilzite sitting at the cave entrance, silent and still.

The storm had loosed the worst of its fury — only occasional, quick gusts of wind persisted. Sonya listened to the wind's dying song, a faint reminder of its former power, and a sad imitation of the storm's angry moment.

She thought about her task — to find the Mountain Dwellers who did *not* have the Image of Corandu (as if the others would show it to her) and give them the Medallion. How could she know which was which? She couldn't just walk up to them and ask, "Hey, are you the bad guys who have the Image, or the good guys who don't?"

She smiled despite herself. It promised to be an interesting trip even if she failed. Failed? Failure hadn't occurred to her as a possibility. Even though she'd never really thought about succeeding, either. What exactly would happen to her if she did fail? She looked around her. Thank God Cowis was there, she knew she could depend on him in any case.

Slowly, sleep managed to overcome her until Bilzite woke them at dawn — his voice booming painfully through her head.

They ate under a clear sky, to the chirping tune of some busy birds rushing about the mountainside. They were birch-tree white with a deep brown strip that zigzagged from the tip of one wing, across the back, to the tip of the other wing. Sonya had never seen any before.

"What are they called, Cowis? They're kind of pretty."

"They are called whides, and they are only found in the mountains, though they are a small bird."

"But they are a sturdy bird," continued Sayeeda, "capable of long, hard flights. Though they are small, they manage well in the cold winds of the mountains." She paused for a moment and smiled a distant smile.

"They are good friends where friends are few."

Sonya watched the birds play with their flying skills — swooping and diving from one tiny vale to the next. She stood on the ridge until they flew out of sight, and she could see Anatawen's towers in the distance.

Straight up from the plain they sprang, specks of security just beyond reach, and almost home. She thought then to ask Cowis where they'd found her but didn't want him to think she'd rush to the spot and wait for fate to take her back. Maybe she would.

Mishwan rode to her side and followed her gaze.

"You do not wish to return so soon, do you, Sonya? The journey has only just begun."

Sonya turned and shook her head. "Just checking out those little whides. They're having such a good time playing with the air currents. I think I'm jealous."

"They look as though it is their only purpose in life."

"Sometimes I wish it were mine, too, Mish."

"I understand, but it is not possible for either of us." He paused for only a moment. "The path is wider now, will you mind if I ride by your side?"

"Sure you can, Mish, you don't have to ask permission for something like that."

Sonya felt some surprise at his request, but didn't think too much about it until they stopped for the midday meal.

It seemed to her that she was the only one who ever talked to Mishwan. Sayeeda always acted amiably, but preoccupied with her task. Cowis had made no secret of his dislike, so while he did his best to be courteous, he didn't go out of his way to be friendly. Bilzite chose to ignore the boy completely, though Sonya did feel a tenseness surrounding them whenever they were together. Bilzite never quite forgave Mishwan for the total disruption of his classroom.

While Cowis and Sayeeda drew maps in the dirt and planned strategy, Bilzite trudged ahead to investigate.

Sonya watched Mishwan as they fed and watered the horses. He had to be the most *alive* person she'd ever met. Something about him — the way he giggled with his whole body — was reassuringly childlike, mischievous. He was just plain cute.

"Has Bilzite been giving you a hard time, Mishwan?"

"No, not really."

His face didn't reflect the meaning of his words. He pulled up hard on the cinch and seemed not to pay attention anymore.

Sonya kept quiet. Why should she pressure him? He'd talk if he felt like it. She leaned against a rock and drank her zukha. Mishwan tried to explain.

"He is not directly hostile. Perhaps that would be easier to address. He is subtle and says only what he absolutely must. You see, he has no humor."

Mishwan tried a smile and shrugged. "He . . . he . . . is just an impossible man. I am still unable to understand why I was chosen as part of this group."

"Zorena wanted you," Sonya blurted out before thinking.

Mishwan's face changed; his eyes opened wide and he talked excitedly.

"I thought, or hoped, that was the reason. Cowis has not liked me since I spoiled his joke on Surriya by letting the skunk loose in the main hall . . ."

"A skunk? You let a skunk go in the main hall? Was it filled with people?"

Mishwan continued, ignoring her questions. "Bilzite never wanted me along and Sayeeda never even knew me, so it could not have been her idea. I thought it might have been Zorena, or Tagor. But I could not be sure. I did not know she knew my name. Did she mention me first?"

Sonya laughed and nodded. "Yup. And she said some pretty good things about you, too."

"She did? Truly? And I thought she did not know my name."

"She knows more than you think, Mishwan. More

than anyone thinks."

He didn't hear her mumblings, but drew himself up proudly and grinned a foolish grin.

"Then I will *not* care what they think. If Zorena wants me here, I belong here!"

He strutted about so arrogantly that Sonya had to laugh. She started to apologize, but he showed no sign of hurt feelings — he seemed to have taken his own advice. When he stopped parading around, Sonya asked a question.

"What's the falling star?"

"You mean, I think, the Fallen Star."

"I guess. But if it's fallen, how can you be born under it?" asked Sonya.

"I do not know, unless, of course, it has not fallen to the very bottom."

"Bottom of what?"

Mishwan smiled a sneaky smile and shrugged, shaking his head.

"Well, it doesn't make any sense," insisted Sonya. "If it fell it isn't there any more and that's that."

"Yet the fact remains that there is a Time of the Fallen Star, and some are, therefore, born Beneath it."

"Well, I wouldn't say it's a fact. That makes it a little too definite. But," she spoke almost to herself now, "to be Born Beneath the Fallen Star. It's a real braintwister, that's for sure."

"You have an interesting way with language, Sonya. Have you ever considered becoming a Tunesmith?"

Sonya laughed and shook her head.

"In any case," he continued, "the legends surrounding the Fallen Star are few and vague, though I tend to think there are those who know more than they tell. I have spent much time trying to learn more about it because I was Born Beneath the Fallen Star. Is this why Zorena wanted me in the group?"

"Well, I guess that could be part of the reason. But I don't know."

Sonya somehow felt she shouldn't elaborate. But Mishwan didn't seem too anxious to know more anyway. He was wrapped up in his own thoughts about the Fallen Star.

"The Fallen Star," he explained it as though reciting a lesson he wasn't really sure of, "bestows some kind of power on those born at the proper time. Everyone born at the Time of the Fallen Star has the potential to hold this power — though what the power actually is has never been explained to me.

"Those born Beneath the Fallen Star are said to undoubtedly have the power — not just the potential for power. I do not even know how it is determined if one is Born Beneath the Star. It is the exact time of birth, I think, that makes the difference, though who decides when that is right, I also do not know.

"Anyone born during a certain time span is born at the Time of the Fallen Star, though what that interval is, and how often it arrives is also vague. Some people say every 25 years. Others say every 125 years. Some just say nothing. My own father does not know. An old man told him I was Born Beneath the Fallen Star. My father says he cannot even remember the man's name. He appeared a few days after my birth and left a short while later.

"I suspect the Ruling Family could say more. There must be some record from the old times. But I cannot read; and so I must rely upon others to find the answer. I will try, someday, to ask the Ruling Family — but I have not yet been able to devise a proper approach to the subject.

"The only belief that everyone agrees upon is that there is *something* special about those born at the Time of the Star's influence."

"So what is a true Starborn?" asked Sonya.

"I do not know. Unless it is one who is surely Born Beneath the Fallen Star — without a doubt a bearer of the power. But I do not know how anyone could know that." He paused a moment. "I seem, vaguely, to recall hearing this word somewhere. I cannot remember where, or when.

Why do you ask?" He looked at Sonya with a puzzled, almost suspicious expression.

"Oh, I just wondered," Sonya hardly believed herself. "I guess I heard it somewhere. And I assumed it had something to do with the Fallen Star thing."

Sonya suddenly felt very uncomfortable with the whole conversation and wished she hadn't started it.

"Look! Bilzite's back. Let's go hear what he has to say."

Mishwan grinned and shook his head as he turned back toward the horses. Sonya didn't try to change his mind.

Bilzite's account only confirmed their fears. Mountain Dwellers had traveled nearby within the last two days.

"Possibly yesterday," Bilzite shook his head. "I had no idea they came this low. I fear they could not have stayed there without discovering us."

They packed their gear quickly. Mishwan's eyes lit up with excitement. Sonya's stomach jumped and turned so much it could've qualified for a gymnastics team; she felt nauseated.

Sayeeda took the lead. Cowis, Sonya, Mishwan and Bilzite followed.

Sonya couldn't remember exactly how it happened. They had been riding long enough for her stomach to calm down a little, but not long enough to stop her from snapping toward every noise off the path. She poked her ears and shook her head, then heard a shout.

Bilzite fought with two Mountain Dwellers and a third moved in quickly. Sonya and Mishwan turned together to help him, but Sayeeda called for order.

"No! Two in front, two behind. Sonya, stay in the middle."

Sonya rushed to Bilzite, not comprehending Sayeeda's words. She pulled one of the Mountain Dwellers away from Bilzite, who kicked another as he ran. Sonya got a good hold on hers, but before she could do anything else, a painful blow from behind knocked her unconscious.

In the White Mountains of New Hampshire, June, 2001
Copyright 2003 Beth David

Chapter Seven

New Friends . . .And the Face of the Enemy

Sonya struggled to get up, but a firm hand on the forehead held her in place.

"Don't move. You got a nasty knock on the head. If you do manage to get up, you'll probably just fall down again, anyway. Keep your eyes closed, too, it'll make the headache seem less painful."

Sonya stopped struggling and tried to relax. He sounded nice enough, and she liked his advice. But what about the others?

"What the hell are you doing up here, anyway?"

Sonya's eyes popped open. *Hell? Hell? It must be him.* She reached for the Medallion. It was safe. She sighed. Her head pounded sharply, and she could barely make out a figure past the spots and blotches. She closed her eyes halfway, but her vision blurred; she closed them the rest of the way, moaning.

What could she do? How should she react? She fought to stop trembling — glad she could be silent. Should she explain about herself? Or let him think she was Anatawen? Her choice of words must be very careful in that case. She felt relieved that she wouldn't have to think about it yet. He told her to sleep, and she did.

An empty room and the sweet smell of rushes greeted her when she woke. She looked around carefully, her eyes slowly adjusting to the dim light from the torch. The room was so small that the tiny cot reached from end to end. A table and two chairs filled the rest of the space — except for a small spot near the door.

She looked for a window, but if there were any, they were covered. She thought she must be in a cave, but couldn't be sure. Large tapestries covered all the walls. She studied them closely — no mountain scenes and no landscapes, all seascapes. Somehow it seemed strange to her.

One of the tapestries stretched several feet along the whole length of the back wall. A great white whale heaved its bulk through the foam, leaving three small boats rocking in its wake. A tiny figure reached out — strapped to the whale's back by countless strands of harpoon rope.

Sonya stood for a long moment, studying this amateur rendition of Moby Dick and the obsession of Captain Ahab. She wondered how long it took him to complete it.

"You like that one, eh?"

Sonya started at the sound of his voice but quickly composed herself.

"It's a whale. That one's a legend where I come from." He giggled at his joke.

Sonya did her best to act like Anatawen royalty; she turned towards him, but only halfway.

"We, too, remember the sea. Where are my

companions?"

He shrugged and sat in the chair by the wall, munching an apple. He threw one to her and Sonya caught it absently, determined not to be caught off-guard.

"My name's Bobby, by the way."

He bit largely into the fruit, and Sonya bit back a smile.

How fitting! It would've been one of her guesses for sure — such a popular Anglo name. He was young 20's, blond hair, delicate features, short, and not handsome, but boyishly cute. He eyed her with the same scrutiny.

Sonya acquired her sternest, coolest manner.

"You have not yet informed me of my companions' whereabouts!"

She threw the apple back at him and held her breath.

Did she lay it on too thick? Overdoing it could be just as bad as not doing it at all. She began to feel suffocated, trapped, and nervous. She needed to get out of there but fought back the panic growing within her. She wanted to run, but held her ground.

"Oh, stow the bull! You've been . . . shall we say . . . out of it for a whole day, and I heard all of your 'thank gods' and other earthly phrases. You," and he pointed with the fruit hand, "and I," he thumped his chest, "are practically related. We're the closest thing to family we've got out here, or up here, or wherever — like long lost cousins. We should stick together."

He paused for a moment and watched her; Sonya didn't move. Now he leaned forward in the chair and spoke in a low voice.

"With the stuff we know, we could literally change this world. They'd think we're magicians or something. We . . . why we could take over the whole damned planet — just like in the *Wizard of Oz:* declared instant heroes!" He waited for her to say something.

She looked at him in disgust. "More like *A Connecticut Yankee in King Arthur's Court.* What are you? Some kind of nut?"

He laughed. "Oh, don't be so serious. We can have a great time while we're at it. We'll make them do all the actual dirty work."

He waited for her answer. Sonya could hardly believe what she'd heard.

"You're nothing but a little kid with a big imagination." Sonya's temper woke fully now. "How can you talk about that like it's some fairy tale? And what exactly do you mean by 'dirty work?' Killing. That's what you mean. Real things, not games. People's lives are at stake. We have no right to interfere."

"Bullshit! We're here and that gives us the right — no, the duty — to help these people benefit from our superior knowledge and experience."

Sonya's mind raced; he could do so much damage, even alone. She became frightened for Anatawen, but kept her mouth shut.

"I mean, look, even the simplest trick — the Trojan Horse. Now, admit it, if you hadn't been there it would've worked," he paused and laughed, "something so simple. The oldest trick in the book. It'll be s-o-o-o easy.

"And the hang glider — hell, they think I'm some kind of magician already. Between the two of us, we could own this place. What do you think?"

He looked on eagerly, and Sonya wondered if it would be better to humor him. She frowned with the thought, and he grinned with a nod; he thought his offer very tempting. But before Sonya could think of an answer, Bobby reached into his pocket, pulled out a chain and held up the Medallion of Corandu in all its splendor.

"What're you doing with this? It looks like it's worth some bucks. When I got here I didn't even have my damned clothes."

A gasp escaped from Sonya's throat before she knew it. He must have seen her reach for the Medallion the first time she woke up; then he must have taken it after she fell asleep again. A wave of anger and fear spurred every ounce of energy she had and aimed it all at Bobby — in the form of a perfect flying sidekick. Bobby and the chair cracked against the wall and fell to the floor. He didn't get up.

Sonya picked up the Medallion and slipped the chain over her head. She pushed back the heavy curtain and peered into the darkness; her heart beat wildly against the Medallion.

A light glowed in the distance and she made for it, scaring herself with her own breath. She listened carefully at each opening along the way. It was quiet, but the silence offered its own kind of fear. She hurried on, longing for a moment to rest.

A quick scuffle from ahead drove her into an opening on the right. She crawled behind a bundle of clothes and waited, keeping her white clothes out of sight. With one eye on the opening, she fished through the pile until she found a dark cloak to wrap around her.

She waited until the silence returned and looked out into darkness. Surely she'd be able to spot those white faces. She drew the hood low over her face and started for the light again. Maybe she'd learn something, anything to help her find the others. And if not? She pushed the thought away; first things first — she had to figure out where she was before she could decide where to go.

Suddenly, voices echoed all around her. She ducked into the darkest corner and waited. A light flickered, casting a shadow that monsterized the man who held the torch. Still, when he appeared before her, greatly diminished in size, Sonya's heart continued to pound out her fear. She held her breath.

A second man followed closely, struggling with a stumbling figure and complaining about it.

"Why do I have to take her to the *back* caves?"

"Because Bobby said to. He wants to talk to her. He said she knows something he wants to know."

Sonya saw her first glimmer of hope; could it be Sayeeda? She caught a glimpse of the face and sighed in disappointment. Both men stopped and looked in her direction. She'd really have to control that.

Before she could decide what to do, the woman broke free. To Sonya's surprise, she didn't run, but pulled a large knife from one of her captors and turned to fight them.

The men turned from Sonya and faced their attacker. The man with the torch pulled his knife and laughed viciously as he spoke.

"You rotten little slime, how dare you?"

He took a slow step toward her, crouched and ready to spring — the torch level with the woman's face. Sonya sprang from her hiding place and kicked him squarely in the back, driving him into the wall with a crack. The woman jumped to the side and deftly sliced the other's throat.

Sonya's throat tightened; her whole body shuddered. A firm hand on the arm pulled her away and she followed — desperately trying not to regurgitate. The whoosh of that slice and the bubbling sound that followed echoed in her brain. Tears burned in her eyes when she reached sunlight.

The woman made her sit in a hole in the rock; that was the only way Sonya could describe the place. She had just enough room to lie down, and that's all she could think about at the time. Her head spun and the rest of her body cried out for sleep.

She vaguely remembered the woman saying her name was . . . what was it? Waylik? She also said she'd be back. Sonya remembered no more.

Z Z Z Z Z

A strong, sweet fragrance abruptly roused Sonya and sent a wholesomeness flowing through her. She woke fully and sat upright.

Waylik laughed, "How do you feel?"

Sonya had been quite prepared to say 'lousy' but she found, upon taking inventory, that she felt good. Her head no longer ached, nor did she feel dizzy; her stomach had settled, and her bruises only hurt when she touched them.

"Much better!"

Waylik raised a brow at Sonya's surprised tone.

"My name is Sonya. Thank you for dragging me out of there." She stood for a second without moving. Shouldn't she bow or something?

Waylik placed her right hand on Sonya's shoulder and squeezed gently.

"It is I who should thank you, Sonya."

Sonya only nodded and smiled.

"What's that smell?"

Waylik held out a handful of tiny, rice-like, blue seeds. Sonya took one and studied it.

"What are they? I've never seen any like these before."

"I never learned their proper name, if, indeed, they have one," answered Waylik. "I have found patches of them — places." She swung her arm to encompass the entire mountain range and the plain below.

Sonya wondered what business Waylik had down there.

"I only discovered them a few summers ago. I have never smelled anything as refreshing — not too sweet, simply . . . rejuvenating." She took a deep breath and let it out all at once.

"I was first drawn to them by their color. Quite unnatural, I thought, but obviously growing. I ignored them for a long time — not knowing of their merits. But I found them everywhere I went. They seem to have been planted by someone. But that could be my imagination."

"Why?"

"Why someone would plant them is obvious," she breathed deeply. "Why I may be imagining?" She paused for a moment and frowned.

"They seem only to grow where there is good shelter, or potentially good shelter. Or," and she smiled slightly, "maybe I decide to camp wherever they are near. It is difficult to decide. In any case, they are a useful seed and have extraordinary healing powers. I simply call them blueseed.

"At the start I did not trust them, until Pingor ate one.

He is much too smart to eat anything that would harm him." A barely perceptible wince hardened her face.

"Well, he was much too smart. Those snakes killed him."

She paused for a moment and Sonya tried to mumble something suitable. But what was a Pingor? Some sort of pet seemed likely. But, how could she be sure?

Waylik interrupted her thoughts. "Which leads me to our problem. We must not stay here any longer. They will undoubtedly search this area soon. Can you walk?"

Sonya nodded and stood up. Her eyes unfocused and she felt a little off balance at first, but she tried not to show it, and the spell passed quickly. Waylik handed Sonya a Mountain Dweller knife to clip on her belt beneath the cloak. Sonya accepted it gratefully.

"I have a stout horse not far from here," said Waylik. "She will bear us both, and we can get away from this place."

Waylik turned to lead the way, but Sonya did not follow.

"I can't go with you."

Waylik whirled around — her face a mixture of doubt and contempt. How could she have been so easily fooled? She drew her knife.

Sonya spoke quickly. "They've got my friends somewhere, and I can't just leave them." Sonya paused, trying to read Waylik's face. Would she believe it? And if she didn't?

"Did you hear anything that might help?"

Sonya's question went unanswered. Waylik's expression became thoughtful. She studied Sonya, who met her gaze steadily, too tired to be suspicious or frightened. Waylik put her knife away and looked about her, measuring the sun and weather.

"How many?"

"Four," answered Sonya.

Waylik became suspicious and confused. Five Anatawens in the mountains? But surely a stranger story wrapped itself around this Sonya. She almost seemed familiar somehow.

"You are not Anatawen?"

"No," Sonya felt no desire to explain further. "Why?"

"Because you would be dead. Your friends are Anatawen?"

"Yes." She wondered if she should explain Sayeeda. No, best to tie her tongue, and fast!

"They have either escaped or they have been questioned and killed."

Sonya's heart sank at the sound of Waylik's words: her tone held no room for doubt. Sonya's very spirit seemed wrapped up in the small hope that Waylik's words made whither and fade away. If ever she really felt like giving up, it would be now. But where would she go?

She looked at Waylik with pleading eyes, hoping for something to hope for. Waylik did her best to sound confident.

"Can you take me to the place where they captured you?"

"No. I was unconscious when they brought me here. Bobby said it's been at least a day." Sonya thought about the Medallion but struck back the urge to feel for it.

"Describe the place to me."

Sonya almost laughed. Waylik explained.

"I know these mountains better than most people know their own homes. Describe the place to me, it is at least worth trying."

Sonya did her best, but she couldn't remember much and to her all rocks looked alike, anyway. Her description just wasn't good enough for Waylik to picture, and the scant hope died quickly.

"I've still got to try, Waylik." Sonya's heart didn't feel the confidence her voice declaimed, but she picked up her failing spirit and resolved to find out what happened to her companions.

Waylik nodded, as if answering a silent question.

"There is one other possibility. I trust your guide knows the mountains well?"

Sonya nodded.

"Then we will go to a place I know. It is the most probable spot for them to rest and decide where to go next — and to plan your rescue." Her tone held little hope for the last part of her statement.

Sonya nodded, too tired to defend or deny. Why should they come back? How could they know she was alive?

She trudged on, scrambling over rocks and through crevices, blindly following Waylik's footsteps. Along the way, Waylik dropped blueseed behind them.

"Isn't that like putting out a welcome mat?"

Waylik laughed. "You have a strange way with our language, Sonya. Have you ever considered becoming a Tunesmith?"

Sonya smiled and shook her head.

"To answer your question — no," continued Waylik. "The fragrance is very mild unless the seeds are opened or heated. It will be just enough to confuse the tracking beasts. Do not fear, Sonya."

Somehow, Sonya didn't fear; she followed without a worry. Why did she trust Waylik so readily? How could she so quickly assume she'd be safe with a woman who'd just slit someone's throat?

Sonya's own actions flashed before her like a movie, completely taking over her thoughts. She might have killed that man with her kick. How could she have done that? What made her do it, anyway — jump out of hiding like a fool? Again, the noises from the cave echoed through her mind in a jumble of confusion. The eerie laugh. The whoosh of the knife. The loud crack of a skull against the stony wall.

The reality of it struck her — the possibility suddenly became a strong likelihood. Her whole body winced. Her knees collapsed and she fell, sliding down the hill in a panic. Her stomach tightened into a solid knot while wild images of death and murder raged through her mind. Water squeezed against the back of her eyes and a cry escaped from her throat.

She concentrated on control — to breathe steadily — to see the things around her. *No time for hysteria. No time for hysteria.* Over and over the phrase repeated itself. She slammed her eyes shut and clenched her teeth with such a vengeance the force of it hurt her ears. Her breath stopped, and she pounded her head with her fists to push out the pain. But nothing helped.

She felt Waylik knock her to her back and force loose her breath by pushing on her stomach. She lay for a moment to take a few breaths.

She decided then that she could have an emotional breakdown later if she wanted; but only when they reached safe quarters. Now, they had to keep moving.

She gave Waylik a grateful look but found no words. Waylik helped Sonya to her feet.

"All you need is some good food and a little rest. We are not far now. I will call Longhair." She made a bird-like noise and they waited.

In just a few minutes, a large chestnut mare trotted in from the south. She stood nearly 17 hands high, her thick neck supporting a slender face. The color of her coat was the deepest, brownest red that Sonya had ever seen; and it shone from pure strength. The muscles in her wide chest bulged and shone in the sunshine as she stomped the ground and tossed her head — excited to see Waylik.

Waylik's face lit up as though she'd found a long lost friend. She slipped a handful of blueseed to the horse and jumped on her back easily. Sonya climbed up behind her and they started for the dell.

They had a long hour of steady riding before they stopped to dismount. Sonya wondered how Waylik kept track of all her little landmarks — there seemed to be no change in the mountains in any direction but up.

What's she doing up here, anyway, thought Sonya, *wandering around these mountains for so long she knows them as well as her own back yard?*

Sonya wondered. But she kept her wonderings to

herself.

They left Longhair in the brush and moved on; nothing to hide them except the shadows of the stunted trees and rocks.

They came to a grassy meadow surrounded by thick firs and tall birch trees. The peaks rose up sharply on all sides and gave Sonya an eerie feeling. She spun around more than once, listening, looking behind her, searching for watchful eyes.

The dell looked like a disk of earth and green that had plummeted from the sky only to get stuck midway through the gap of these slowly tapering mountains. It sat well above the plain, yet well below the peaks — protected by them, hidden by them — its ring of green further guarding it and sending out a welcome, an invitation to explore this cozy, overgrown outpost where tired travelers could rest and warm themselves before the steep, cold climb.

Sonya's muscles creaked from weariness.

Waylik pointed to the far corner of the meadow and motioned for silence. Sonya followed carefully, without a word. They circled the entire field once, Waylik's face in frowned concentration as she studied everything around her. Then they traveled back a short way to Waylik's special place in the woods. Here, the trees grew apart just enough to let a little sunshine warm the floor of pine needles.

"Travelers camped here not long ago and made a good meal of something — smells like bushytail. I think they are not far away."

Sonya's heartbeat quickened, but she tried not to hope — Waylik said *travelers* had camped there; she didn't say who or how many.

Waylik told Sonya to stay hidden while she sneaked off to explore the area. Sonya stretched out, gladly taking advantage of the chance to rest.

At first she tried to listen, to be ready if Waylik needed her. But minutes after she lay down, her whole body turned limp. Sleep nagged at every muscle, and she slowly succumbed to it.

Sonya woke to a cool, crisp night. The stars shone clearly through a deep blue sky, the quarter-moon sharp against a cloudless backdrop. A tiny fire, well protected by a wall of rock, glowed softly beside her. Waylik sat at the edge of the flickering light, still and silent as though in thought so deep she'd never come out of it.

The sweet smell of tender meat filled the camp and Sonya's stomach churned hungrily. Waylik laughed at the sound and retrieved a generous pile of bite-sized morsels warming under the coals.

Sonya sat up and gratefully accepted the food Waylik offered. Her stomach quieted — full and satisfied — long before she stopped eating. She tried to remember her last meal, but the past few days only blurred into a confused mass of unconnected events. And concentrating hurt her head.

She moved closer to the fire, sipping a hot drink that tasted like tea. Slowly, steadily, Sonya's mind cleared and her head stopped its relentless pounding. She felt more like herself — but still not right. This Sonya lacked something, something vital to the old Sonya.

Sadness, depression, or plain old exhaustion had tarnished the very spirit that was her lifeblood. The stubbornness that always pushed her to the limit had been spent. The relentless naivete that always picked her up and gave her hope had seen enough. And the one-last-try-mentality that always saved her in the end, when everything else had failed, had been tried out. But worst of all, the instinct to find these things and bring them back to life had ebbed away.

She tried to think about the next step. But the strength to continue had been drawn from her, sucked out by one disaster after another, leaving her with neither the desire to go on, nor the energy to go back. She thought she might cry, but even that required strength that she didn't have.

She turned from the fire and faced Waylik who lay

propped against a rock, watching the moon.

"How long was I asleep this time?"

Waylik turned towards Sonya.

"Not long," she answered, "a few hours." Waylik moved closer to Sonya and sat up.

"I found signs that someone stayed in the dell for at least one night."

She paused and continued cautiously, "I fear there was only one."

Sonya listened to her words, and slowly absorbed their meaning. She kept surprisingly calm.

Waylik watched her, studying her reaction, trying to read her face.

"You think it was one of my friends, then?"

"I cannot guess who else it would be," answered Waylik.

But this time Sonya's heart didn't jump. Not the slightest ripple disturbed its slow, steady rhythm.

"The signs," continued Waylik, "are not at all like those of Mountains Dwellers. Therefore, it is most likely one of your companions."

Sonya noted with mild surprise the tone Waylik used when she said 'Mountain Dwellers.' It sounded much like 'they.' Wasn't Waylik a 'they?'

"Whoever it is may still be close by."

Somehow Sonya didn't believe that and was glad of it. She closed her eyes and lay back, thinking of nothing in particular, resting without care. Waylik watched her.

Obviously, Sonya needed some kind of incentive before they could go anywhere. She needed new hope, and Waylik had to find a way to give it to her. Or leave her. Sonya looked so depressed, she could barely move. Suppose she had to defend herself? She may not even bother.

Waylik decided to stay in the dell an extra day. She needed to convince Sonya to go with her, or back to Anatawen, but not back to the caves.

Sonya would not last a day in those caves. And her chances of finding anyone alive were practically nonexistent. Even the person who camped in the dell had left. If tey was smart, tey left the mountains completely.

"I suppose one of us has to stay awake and keep watch," Sonya didn't open her eyes when she spoke. "Since I just slept, I'll go first if you want."

"That will not be necessary," answered Waylik, glad that her safety did not depend on Sonya's vigilance. "I will wake at the first disturbing noise. A childhood malady — and the reason I have often been chosen for these . . . misadventures."

Sonya didn't answer. It meant she could sleep and that was the important thing. It didn't matter that she'd just had a long nap. Her mind was still tired. And when the mind is weary, the body will sleep.

The pre-dawn greyness greeted Sonya when she woke. The sun still hid behind the peaks, but its light crept slowly through the little dell. Some whides perched themselves in the trees above her and chirruped noisily. Sonya didn't notice them. She groaned and wiggled her toes. Her legs felt so weak they seemed not to belong to her.

Sonya leaned forward on her elbow as Waylik carried an armload of wood towards the sadly diminished fire. Suddenly she spun around, dropped the wood, and reached for her knife — but too late. A large mountain lion knocked her to the ground before she drew it. Sonya pulled her own knife and ran to Waylik. But the cat lay still.

Waylik crawled out from under it and pulled a throwing knife from its neck. A voice called from the trees.

"I often dreamed of making such an entrance, though I never believed it would happen."

Sonya raced towards the voice with a shout, her heart beating so wildly she could hear it. Mishwan jumped from the shadows and lifted Sonya right off her feet in his excitement. She thought his face would break from the largeness of his smile.

Sonya hugged him so hard her arms hurt. Every muscle in her body pulsed with a new energy, and she couldn't stop giggling. Even her stomach jumped up and down — but now she welcomed its familiar twists and turns.

Waylik approached slowly and bowed slightly when she spoke. "I am grateful for your timely arrival and quick action. May your weapons always be as well-guided."

Mishwan became serious and bowed in return. Sonya sighed.

"I am happy I could assist you," answered Mishwan. "May you never again be in need of such assistance."

Sonya and Mishwan sat by the fire while Waylik took care of skinning the mountain lion. Mishwan told his story slowly.

"After we beat off the first assault, we realized you were missing. Sayeeda told us to meet here if we lost each other while looking for you. For a whole day we searched. But even Sayeeda could find nothing to follow in those rocks," he shook his head and looked to the ground. "Now it is she who is lost."

Sonya watched him. His face went tight; and he frowned — much too serious for the Mishwan she knew.

She dared a question to break the silence.

"How did you get separated?"

Mishwan stared into the fire with unfocused eyes.

"I do not know what it was. We came to a large waterfall and searched for a rope bridge, or something to get across. We heard an incredible noise. It sounded like four bears at once and all around me. I rushed back and saw the most frightening creature I have ever seen in my life. It looked like a huge, mutilated plains cow on two legs, but three times as large. I think even Bilzite did not know its name."

He paused and shook his head as though trying to knock something off. Sonya had never seen anyone look so helpless. She wished she could do something — anything. But she didn't know what to say.

Mishwan threw his head up in a forceful demonstration of control.

"We prepared to fight it. But Sayeeda ordered us

back, saying that she knew its weakness and could succeed where we would fail. We stood behind her nonetheless. Cowis never left her side.

"Suddenly, she ran within its grasp with only her throwing knife drawn," Mishwan bit his lip and closed his eyes. "I was terrified beyond anything I have ever known before. My legs refused to move except to tremble. I tried to follow her, to help. I *did.*"

He didn't look at her as he spoke, as though she was not the one he tried to convince.

"The next thing I knew, Mountain Dwellers swarmed all around us. I tried to keep track of Sayeeda, to go to her. But soon all my attention went to my own defense.

"Then I heard a terrifying shriek. Even the Mountain Dwellers stopped for a moment. Sayeeda and the beast were gone."

He nearly whispered now, as though it didn't matter if anyone heard him. "I suppose they fell into the water. I do not know."

He stopped talking and Sonya remained silent. She almost wished he hadn't told her.

"I think I went insane with anger then," he looked at Sonya now. "Because I cannot remember much more. I swung that Mountain Dweller sword until I thought I would drop, and then I slashed some more. I fought the empty air for some time before realizing I was alone.

"I found Bilzite's body and buried him as best I could, though the grave could not be too deep among those endless rocks. He was a large man; and I had difficulty moving him far. But I managed it. And I covered him with rocks — calling upon my training with the Builderkhan to build a cairn that I hope will stand the test of weather and time, and protect his remains from the animals of the wild. The Mountain Dwellers I left for their own kin to attend to.

"I looked for the others everywhere. I ran along the waterway. But it was useless. I shudder to think of Sayeeda's fate if she fell into the swift current. Though it is probably a better fate than the creature would be.

"I made my way here two days ago, hoping to find someone waiting for me. When I did not see them I traveled back a short way hoping to find something.

"I feel restless in these mountains, Sonya. I feel I must keep moving or be trapped.

"No sign of them?"

"No, no sign," answered Sonya.

They sat in silence as the sun rose above the highest peak. Sonya stared at the fire thinking about all that had happened since she arrived in Anatawen.

Now what? She still didn't know where she was or where to go from there. Her guides had tragically disappeared, and she couldn't be sure about Waylik yet. How much could she be trusted? Neither of them had asked or answered many questions.

At least Mishwan was with her now. His timing couldn't have been better. Sonya felt a new vitality because of him. She felt she could go on now — though she didn't know where to go.

Waylik threw some wood on the fire and startled Sonya out of her trance.

"Now that's weird," Sonya told Waylik. "You're cold, and I'm not. If we're so high up, how come I'm not cold?"

"It is the cloak," answered Waylik. "You found it in the caves?"

Sonya nodded.

"It is made for traveling in these mountains — light and warm. You were fortunate to find one."

Sonya looked at the cloak. It didn't seem like anything special to her. But she felt perfectly comfortable where she sat while Waylik and Mishwan leaned close to the fire sipping hot tea.

When Waylik slipped off to find some herbs for the meal, Sonya told Mishwan her story quickly.

She held up the Medallion and examined it closely: her first chance to inspect it since taking it back from Bobby. It seemed the same as always. It looked as though it changed shape and size and hue, but it didn't feel any different.

Mishwan gasped. "I have never seen it so close. It is marvelous! See how it changes hue!"

Sonya smiled at his tone and watched the Medallion's magnificent display. Waylik's angry snort turned them both around.

"The Medallion of Corandu. How very fortunate — but not for you, I fear," Waylik shook her head in mock disappointment.

"How sad, Sonya, I was beginning to like you."

Mishwan drew his sword and jumped to Sonya's side. Sonya motioned for him to wait, and Waylik continued.

"You see, I have been trying to find the Medallion — to return it to its rightful owners," Waylik laughed. "I have been searching these ghastly holes for months, and you had it."

Sonya put a restraining hand on Mishwan's shoulder, but he had heard enough. He pulled away and attacked. Waylik relieved him of his sword with a single stroke and threw him to the ground.

Sonya screamed and threw herself on top of them both, holding back the knife that nearly cut Mishwan's throat. Sonya spoke quickly.

"Hold it, Waylik. You're jumping to the wrong conclusion here. We didn't take the Medallion. We're returning it," Sonya waited.

Waylik listened, holding the knife in place. Mishwan kept still, eyeing the sword just beyond his reach.

Sonya continued. "I'm supposed to be taking it to its rightful owners."

Sonya's breath came in spurts. She held onto Waylik's wrist with trembling hands.

What else could she say? Either Waylik believed it or she didn't. She *had* to believe it! Why couldn't Zorena have come up with something brilliant to say or do at times like these?

"Who sent you?"

"Zorena."

Waylik looked surprised. She tilted her head toward Sonya.

"Why?"

Sonya sighed. "She said it's time to give it back. That's all I know."

Waylik laughed and loosened her grip on the knife. Sonya let her go, and they stood facing each other. But Waylik smiled and shook her head with a why-didn't-I-think-of-it look on her face.

"So Anatawen had it all this time. It would be comical if not so dangerous. Zorena," she shook her head and laughed softly.

"She is wise; her timing sound. Perhaps her reputation is deserved," she paused a moment and handed Mishwan his sword.

Mishwan took it without speaking.

"And Sayeeda," asked Waylik, "she is the same whose father was Anatawen and whose mother was Mountain Dweller?"

Now Sonya was surprised. She nodded.

Waylik put her knife away and announced, "I believe you. You are both young and I think you could not easily deceive me."

She said it with such seriousness, such finality, that Sonya thought it might call for some official response or something.

"Come," said Waylik. "We will discuss our course."

She led them to the fire and sat. Mishwan eyed her suspiciously, but Sonya pulled him along, more than relieved to have Waylik as a guide . . . and a friend.

"Tell me," started Waylik, "why have you come to this part of the range? Does not the great Zorena know where to send you?"

Sonya hid her resentment at Waylik's tone, and thought for a moment. How could she tell her enough without telling her anything?

"All we know for sure is that there are two groups of

Mountain Dwellers. Which is which and where, I had to find out for myself."

Waylik's eyes twinkled, and the faintest hint of a smile grew on her face.

Sonya sipped her tea and ignored Waylik's stare. Should she tell Waylik about Bobby? Maybe she already knew? She obviously had guessed something. But what?

"Let me give you counsel," Waylik said. "You are fortunate that I am more understanding than most."

Sonya almost choked at Waylik's description of herself.

Waylik continued. "We are not Mountain Dwellers," she enunciated each syllable as though it had a sour taste. "We are the Zukulan. Refer to us as the Zukulan at all times if you value your lives."

Waylik turned her attention to her meal — bushytail and mountain lion. Sonya decided to stick with the bushytail. Mishwan sat across from Sonya, a blank expression hiding his thoughts. Sonya tried to understand what he felt, but too many other things occupied her mind.

"We will start as soon as we eat," Waylik said.

She looked around, measuring the sun.

"The weather should stay clear for at least two days, although these mountains can hardly be trusted at this time of year. By then, we will be close enough to good shelter.

"Our safest route will be to cross along the length of the range for a while. We can follow a fairly direct path that I know. It will bring us south, then we will climb and cross over the top to the other side, to my people."

Waylik looked to Sonya for approval and Sonya agreed, although she had only a vague understanding of what Waylik meant.

Mishwan said nothing and Sonya was glad. She thought she could guess his opinion.

They followed Waylik to the other side of the field, and she called Longhair.

"The three of us cannot ride her, and we will be taking a road she cannot. I will send her home."

Waylik rubbed the horse's ears and slapped her neck and rump in some predetermined signal. Longhair tossed her head and trotted off the way she had come.

"We must climb for awhile. The path we need passes straight above us. But be silent, and keep careful watch. We are clearly exposed to the heights until we reach the trail."

Sonya looked around nervously. She half-expected to see an army of Mountain Dwellers silhouetted on the peaks. But nothing moved at all; even the wind made no sound.

Sonya suddenly realized that since they left the dell, she hadn't seen or heard any animals at all — not even whides. But before she could mention it, Waylik stopped and stiffened. Sonya followed her gaze.

"What is it?" Mishwan stood behind them, shading his eyes from the midday sun.

"I do not know." Waylik sounded worried. "It seems very large, though far away. I think it is too large to be a bird."

Sonya squinted hard to find the tiny dot in the sky. It didn't look like anything to her, but she didn't need to see it to guess its origin.

"Is it coming this way?"

Waylik nodded as she watched it.

"We should hide," said Sonya. "Is there a place nearby, Waylik?"

Waylik turned slowly toward Sonya. "You know of this thing?"

"Well, I'm not sure. I can't really see it yet. But I think I do know what it is."

Sonya paused for a moment. Should she explain? No, they'd never believe it.

"We really should hide," was all she said.

Sonya fidgeted, but Waylik nodded and led them away quickly.

"I agree," said Waylik. "I saw one for the first time a few hours before I was caught. And they seemed to know right where to find me."

She led them to a shallow opening in the rock face.

An overhanging ledge hid them from above, and a careful peer from the proper angle commanded a good view of the bird-thing. Waylik took this place and Sonya explained in answer to Mishwan's expression.

"Although my eyes don't seem to measure up the way they should, I'm pretty sure there's a person up there."

Mishwan and Waylik both laughed.

"You said yourself it's too big to be a bird."

"A bird known to me," answered Waylik. "But there are many ancient beasts that may have survived unnoticed in these mountains. When I said I did not think it was a bird, I did not intend to imply that it was human," Waylik's tone insulted.

Even Mishwan bit back a smile. Sonya's irritation spoke for her.

"Listen, where I come from it is very common for people to use certain structures for flight. We have, in fact, the capabil-, oh forget it. The point is, it can be done. This bird-thing of yours is primitive, a toy compared to what we do. And," she turned angrily to Mishwan, "Bobby's from the same place — in case you've forgotten. As a matter of fact, I think he even told me about the damned thing."

She regained control and moved to Waylik's side.

"That, my friends, is a hang glider, controlled by a person who is hanging on for dear life. Even I can see that now."

They watched as it circled around the dell. It sailed above them, slowly losing altitude. Soon they all could clearly see the human figure clinging to it. Sonya couldn't get the smug grin off her face. Waylik spoke first.

"Can you build one of these?"

Sonya laughed. "A minute ago I was nuts. Now, can I build one?" She shook her head.

"No, I can't. But now that you believe me, I'm sure any skilled builder could. I know what it's supposed to look like and basically how it's supposed to work."

They waited in silence until the glider had been out of

sight for a long while. They said little as they climbed and reached the path quickly.

The Mountain Dwellers seldom used it, explained Waylik, because it did not give them direct access to the caves. It strayed along the upper part of the lower peaks; rocks gutted the whole trail and in some places the fir trees nearly blocked the way.

Sonya breathed in the sweet smell of pine. The crisp air felt clean in her lungs and almost made the steep ups and downs pleasant.

Sonya scrambled along, trying to keep her feet on the path, following Waylik's lead. It occurred to Sonya that liking Waylik, and wanting her to be a friend, did not justify trusting life and limb to her. Waylik could easily be leading them to their deaths. Then it occurred to Sonya that that had already occurred to her.

Her thoughts spun around in her head. She tried to untangle them, to think of reasons — logical reasons — for and against trusting her guide. If Sonya were dead, or alive, how would Waylik and her people benefit? How would they not? Again, Sonya took comfort in Mishwan's presence. Not for being the mischievous child of before — he no longer was — but for being someone she could trust, absolutely, without question.

Mt. Whitney, Sequoia National Park, California, 1991
Largest peak in U.S. outside Alaska. © 2003 Anthony David

Chapter Eight

Behold Zukulan In All Its Splendor

The trail took them on a winding course around the tree lined edges of the mountainside — the most concealing way.

Waylik led them cautiously, often climbing to a higher point to check their position.

On the second day out of the dell, a huge rockface crossed their path. A narrow ledge, hugging the bottom of this boulder, hung over a deep recess in the mountain's side — a fall would be long and final.

As though by verbal command, Sonya sprang forward and pulled Waylik so violently that they both fell backwards groaning. Waylik grinned sarcastically.

"I presume you have prepared an adequate explanation?" She lay without moving, waiting for an answer.

Sonya turned to Waylik with a dumbfounded stare. It

would have been comical if Sonya hadn't been so scared. She tried to smile; she felt foolish.

"I guess . . . I well, it must've been . . . I don't know! Maybe . . . I can't even guess!"

Waylik stood up and walked carefully to the ledge. Slowly, she studied the length of it while Sonya and Mishwan stayed back, watching and waiting. Waylik found a suitable rock and heaved it toward the ledge. It landed safely in the middle.

Waylik shook her head and gave Sonya a stern you're-a-bad-girl look. Sonya detected no real anger in that look, and she laughed as they went on. But Waylik stopped abruptly one step before the ledge and pointed. A long, narrow crack grew from where her test-rock had landed, traveled along the base of the boulder, and spread to the outer edge of the shelf. Sonya's eyes asked the question for her.

"Do not question good fortune," said Waylik. "It is a gift. Accept it."

Sonya and Mishwan stood facing each other, neither one satisfied with the answer. Sonya had known nothing about the weak ledge, so how did she know to stop them? She stared dumbly at the crack.

"Zorena sent you," said Waylik. "And yet you do not even know her. Can you truly be so ignorant of her Power?"

Sonya looked to Mishwan for help, but his expression matched hers.

Waylik shook her head. "She must indeed be worthy of her renown if she can persuade people to endanger their lives for her cause without even telling them all the details of their task — especially when they do not even guess the extent of her Power."

Sonya didn't like the sound of it. "What are you talking about?"

"There are many questions you could not answer," said Waylik. "Some you would not. You obviously do not know the capabilities of the person you serve — Zorena, the most powerful person on Loraden."

It took some time for the description to sink in. Sonya snapped her head towards Mishwan, then back to Waylik — as would a child who has just discovered a secret. Waylik laughed at Sonya. She closed her mouth.

Waylik led them back along the trail until she found a way up and around the rockface. They climbed in silence, too busy with their own thoughts to say anything.

What's to say, thought Sonya. She felt both amused and frightened at the thought of Zorena's intervention. A keen excitement swept through her until a dull fear grew from within.

What exactly happened back there? How did it happen? How . . . that damned word again. Sonya smiled as she remembered the twist in Zorena's grin when she'd said "It is a matter of birth."

Sonya should have been more suspicious about the things that happened in Anatawen — the way Sayeeda showed up at the meeting; what Zorena said about Mishwan "reaching" her from the bell tower.

But they were such little things. Sonya never would have thought they meant *power.* She automatically attributed them to some natural, explainable thing — even if she couldn't explain it. It simply was not in her nature to think of . . . Magic? Sorcery? Witchcraft? Whatever. The implications sent a bolt of fear right through her. But at the same time, she thanked Zorena.

They spent the night in the most protected place they could find: three pine trees growing a few feet apart for enough years to form a cozy little room.

A thick blanket of pine needles covered the ground and made a soft bed. Sonya leaned against a trunk and soaked in the warmth and fragrance. The wind pushed and pulled at the branches outside, but only thin wisps got through.

Sonya laughed. Not long ago it would have horrified her to even think of facing a storm in such a place — a couple of trees for protection! But now, she could think of no cozier little room anywhere.

She wrapped the cloak around her and closed her eyes. The thick branches muffled the wind's howl and even gave the thunder distance. She slipped off to sleep, undisturbed, until Waylik woke her.

Clouds still blocked the sun when they started next morning. The worst of the storm had moved on, but a drizzle soaked the air, and the wind blew with a biting cold that caught Sonya's breath; impossible weather for traveling — by her standards.

Waylik disagreed.

So they trudged along the trail as well as they could; Waylik leading and Sonya following, keeping the bent back just within sight of her half-closed lids. The wind whipped through the cloak, and Sonya cursed her "luck" at having found it. A cheap parka and ski hat would've served her better.

One day, quite suddenly, the foul weather ended and the bright sun strained to make up for the gloom of the past week. Sonya stopped in the mid morning brightness and looked up to see the clear, crisp blue of an autumn sky stark against the green of leaves not yet feeling fall's bite.

For six days they scrambled across the mountains. Every morning Sonya looked for their end, but her eye couldn't reach it.

Fir trees filled her sight — thousands and thousands of fir trees. Some stood only three feet high, their growth stunted by the altitude. Others climbed higher according to the twists and turns of the trail.

But everywhere smelled of pine. At first, Sonya gladly breathed in the aroma. Now it nauseated her. Every moment of every day filled her nostrils with the smell of evergreen trees. Her clothes and hair smelled like pine, even her food began to taste sappy. She wished for an end to them, even if they did give the best cover the mountains offered.

They had seen no Mountain Dwellers since the hang

glider incident, but Sonya watched and listened. She also hadn't seen anything to show that Mountain Dwellers were not there.

Still, it had to be a good sign when Waylik slowed their pace a little. Sonya tried not to think about it. She just continued to trust Waylik's instincts and turned her own thoughts towards bringing out the old Mishwan.

But he was lost in a fog of chronic introspection. He plodded along behind them, hearing little of their conversation and saying less.

On their seventh day out of the dell, Waylik changed direction. Instead of heading straight south across the side of the mountains, they turned west and climbed.

After an hour of merciless scrambling Sonya collapsed on top of a wide peak. But Mishwan slapped her shoulder and made her stand dangerously near the edge.

The sudden cold felt strange to Sonya. A cutting wind nearly knocked her down. She pulled herself up over the rock and jumped down beside Waylik. The tingling pain of a million little aches bunched up in Sonya's toes and traveled through her feet, up her legs. She stomped and shivered, trying to shake off the feeling. A thick wind blew hard and numbed her face. Snow swirled around her — real snow! She giggled and held out her hands to catch it.

An orange sun hung below eye level and the snow glistened from it, sending little sparks of light towards the sea.

And what a sea that stretched before them. The waves broke unevenly, spotting the distance with white foam — as the manes of Palominos pushed by the wind.

Near the shore the waves seethed and crashed against the rocks, spraying the mountains with salt. To the left the rocks gave way to a long, sandy beach. Sonya's eyes followed it as far as they could.

She forgot her fatigue in a moment. She wanted to rush down and hear the ocean's thunder, to feel the water's spray. She breathed in the salt air. Damn the winter! How she'd love to ride the waves and let a hot and humid sun dry her. Hot, sticky, uncomfortable, and familiar humidity — she promised never to complain about it again.

Waylik led them to the left and down, along a rocky path. They didn't get very far before an armed group stopped them. Waylik spoke quietly to the soldiers for a few moments, and they let Sonya and Mishwan pass with her.

As they moved away, Waylik whispered, "Remember, we are the Zukulan. Call us nothing else."

Sonya and Mishwan nodded and followed her silently to the City By The Sea — a series of houses, shacks and other strange structures set on slabs of stone that jutted out from the mountainside.

Sonya couldn't think of it as a city though. It seemed a dangerous place to live, especially for children. But Sonya saw no children. This was an extension of a larger city, an outpost to keep the wilderness away from Zukulan and its people.

They took horses there and rode leisurely to the city of the Zukulan. It lay about two miles south of the City By The Sea, and just below it.

A huge recess pocked the mountain here, and the houses of the city filled the little valley from end to end. A calm beach stretched along its length and beyond.

Waylik took them to a small, empty cottage at the near end of the city.

"Where's this?" asked Sonya

Waylik smiled a sly smile and answered. "This is my cottage. I live here alone — that is unusual in Zukulan. But I need a place away from the others, where I can slip out quietly." She paused and smiled. "I am becoming quite the loner."

They sipped some tea and Waylik asked the question Sonya had been waiting for.

"What is it you need first. We must see Arkola soon."

Sonya looked up hopefully, and Waylik waited.

"Can I wash my hair?" Sonya pulled at the straggly ends to emphasize the obvious necessity.

Waylik motioned for Sonya to follow and led her to a small room. Waylik heated water and filled a tub.

Sonya didn't think about time. She didn't think about the others having a turn. She just enjoyed the clean.

Her new clothes fit loosely and felt light and cool. Waylik gave Sonya a cloak and she wished for a full length mirror. The cloak's silvery off-white color lent sleekness to the garment and created a striking contrast to her black hair.

She smiled: a cloak? She always thought they were impractical; now she wished she could see how it looked.

They walked through the city, away from the beach, to a house that seemed to be carved out of the mountain itself. Higher than any other house it stood and looked out upon the city, the beach, and finally the sea. The thick walls seemed perfect for keeping the inside cool in summer; Sonya shuddered to think of it in the dead of winter.

The King of the Zukulan sat in a chair worthy of the word "throne." The backrest climbed ten feet up the wall behind him. The armrests spread to twelve inches wide, covered with detailed carvings of plants and animals. The finest velvet covered the seat and back.

Arkola's face did not reveal his age. His eyes shone dark and bright, sparkling and bursting with energy. Sonya had become accustomed to long, searching stares, but Arkola's eyes drove deeper than any of the others, steady and strong. His power was rooted in this ability to calmly look into people and yield the truth. After a few scant seconds, Sonya turned away.

Arkola smiled, motioned for them to sit, and they moved to a table laden with meats and zul.

Waylik recounted the stages of her journey with tedious detail. Sonya listened, surprised at her own interest; had she been in Anatawen, the report may have been the same. Except Anatawen had no reason to seek out the Mountain Dwellers that Waylik espied. She told of her capture and Sonya's timely arrival. She told of the hang glider incident.

"It seems that Sonya knows something about Bobby that we do not. We have not discussed it."

Arkola's gaze fell upon Sonya, waiting for reply. Sonya looked at him with innocent ignorance, determined to say nothing. Waylik laughed, and Arkola spoke.

"You will thank Zorena for saving the life of my best scout, please."

Scout? Or spy, thought Sonya. But she nodded and laughed quietly, grateful for the reprieve.

He questioned them but did not press for details. Sonya waited for him to demand the Medallion. He was, after all, the rightful owner, and there was little chance she could successfully refuse. And wasn't she sent to give it to him? Zorena should have told her *something* that would help her at this critical time.

After a few more questions, Arkola asked to see the Medallion. Sonya's nerves did the talking.

"How do I know for sure that you're the one I'm supposed to give it to?"

Before he could answer, Mishwan spoke. "He is the one, Sonya. Do not worry," he looked at the others. "Give her time, and she will see it for herself."

Sonya raised her brows in feigned indignation, but she said nothing.

"You can show me the Medallion when you are ready to give it to me and no sooner," said Arkola. "You still do not understand! Zorena will let you know. But she must wait, she has been busy in many places these past several days."

They left, Sonya trying to make sense of everything. She learned, among other things, that Waylik had been to the mountains many times looking for the Image of Corandu. No one had any reason to believe that the Medallion had been separated from it. Arkola had assumed that the Mountain Dweller Ruler did not know the secret of its use, and the Ruling Blood was too weak to overcome that lack of knowledge.

Now that he knew the Medallion and Image were not together, Arkola worried about the condition of the Image: did it lay forgotten in some dank place, slowly crumbling from neglect?

Without the Image to support it, the Medallion's power diminished greatly. But the Medallion could aid in finding the Image. How to use it posed another problem. Waylik was best suited for the task. But now that she had been caught, her future was uncertain.

They walked silently down the long hill in front of the house. When they reached the bottom, Sonya turned and looked back.

Arkola's house seemed to float in the sky. Set back inside the crook of the mountain, it sat high above the city, a guardian of the people. *Or maybe a watchdog,* thought Sonya.

Waylik brought them to the tavern for food and drink. There, Sonya tasted wine rivaling that of Anatawen. It surprised her how quickly she'd come to appreciate the taste of a good vintage.

She sipped the wine and ate the food Waylik brought — bite-sized chunks of tender meats, bread, butter and assorted fresh fruits and vegetables.

But the Zukulan specialty — smoked fish — stole the hour. Served in long strips of varying thicknesses, a delightful assortment of fish from the Zukulan Sea revealed an endless variety of tastes. Differing methods for smoking fish using just exactly the right herbs remained a favorite topic among the Zukulan. Sonya found herself eavesdropping on a heated discussion of the best technique for smoking large pieces without the edges going dry.

"You've got to use the fish's own oil," growled one burly man.

"Bah," snorted another. "You've got to use the flavored oil my old grandma makes, and you've got to wrap those fish."

"Wrap the fish? What are you, daft, man? You have to let the air at 'em. That's what makes them smoked!"

And so the conversation went back and forth.

All the while, Waylik and Mishwan gulped from huge mugs of beer while Sonya sipped at her wine.

All around them music and conversation filled the air — noise that reminded Sonya how much she missed the company of people engaged in superficial talk and meaningless fun-making. She felt refreshed by it.

Most of the songs had simple, sing-along tunes with words easy to learn. Many told well-known stories from Zukulan's past. Three Tunesmiths played a variety of instruments — flutes, guitars, banjo-like instruments, a zither, and even a harp.

Sonya had never heard a harp before. The harpist sat in a low chair, the top of the harp reaching past his shoulder. He stretched his arms far to pluck the strings, exaggerating their resonance with elaborate motions — much like a concertmaster absorbed in the music of the orchestra.

Most of the people in the tavern seemed to know each other. They moved about from table to table, talking and joking, or just singing confidently. Many came to Waylik to pry bits of information from her — they had not seen her in such a long while. Had she been away again? Where to this time? Did she go alone *again?* Or had she been in the City By The Sea?

Waylik skillfully deflected each comment and question. Sometimes, she simply ignored them altogether. Sonya watched her. How strange Waylik looked, sitting at a round, wooden table, holding a large mug of beer in one hand, leaning against the wall of a dimly lit, smoke-filled room crowded with the noise and movements of too many people.

Sonya suddenly saw the quaint, hand-hewn wood of these walls as confining, crowding. Waylik looked so out of place — as a caged bird trying not to jitter. Sonya remembered their guide — relaxed, controlled, confident when facing even the most vicious animal. Sonya moved to the seat next to Waylik.

"Are you ready to leave?" Sonya asked.

Waylik tried to smile, revealing a slight touch of embarrassment.

"Does it show so much?"

Sonya laughed and nodded. "I'll find Mishwan and tell him he can meet us at the house."

It took some time for Sonya to find Mishwan. He danced vigorously among a crowd of people, totally entranced with the woman showing him the steps. As Sonya told him, he only nodded, never taking his eyes off his teacher.

When Sonya returned to the table, Waylik stood waiting. She held a small barrel in one hand and a large wineskin in the other. Sonya smiled in appreciation.

"There is no reason to leave everything behind," said Waylik. "I am no tunesmith, but I am adequately entertaining with the lute."

They left the noisy tavern and walked into a quiet night. Infrequent lights scattered themselves through the eerie quiet of the city. Sonya's own steps echoed in her ears while Waylik's walk melted into the silence. Sonya watched her, and Waylik tried to explain.

"It has been three months or more since I have been in the city. On this last trip, I spoke to no person until they caught me, and then I met you. It is strange, but I feel . . ." she hesitated and Sonya said nothing.

"I feel afraid when many people are close around me. There is no escape, no fast exit. I feel trapped and must fight not to run. I am unaccustomed to running."

Sonya listened and watched the night. The stillness was so complete. How had she left the crowded crowds of the cities to find her way to this female mountain recluse?

Inside the cottage, a dwindling fire still burned and spread cozy warmth through the room. They settled in this front room and Sonya looked around, something she'd had little time for earlier.

On the walls hung fine tapestries of nature's best: blue and white mountains rising from green and yellow plains; seascapes that included rocky coasts, sandy beaches, and boats swaying in unsteady waters.

The smallest one impressed her the most. It was a seafarer's viewpoint of a raging coastline. Powerful waves crashed against the rocks, sending a spray of water high into the air to fall upon rocky hills. A lonely palomino stood still amidst the spray, silhouetted against the white peak behind him. Above, clouds formed odd configurations.

Sonya stared at this one for a long time, taking in every detail, seeing through the eyes of the horse, imagining the coolness of the water's spray, the sound of the tide.

Waylik picked at a lute as though practicing alone. Sonya settled into a large chair across from Waylik and broke her concentration.

"Waylik, how do you know Sayeeda?"

"We met in the mountains. A comical first meeting, and rather violent." She smiled and paused.

"We had both strayed into the same area while trying to evade the same watchful eyes. We almost banged into each other. Then we tried to kill each other. We were rudely interrupted by the Mountain Dwellers. We . . . united against them and became friends.

"I wondered often what became of her."

"So do I," said Sonya.

Waylik ignored the remark and started playing a bouncy, happy tune.

> A drinking song my heart desires,
> One to stoke and feed the fire
> That burns within my very brain,
> To heal my heart and ease my pain.
>
> More beer! More ale! More wine divine!
> To help me sing and dance so fine.
> Oh, praise the night and when I wake
> I'll curse the morning's sharp headache.
>
> But when the long day's work is through,
> And beer and ale are brewed anew,
> Happy then the hour indeed
> And the public house is filled in speed.

"That's just the kind of song I bet Sayeeda would love," said Sonya. Her thoughts strayed to Anatawen and the "how" question.

"Tell me something, Waylik," Sonya started slowly. "You called Zorena the most powerful person on Loraden. How would you know that? I mean, if the Zukulan and Anatawen have had no contact for generations."

Waylik rested her lute and drank from her beer mug. She eyed Sonya carefully for a few moments before answering.

"I have spent much time traveling the Vastness that we call Loraden. I have met and talked to many people, I have heard many conversations — some without permission of the speakers."

"Arkola also seemed to know more about the nature of the Ruling Family's power than I thought anyone knew. Can you explain that?"

Waylik grinned. "I can explain many things. However, I choose to keep much of this information to myself.

"Ancient lore states that the Rulers of Anatawen and Zukulan had a secret way of communicating and combining their powers. This is well known among the Zukulan.

"I will also add this. I knew from the start that you were not Anatawen, although I could not quite imagine what you were. Finally, I recalled another traveler. A man. I believe he was from the same place as you. We became friends, and I learned much from him. He came to us, not to Anatawen, in our hour of need. He helped us build boats that weather storms well; he taught us to build our houses high off the ground and even into the ocean. I believe he brought his knowledge from the place of your home."

Sonya sat quietly while Waylik played another tune — this one slow and melodic.

"Do you know why I'm able to understand your language? And what about time? If I ever do get back, will the same amount of time have passed?"

"I cannot believe that time is different in many places.

This other time theory has been explained to me many times. But it is beyond my capacity to understand. So I cannot answer that question.

"Language is different in your world. All of Loraden speaks the same tongue, although in different manners. It is probably why Sareema's people arrived here in the beginning. It is also a factor in your travel here. Zorena needed you. Zorena found you. Zorena brought you here through the Power in her from her birthright. It would do no good for you to end up where you understood no one and no one understood you.

"I do not understand the details of this travel. But your looks are Anatawen — your hair color, your skin tone. And so you land in Anatawen, or where they can find you. So do not worry that you may have fallen in with the rogues of this world. This would only happen if you are yourself a rogue. At least this is my understanding."

They drank and sang and talked until both their drink and their energy were spent.

Sonya collapsed on the bed, reveling in its softness. But she found she couldn't fall asleep for a long time. Almost, she wanted to move to the floor, but couldn't bear to do the injustice to her body — no matter how sleepless the night promised to be.

Mt. Denali, AKA Mt. McKinley, in Denali National Park, Alaska. Denali is the highest mountain in North America at 20,320 ft. Summer, 1982. © 2003 Anthony David

Chapter Nine

A Task Completed

Sonya woke at the first ray of light and cursed the bad habit. Mishwan slept soundly while Sonya and Waylik drank zukha and ate fresh fruit.

During breakfast, Sonya made the decision to give the Medallion to Arkola. She felt as though she'd known it all along. But until then she didn't feel right about it. She didn't understand why, but all at once she knew it was the right thing to do. And suddenly she couldn't wait to head back to Anatawen.

They woke Mishwan and the three of them went to Arkola. No one questioned Waylik when they arrived; she seemed always welcome at the Ruler's house. They waited only a few minutes before Arkola met them.

Sonya noted his informal dress: a simple, loosefitting smock of deep blue, and white trousers that had seen better days.

She laughed quietly. Arkola shed his royal awesomeness as casually as he changed clothes.

He led them to a small room at the back of the house. Here, very little natural light leaked through a high, small window. This part of the house dug itself into the hill, and this particular room was mostly underground. Tables of different sizes crowded every corner and were stacked with carefully transcribed documents bound by patient hands.

Sonya longed to examine such primitive bookbinding, but she confined herself to staring. Arkola motioned for them to sit at a less crowded table against the far wall.

Sonya's oratory for such occasions was, she knew, rusty. So she handed the Medallion to Arkola with few words.

Arkola grasped the chain between the fingers of his right hand and let the Medallion rest on his palm. His bright eyes opened wide and Sonya saw the flickering Medallion reflected in them. She smiled at his expression.

Arkola slipped the chain around his neck and hid the Medallion behind his smock.

"You, Sonya," he said with much authority, "will be remembered in the annals of our people. You will be remembered in our history as a friend. It is appropriate that we meet here, in the Record Room of the Kings. Here, the entire history of the Zukulan is stored."

He said other things that Sonya didn't care much about. The world of the Zukulan and Anatawen and Mountain Dwellers was not her world. Its magic seemed unreal even as she stood among the rocks of this otherworld. It didn't matter who remembered or forgot her. And the dingy, cave-like room made her nervous.

Now he told her that the Medallion must continue to be a secret, at least until the Image was found.

They left Arkola in his dark room of chronicles. Sonya sighed heavily as they stepped into the sunlight. The Medallion must remain a secret; her good deed sadly lacked ceremony and attention. Self-satisfaction would be her only reward. Who was it that said knowing within oneself was as good as telling? And what did they know? She turned her thoughts to those around her.

"You stayed out till a respectable hour last night, Mish. Have a good time?"

Mishwan grunted and shut his eyes as she slapped his back.

"So sorry!" she said too loudly. He frowned in pain.

"Yes. I did find unexpectedly delightful company," he answered. "The people of Zukulan have won my admiration and have charmed me with little effort.

"I trust the two of you enjoyed your quiet, uneventful evening?"

"Ah, yes, delightful," mocked Sonya. "Absolutely marvelous!"

Mishwan's tone suddenly took on a concerned note. "Does this mean we must leave? Now that we have accomplished our task?"

Waylik laughed, and Sonya welcomed back her old friend Mishwan.

"You will leave in a day or two," answered Waylik. "No sooner. First, Arkola must thank you in proper fashion and give you a proper farewell. Second, a storm is preparing its fury for Zukulan tonight or early tomorrow. You cannot, of course, travel in unfriendly weather." She smiled and continued walking down the hill.

Sonya shook her head and followed. She remembered much unfriendly weather during their trek through the mountains — it didn't stop Waylik then.

Mishwan excused himself abruptly and went off towards the city. Sonya headed for the beach, leaving Waylik free to go her own way. Sonya didn't ask where.

A special set of rules governed privacy here, and Sonya liked it. Respectable people didn't ask a lot of questions in idle conversation. If somebody wanted you to know something, tey told you; if not, tey said nothing. And that was enough. No one feared silence among friends.

Of course, some, like those at the tavern, were less discreet than others. But they were few, and it seemed more like a game — a game they didn't play very often. Sonya remembered the way they fumbled around inside their heads, trying to find the words to make Waylik tell them what they wanted to know.

In the past, Sonya would've found it difficult to trust someone who hid so much from her. But now, it seemed that these were the only logical people to trust, for they could understand the genuine, honest need to keep a secret safe.

She thought of Zorena and the secret of the Medallion kept for so many years.

She thought of Cowis, and a sharp sickness tore through her. Was he alive? And Sayeeda? Where could they be? She wished for a telephone, even an old fashioned telegraph system. Then she laughed — she didn't even know the Morse Code.

Walking along the beach, Sonya let the action of the waves fill her senses. She found herself climbing the rocks and sitting amidst the spray of an approaching tide. The sun hung close to the water. The air cooled. She left the beach at dusk.

Sonya started toward the pub for a glass of wine, but realized she had no money. She wondered if the Zukulan used money. She didn't even want to ask; suppose they'd never heard of it, and she became responsible for introducing such a thing?

The cottage's front room caught the last rays of sun, but Sonya sat on the porch with Waylik until the dark surrounded them.

Sonya learned that a form of currency did exist though barter was more widely accepted. She could've gone to the tavern and taken whatever she liked — on Waylik's name, or maybe for the price of a good story. Everyone knew her as the Anatawen Waylik had found.

Sonya didn't realize how famous she was.

Still, she felt restless and wanted to get back to

Anatawen, hoping against logic that the others would be there.

The next day they saw Arkola and spent a farewell feast with select members of his household. Sonya was introduced to everyone and thanked a hundred times. She didn't understand much of what anyone talked about, but Waylik provided endless stories about each person's background, fame and position. Sonya sat fascinated; these people could be out of Camelot, she mused. And their quest? She hoped it was a noble one.

The day after the storm, Arkola came to the cottage early. He made all the proper farewell speeches, and Sonya tried not to mumble her poorly thought out responses. Arkola gave Mishwan a scabbard and a sword to replace the one he'd acquired from the Mountain Dwellers.

Sonya received a well-honed throwing knife and scabbard.

Both gifts bore Arkola's mark — a clear sign for all of the Zukulan to treat their owners as trusted friends.

Waylik joined them for the first leg of their trip, and Sonya tried to convince her to go to Anatawen with them.

"C'mon, Waylik," argued Sonya. "You can use the vacation. And we wouldn't mind a guide. Would we, Mish?"

Mishwan stood without saying a word.

"You will manage without my help, I assure you," said Waylik. "Watch for the snakes, they are the most dangerous. And if Mishwan can wake himself up, you will have no problems with anything else."

Mishwan didn't acknowledge. Sonya rapped him on the shoulder, and he caught his balance just in time. He'd been oddly broody since they left Zukulan.

"What's the matter, Mish? Miss your little honey?"

He wrinkled his brow in exaggerated puzzlement.

"Y'know," persisted Sonya, "the sweetheart from the tavern."

He continued his puzzled expression, but Sonya waited.

"I prefer to call her my little Zukulan seaflower."

"Oh, Mishwan, that's much too corny."

They climbed to the top of the mountain near The City By The Sea and started down the other side. It was here that Waylik would leave them.

She advised them to travel well into the plain before heading north to Anatawen. They stood for a moment at the start of the next descent. Mishwan made all the proper farewell responses. Then he moved a short way down the trail and waited. Sonya hung back and tried to find the proper way to say good-bye to her friend.

"I don't know if I'll ever see you again, Waylik. I'm not from a place that I can even explain to you." Sonya paused.

"You can always feel free to go anywhere in Anatawen, though. I'm sure Zorena will make it official — however that's done."

Waylik smiled, thanked Sonya, and quickly sent her on her way. Sonya turned and followed Mishwan.

Waylik watched them descend for awhile. Then the trees closed in around them and she could see them no more. She felt a strange aloneness that she didn't like. She turned and went back to her cottage.

Sonya caught up with Mishwan quickly, and they started down the path together. Mishwan broke the silence first.

"You had no right to extend the Right of Travel to her, Sonya." He sounded angry.

Sonya's reaction was fierce. "Why the hell not? They gave it to us!"

Mishwan stopped and turned to face her. "Because you do *not* have the *power,* therefore, you have no right."

"Y'know, Mishwan, I could belt you sometimes. I realize that you're caught in the throes of love, but that doesn't mean you have to hate the rest of the world!"

Mishwan's anger peaked quickly and dissipated into slumped shoulders. He sat and looked up at her.

"You are right. But so am I."

Sonya calmed herself and sat by him.

"It just kind of came to me to say that stuff. It seemed right at the time. Besides, you're just mad because she almost killed you once."

"Well," said Mishwan, "I think that *that* is a very good reason to dislike someone!" He looked at her, surprised, but no longer angry.

Sonya realized what she'd said and stopped smiling.

She remembered the caves, her first sight of Waylik, but pushed it out of her mind before reaching the fight. Mishwan watched her silently as she frowned, shook her head. Suddenly, she stood up and started down the trail. She walked fast and hard, shutting her eyes to keep out the images. Mishwan followed and said nothing for a long time.

They saw no signs of anything except bushytails and foxes. They took turns hunting for food and Sonya was impressed with her new-found skills. But she was tired of bushytail. She couldn't wait to get back to Anatawen for Homak's Delight. And the snakes worried her more than they should have. She worried more when she didn't see any than when she did.

They steered by the sun and could see the outlying towers by midday on their fifth day out. Sonya stared at them — tiny specks never seemed so real to her before.

She and Mishwan walked steadily, but slowly. They knew that someone would come to meet them on the plain. Tagor and Barska met them with fresh mounts long before the outer defenses. Sonya hugged Tagor until he actually laughed. She laughed, too, remembering their first meeting. Barska kissed her till she blushed.

They went directly to Zorena's rooms where Zorena and Anatawen's best wine awaited. Zorena greeted them warmly and Sonya felt part of a real homecoming. She tasted the wine and savored every drop.

The five of them sat for a few painful, quiet moments. Sonya refused to ask the question. Wouldn't they ask her something? Wouldn't they tell her something?

Tagor and Barska thought of some excuse to take

Mishwan away and leave Sonya with Zorena.

Tagor and his sister exchanged knowing looks, and Sonya refilled her glass shakily. She knew the answer, but still had to steel herself to ask the question.

"They're not here, are they?"

Zorena shook her head and poured herself some wine. Sonya stood and walked to the window briskly. She took a deep breath and cursed the heat.

"Tell me everything that happened," Zorena said.

Sonya sat, feeling defeated, guilty, and too tired to tell a story. But she recounted the tale from the beginning.

Zorena nodded at certain points in the report and Sonya asked how she knew about the ledge. Zorena grinned cunningly and shook her head.

"I do not answer 'how' questions," was all she said.

Sonya nodded without being amused; instead, she tried not to be angry. What happened was no one's fault. It just seemed so easy to blame Zorena for things that happened in this crazy world.

Sonya went to the garden and watched the sun set. Cowis was right. She didn't remember a single sunset from the mountains. She curled up on the mat and slept till past dawn.

Upper Turkey Pond in Dartmouth, Mass., 1975. © 2003 Beth David

Chapter Ten

Found . . . But Still Lost

Sunshine filled Sonya's eyes when she woke. She rolled over with a sigh, but felt refreshed, and happy that she could lie still for a minute. Slowly, she allowed her body to wake instead of jumping up and charging off to some unknown danger.

She walked around the early morning garden searching for breakfast. But except for a few rotten leftovers, the trees had emptied themselves for what little winter Anatawen would get. Sonya took her growling stomach to the kitchen, and Surriya cooked up a king's feast — eggs, cakes, meats, zul and zukha.

Sonya sent a servant to find Mishwan and took a fresh cup of zukha to the fireplace in the main hall. A small fire crackled, sending a dim light through the empty room. Sonya sat on the floor, where she and Cowis often sat, and watched the flames. She sipped her zukha quietly.

Mishwan arrived — one eye closed, the other one squinting as though he'd been roused out of a sound sleep. But Sonya only laughed. She knew he was as anxious to see her as she was to see him. He grabbed a cup of zukha and joined her by the hearth.

"Did you get anything out of the guys," asked Sonya. "Zorena pumped me for information all afternoon, and she didn't tell me anything."

Mishwan shook his head. "They don't *know* anything. But they think Sayeeda and Cowis are alive."

"Why do they think they're alive," asked Sonya. "Or . . . *how* can they guess? What is it with that damned word?"

Sonya refrained from pounding the floor. She needed a less painful way to vent her frustration. And since Mishwan knew as little as she, their talk had too many ifs and maybes. Sonya couldn't stand it. She knew that Zorena had more to tell, but what would make her tell it? Sonya left Mishwan abruptly, determined to stop playing this game and demand that Zorena tell her everything.

Sonya knocked at Zorena's door and waited. She listened, barely breathing, but couldn't hear a thing. Slowly she lifted the latch and quietly opened the door. She stood in the doorway for a few moments before looking around. She knew she shouldn't be there, but it just seemed like the only thing to do under the circumstances.

She checked each room, but didn't find Zorena. Sonya laughed. She should know better — as if Zorena would let her snoop around like that. So Sonya went to Homak's rooms, determined not to give up so easily. He'd be able to tell her what she wanted to know.

Homak answered the door but slipped out and quietly led Sonya back along the hallway. He sent someone for zukha and they settled comfortably in Zorena's room by the big window.

"Ask what you so desperately need to ask, Sonya."

"Where's Zorena?"

"She is in my rooms and cannot be disturbed."

"And why can she not be disturbed?" Sonya didn't hide the bite in her voice.

Homak sighed and nodded. Then he smiled and looked at Sonya.

"She is Removed," was all he said.

Sonya waited for further explanation. Homak couldn't possibly expect her to understand what he said. She tried to be patient, not to shift around in her seat. Homak smiled again.

"You have wondered, I know, how Zorena saved you at the ledge," he told her. "You have made many comments expressing your surprise at several incidents you cannot explain." He paused for a moment.

Sonya's expression promised her undivided attention, and Homak continued.

"The members of the Ruling Family have a special ability passed only to heirs. We can extend ... our minds, reach into the minds of others." He stopped, waited for a response. But Sonya held fast to her silent listening.

"When Zorena called Sayeeda to the conference," he explained, "she used a light mind touch to suggest Sayeeda come to us. Sayeeda is attuned to these suggestions and so responded immediately. This is a simple, non-taxing thing to do.

"When Zorena Reached you at the ledge, it was very different. She had been Removed for nearly two hours before she found you." He shook his head slightly.

"It is dangerous to be Removed for such a long while. And she sapped nearly all of my strength as well as her own. I am older than you may believe, Sonya."

Sonya listened carefully and quietly to let his words sink in.

"Let me explain this carefully, from the beginning. As the first born of a Ruler, I was born with the largest amount of Power — compared to my brothers and sisters. This Birth Power will stay with me until I die. Then it will pass to my first born, along with any other Power I may have. As I grew, I received more Power from my mother, the Ruler. And I developed what Power I had — Power that grew with me, and with every discovery I made.

"As Ruler, I am able to give my Power to my successor gradually, rather than waiting until my death. A sudden surge of inherited Power can be very unsettling. And so I have chosen to give Zorena my Power piece by piece over the years.

"Zorena, of course, was born with a healthy amount of her own Power. And she has developed it as well as I could hope. She is, I believe, the most powerful person on Loraden."

Sonya smiled at the familiar description and wondered how this news had reached the Zukulan.

"But you didn't give her your Birth Power?" she asked. "That's different?"

"Yes," he said. "This I cannot control. When I die, my Birth Power will go where it should, not sooner and to no one else.

"We all have the Power, but it lessens with each child, and lessens further with their children. Yet we can combine our efforts and share the larger Power of two or three persons. This is an awesome possibility. It is why Tagor insisted that we all agree so wholeheartedly to your journey. A weak link can be very dangerous when you depend upon it.

"Zorena's responsibility was to keep her mind with you, I with Bilzite, Barska with Mishwan, and Tagor, of course, with Sayeeda. We depended upon Cowis to Reach us if needed. When you were separated, Zorena's and my responsibility included both you and Cowis.

"We should not Reach such long distances more than a few times a day, for a few short minutes. Zorena has been overburdened." He paused and smiled slightly.

"I have good reason to be happy you are safe."

Sonya smiled nervously. *Nothing like a lopsided compliment to lift your spirits.*

She drank her zukha in silence, happy for Homak's

cooperative manner, but uneasy with this information.

"Can you read my mind?" she asked.

Homak chuckled softly. "No. And yes. It is very difficult to know another's thoughts. Especially if tey does not want us to. Most people react suspiciously; one reason for keeping our Power a mystery. But reading is an inaccurate description. It is more like focusing on a place or a thing."

Homak left her sipping zukha and watching the birds from the window. Sonya tried to think about all he said. But none of it seemed real to her and she couldn't get past the words. So she got Appy from the stables and spent the afternoon riding.

She and Appy explored the area by the pond and the patch of woods before the ravine. Soon, she found herself straying towards the hills east of the city.

Bushes and trees, rocks and hills, spread themselves over a wide area. Sonya found a comfortable spot in the shade and leaned back against a tree to face the peaks.

Was Waylik up there? She wondered. Was Cowis up there? She had been so sure she'd find him here. Mishwan told her there'd been no ceremony for anyone's death. Did that mean Zorena *knew* they were alive? Or was she still not sure? Certainly by now she would've found one of them? And with Barska to help her, since Mishwan was also safe, she must know *something*? And if Cowis could also Reach out, it would be much easier, wouldn't it? But he could be hurt, she knew.

The sky slowly turned pink, and Sonya rose with a sigh. If she went straight to the garden, she could catch the sunset in its full glory. She rode slowly, thinking of a chilled glass of wine but thought she'd eat first since breakfast was her last meal.

She decided to find Mishwan and see if he'd join her at the public house. She longed to hear the noise of the pub and the sounds of good old fashioned merrymaking.

Sonya left Appy by the gate and walked into the garden. There, Mishwan greeted her with a big smile.

"I thought you would return for the sunset," he said. "I, too, missed its many colors while we were away. Are you hungry?" He pointed to the shade of the grapevine and Sonya sat down gratefully.

A feast covered the small table: meats and steaming breads, pastries, zukha, a carafe of Anatawen's best wine, and a cold pitcher of beer. They ate leisurely, enjoying each other's company and their free time.

The sun set as brilliantly and as mysteriously as ever. Sonya watched it quietly, spending the time as though it had been set aside from the rest of her life for that purpose alone. The sky became dark but studded with bright stars . . . diamonds in the sky, reflecting white light. Soon the air cooled and Sonya felt new energy.

She returned Appy to his stall and followed Mishwan to a pub in the city. Here, she laughed, joked, made up stories, and drank too much wine. Mishwan taught her an old folk dance that she couldn't get right; she sang, though she didn't know any words, and she made quite the fool of herself. It was the most fun she'd had in Anatawen.

The next morning, Sonya woke with a start and jumped out of bed. Her head hurt from too much wine the night before, but she ignored the pain and dressed quickly. The knock on Zorena's door went unanswered. Sonya waited a moment then slipped in quietly.

The room was dark, except for a small fire. Zorena sat at the table, staring straight ahead, and didn't move at all — even when Sonya sat next to her.

Sonya didn't dare move; she barely even breathed. Zorena's face was drawn and she looked tired. Somehow, Sonya knew it wouldn't be very long, so she waited.

Slowly, Zorena turned, and then suddenly came out of her trance. She gasped to control her breath and her whole body trembled with the effort. Sonya poured zukha for them, but Zorena grabbed a wine goblet and drank fully. She rested her head in her hands — not, it seemed, out of distress, but simply out of exhaustion, as though her neck tired of the weight.

Sonya watched quietly, not knowing what to say. Zorena picked up her head and smiled weakly.

"Have I been Removed for long?" she asked. "Sometimes it is difficult to know time."

"I don't know. I woke up only a few minutes ago."

Zorena nodded slowly but said nothing. She fiddled with a blue medallion she wore and sipped at her wine.

If it had been anyone else, Sonya would've sworn Zorena fought back tears. But Zorena? Cry!? The thought frightened Sonya, but she had to admit that even Zorena must have a breaking point.

"What did you see, Zorena?"

Zorena's eyes met Sonya's, but didn't answer the question for her. The deep, probing gaze was gone. The eyes were just looking. Sonya knew it had something to do with her. Why else would Zorena study her so? Why else would she even be there?

Zorena poured more wine, and Sonya shuddered to see the glass shake in Zorena's trembling hands. Zorena walked to the window and spread wide the drapes. The full morning sun burst through the room.

"It was Cowis," said Zorena.

Sonya couldn't begin to identify the onrush of emotions she felt.

"He's alive?"

Zorena nodded.

"And you knew? You knew the whole time?" She turned to face Zorena who stood above her facing the window.

The light of day behind magnified Zorena's presence. But anger surged through Sonya with every breath.

"Well, where the hell is he?" she demanded.

Zorena shook her head. "In a very dark place." She went to the table and sat.

Sonya watched in disbelief. How could anyone be so unfair? After all she'd done to help, didn't she deserve honesty at the very least?

"You knew and you didn't tell me!"

Sonya went to Zorena, grabbed her by the shoulders and pulled her around so violently that the chair moved with her. Zorena's face showed only weariness. At first, Sonya wanted to curse Zorena with whatever horrible names came to mind. But words could not express her rage. Sonya lifted her hand to strike, but pulled back in shame and confusion. She smashed her fist on the mantel, whirled around, and shouted.

"Why didn't you tell me? Who do you think you are? Damn it! And damn you! I want to know why you didn't tell me. I demand to know!"

Zorena's eyes flashed at the commanding tone. But her bearing remained unchanged. She simply didn't have the energy to act otherwise.

"I could not tell you, Sonya. You will realize that yourself if you think for a moment."

"But I left him there," Sonya waved vaguely at the window, her voice cracking faintly.

"I would've stayed if I knew. I could've gone back and found him." Her voice cracked again, and she inhaled deeply, refusing to cry. She straightened and leaned against the stone of the fireplace.

Zorena stood slowly, wearily, one hand on the back of the chair.

"That is precisely why I could not tell you. You had the Medallion, not he."

Sonya rested her head on the mantel. No, she wouldn't cry, she was much too angry. Zorena placed a hand on Sonya's shoulder but she pushed it away and ran out the door.

Zorena went to her bed and sat. She tried to Suggest to Sonya that she see Homak, but she was too far away. Zorena couldn't even Reach Homak. She put it out of her mind and slept.

Sonya went to the outer defenses to find Barska. Maybe he would tell her something, anything. But she couldn't find him anywhere, and Tagor had left instructions not to be disturbed. She rode back to the city and burst in on Homak. He smiled as she entered.

"You look angry, Sonya. Sit down and tell me why."

"As if you didn't know. You knew Cowis was alive. I want all the details. Why wasn't I told? Where is he? And has anyone gone to help him?"

She stopped for a moment, then added. "Please answer, Homak. I'm about ready to smack Zorena upside the head."

Homak shook his head and smiled. "Well, that would not be good, would it? Sit, Sonya, relax. I will answer your questions . . . over breakfast."

He was so slow about it, Sonya wanted to scream. But she knew he did it to teach her patience . . . so she tried to learn the lesson. He'd tell her when he wanted to . . . not a moment sooner. So Sonya sat in the chair and tried not to fidget.

"Zorena only found Cowis this morning. We knew he was alive because his Birth Power did not pass to me. We have not found the others.

"When I say found, I do not mean that we actually know where they are, physically. Cowis must have been unconscious; we cannot Reach anyone who is in that condition. He woke this morning. You were alerted by accident. Zorena and I found him together. He cried out with all of his Power for you when we connected. That is why you woke. Neither Zorena nor I expected that or we could have blocked it. He over-exerted himself in his weak state. Zorena passed much of her energy to him to save his life," he paused. "She went too far, again." He sighed angrily. "She is still young . . . and impulsive at times."

Sonya choked on her zukha. *Zorena, impulsive?*

He smiled. "Do not be hard on her, Sonya. She has her reasons for doing everything she does, and everything she does not. And do not try to see her for a few hours. She *must* sleep and regain some of her strength. Meet us here, tonight, after the evening meal."

Sonya got up to leave; she wanted to run, scream, anything to release her anger and frustration. Every muscle strained with tightened, controlled energy. As she reached the door, he called to her.

"Sonya, when you talk to Mishwan, be sure you go to a safe place."

Sonya nodded and left to find Mishwan. She spent the afternoon with him, but alone in her thoughts.

It embarrassed her when the full extent of the Ruling Family's Power became clear to her. *And I tried to teach them concentration?*

Mishwan agreed that they should go to find Cowis and Sayeeda. They never considered consulting Zorena or Homak. Sonya knew Zorena would never allow it. Mishwan promised to be ready first thing in the morning. Sonya tried to convince him to go with her to Homak's rooms as well.

"I was not extended the invitation," he said. "If you could arrange for me to be a spider in the corner — this would be a different story."

Sonya shook her head and dragged him to dinner in the hall. Afterwards, she climbed the stairs slowly, wondering what she'd say, and how she wouldn't say it. She heard voices before she knocked on the door and couldn't help but listen. Homak was speaking.

"It was foolish, you could have killed yourself."

"My life was not in danger," answered Zorena. "You were there to sustain me."

She paused for a moment, then called out, "Sonya, come in." She said it in a lighthearted voice, and Sonya walked in wearing a stupid grin.

"Hi, all . . . sorry about the eavesdropping . . . but — ah, well, I was afraid you'd change the subject."

Zorena laughed. "You are correct," she said. "Eezdropping?"

Sonya wanted to explain, but knew it wouldn't make sense. She faced the two silently. She'd never felt so nervous before. She remembered the exhaustion she saw on Zorena that morning. She looked fully recovered now, her old intimidating self again.

Sonya remembered their conversation. She wished she could do something, say something. She stared at Zorena, and worked herself into a fury in less than thirty seconds. But she couldn't say anything! Not because Homak had asked her to be kind, but just because Zorena was . . . Zorena.

Damn, thought Sonya. She knew she was right. But she couldn't bring herself to do anything about it. She couldn't tell who stopped her — Zorena or herself. She tried not to care, and found herself staring out the window. When she turned around, Homak was gone. Zorena held out a glass of wine, and Sonya took it without a word.

"How long do you intend to stay angry?" Zorena asked, her manner cautious, not the haughtiness Sonya expected.

But Sonya had, by now, gotten herself fully incensed. She tried to act cool and uncaring.

"It doesn't matter, Zorena. I don't plan on imposing on your hospitality much longer."

Now Zorena took a turn at anger — as Sonya had expected but could not possibly have been prepared for. Zorena held herself solidly, imposingly, where she stood, and Sonya couldn't look her in the eye.

"Do not be a fool, Sonya. You have no idea what you are up against. You will not go home now, I know that. But if you expect to go to the mountains to find Cowis, you would be wise to go back where you came from."

Zorena's eyes opened wide now and her expression betrayed both rage and derision.

"Do you truly believe that *you* are capable of conquering the forces that Cowis could not? You are an able person, Sonya, but such self-flattery will only get you killed! One journey does not make you a seasoned adventurer. I will not let you leave Anatawen until you have recovered what little sense you once had."

Sonya watched, frightened, and angry. She listened

and felt her body begin to tremble from her effort to keep still. Zorena stopped talking, and in the moment of silence that followed, Sonya shook off her trembling fright and fully loosed her anger. She hurled the wine glass into the wall and shouted.

"You go straight to hell, you bitch! I'll leave Anatawen if and when I damn well feel like it. I've had enough of Anatawen royalty and the wicked old witch of the Great Plain. I'm sick of playing your mystery games. How dared you not tell me about Cowis? How dare you try to stop me from finding him? If I don't find him I'll gladly die trying — knowing I *tried* to do something to help him."

Sonya started for the door, but Zorena grabbed her arm. Sonya steeled herself.

"Get your hand off me, now." Sonya spoke softly but sternly.

Zorena shook her head. "Sit down, Sonya. You cannot go storming out of the room every time you get angry."

"I fail to see the logic in that. The best time to leave a place is when you don't want to stay. And I do *not* want to be here."

She pulled to get free, but Zorena's grip held fast until Sonya knew she couldn't get loose. Zorena let her go then, and Sonya charged out the door.

Z Z Z Z Z

Mishwan caught up to her in the Main Hall. He took long, fast strides to keep up as she pounded out each step and burst forcefully through the door. They rode out to the woods past the pond. Mishwan followed silently while Sonya's voice echoed in the Anatawen night. She paced between the trees and pounded them with her fists.

"She," and she pointed, "got mad at *me!* At me! I should've smacked her upside the head the minute I found out — and I'd have been right to do it. But I didn't. I stayed calm and cool. And what do I get?" She threw up her arms, pointed, paced, and muttered.

Mishwan watched until it seemed that she would make him angry at someone. He tried to calm her.

"Sonya, you are letting your temper rule your mind. We are not in the mountains now, with our enemies, the Mountain Dwellers. Things are different in Anatawen — you cannot go around punching people every time they say or do something you dislike — especially people like Zorena. You are lucky she has not done anything to you up till now. So ease your temper. Tell me what happened," he paused. "Then I'll tell you what you did wrong."

Sonya whirled, and Mishwan jumped up.

"See? Look at what you are doing! You want to attack me for saying something that should make you laugh. It is not Zorena, Sonya, it is you. Now sit. Try to relax for one minute."

He pulled her by the arm and forced her to sit on a stump. Sonya gritted her teeth.

"If there's one thing I hate when I'm upset, it's people telling me not to be upset." She knew he was right but struggled not to admit it.

"Because if I'm upset, I have the right to be, and, therefore, should have the full benefit of uncontrolled rage and tears, or whatever else I feel is necessary."

Mishwan shook his head and waited. Sonya sat on her stump and kept her mouth shut. He had to be right. And she knew it. It wasn't being wrong that upset her as much as Zorena being right — again.

Sonya sighed and relaxed herself muscle by muscle until she calmed down enough to tell the story.

"Do not worry," said Mishwan. "I will not leave without you."

Sonya's anger flared up once more. "You bet you won't," she said. "We're leaving in the morning. She will *not* stop me."

Mishwan laughed mirthlessly. "Maybe not," he said. "But she could. And I tend to believe she will. At least until you stop acting like a lunatic."

Sonya ignored him, and they rode back to the city.

"You just meet me a little after dawn," she told him.

Mishwan agreed and left her to get ready for the journey. Sonya slept well for the first time in more days than she could remember.

The first light of dawn woke Sonya; she dressed and slipped out the door soundlessly. But Barska stood in the hallway waiting for her.

"Zorena would like to see you," he said.

Sonya kept walking and didn't look at him when she answered.

"Well, you can tell Zorena to stuff it," she said. "Because I have something better to do."

Barska's eyes darted through the hallway and he laughed. "Do not be hostile, Sonya. You may not be unhappy with what she will say."

"Oh, really?" Sonya stopped to face him. "I can't imagine she has anything to say that I want to hear. But if she does, why does the all-powerful Zorena not come here to tell me?"

"Because her rooms are more comfortable than yours and she is spoiled." It was Zorena's voice that came from behind; Sonya turned as slowly as she could. Zorena smiled warmly.

"Come, Sonya. I will only delay you for a short while."

Sonya followed her suspiciously. She walked through the door and found Mishwan sitting at the table.

"Thanks a lot, fink. What did you tell her?"

Mishwan turned to Zorena with a helpless, I-told-you-so expression. Zorena took Sonya by the shoulders and gently guided her to the chair. Sonya sat and poured herself some zukha.

"I'm going, Zorena. Don't even try to stop me."

"I understand, Sonya. I will not try to stop you. I simply want you to take Barska with you."

"No. Mishwan and I will do just fine, thank you." She stood up to leave.

"Sonya," said Zorena. "I will not permit you to leave

without Barska."

"What'll you do to stop me? Or should I say *how* will you stop me?" Sonya felt a grin growing beneath her face, but she held it back. She knew Zorena could stop her somehow.

Zorena shook her head. She was an amusing child, this Sonya.

"You are very stubborn, Sonya. But there are many ways available to me. Besides the usual — having the guards stop you at the border — I could make you fall asleep midstep. Use your imagination, you can surely think of other ways."

Sonya buried her smirk before it surfaced. Her anger of the day before seemed so foolish to her in the morning light. Maybe the good night's sleep was responsible. She couldn't tell why. She just knew that taking Barska along wasn't such a bad idea. But she began to enjoy the game.

"But you can't stay with me constantly," she said. "And the minute your mind leaves mine, I'll bolt so fast you'll never find me. Of course, you could always bind and gag me."

Zorena laughed, that clear, sing-songy laugh straight from her heart. Sonya could no longer stop the smile from reaching her face.

"I assure you that *that* will not be necessary," answered Zorena. "Besides the shackles in Anatawen are so rusted they could not restrain a child."

Moosehorn National Wildlife Refuge, Washington County, Maine. June, 2002. © 2003 Beth David

Chapter Eleven

A New Journey

The horses stood packed, quiet, and tethered at the far end of the garden.

Sonya shook her head, musing over Zorena's certainty as she snatched some breakfast from the kitchen. Homak and Zorena joined her beneath the grapevine. They used very few words of farewell at their departure. Tagor stayed at the house. Sonya did not look back.

The travelers followed the path along the garden and around the pond, their horses stepping on the same worn way as the first time. But this time, Sonya and Mishwan were not the same. This time, they knew what lay ahead, they knew which dangers to watch for, and they knew what action to take when facing every one.

Each hour passed slower than the last as Sonya's anxiety grew. By the time they reached the spot where

Sayeeda killed the snake, Sonya had to fight to keep control — to keep from trembling or jumping at every sound. But this time, her trembling hand gripped a weapon; and if she jumped, she jumped into a fighting pose. She wouldn't get caught unawares this time.

And so they arrived without mishap to the place of their first confrontation with Mountain Dwellers.

Sonya stopped her horse and looked around suspiciously. She listened, but the shuffling horses suddenly drowned out all else. Could that have been their first mistake? How could they had avoided it?

Mishwan rode ahead while she and Barska prepared the midday meal. Did Mishwan feel the same stomach-rending terror? Did he struggle with the same desire to go back, to forget the whole thing, to admit the task was beyond them? She studied him when he returned, but she couldn't read the thoughts behind his bright eyes.

"Hurry, Barska," said Mishwan. "I do not like this place. It brings to mind unpleasant memories."

Sonya nodded her agreement. Barska sighed and took on a serious air that Sonya thought unbecoming.

"I need to search the place where you were separated. Then, especially the place where Sayeeda and Cowis were lost."

Mishwan nodded, feigning courage. Sonya made no attempt to hide her feelings.

"Well, I hope your thoroughness doesn't add more than a minute or two. This place gives me the creeps, and as we ride up the trail, it'll only get worse."

They rode slowly, cautiously that afternoon, camping in the same cave as the first trip.

The others slept while Sonya took her turn on watch. She studied the sky as the stars popped out, wondering at how much it looked like any other star-filled sky from her past. But she knew nothing of the constellations. And it seemed she'd missed many hours of splendid light-watching by not studying about them — or even enjoying their brightness. No night sky ever seemed so brilliantly lit. *Smog,* she thought. *Must be smog.*

The wolves started their eerie howling as the moon climbed. Sonya remembered them well, her throwing knife from Arkola at the ready. She studied the marvelous Zukulan ornamentation glittering in the firelight and wondered where Waylik's roamings had brought her.

Barska took his watch as the wolves prowled outside. Sonya fell asleep within minutes — the yelps and barks no longer cause for losing sleep.

A hard rap on the bottom of the foot woke Mishwan, who in turn woke Sonya. Barska signaled for silence. They listened, but no wind, no wolves, no rustling of small animals disturbed the night.

Sonya held her throwing knife loosely in her hand — it seemed even the stars had lost their brightness. For several minutes they all listened to the silence. Then a voice cried out from the darkness.

"You move around too much in your sleep, Sonya. Did I never tell you that?"

Mishwan sheathed his sword and gently pushed down Barska's knife hand.

"Waylik? That you?" Sonya called into the darkness without moving from her place in the shadows.

Waylik appeared at the edge of the failing firelight, a wide grin decorating her face. Sonya embraced her with happiness and relief. Barska watched impatiently as Mishwan extended a more dignified greeting.

Sonya formally introduced Waylik and put on a pot of zukha while Mishwan asked about "the people he'd met."

"Y'know, Mish, it occurs to me that we never learned the name of the fair lady who so occupied your time in Zukulan."

Mishwan laughed. "That had also occurred to me. But as you never asked, I never had cause to tell . . ."

"Well, then?"

"Well?" he teased. "Well, since you have obviously

survived thus far without the knowledge, it is my humble opinion that your survival will not depend upon it now."

"I think that means he's not going to tell us." Sonya declared in mock horror as she poured a cup of zukha for Waylik.

"Waylik, is there any way you can think of to repay him this kindness?"

Waylik shook her head laughing. "No, I think I will take Barska's example and leave the two of you to your games."

"A wise and honorable decision." Mishwan raised his cup in salute.

Barska and Waylik quickly turned to business.

"You have come to find Cowis?" she asked. They agreed.

"He is not up there."

"Well, where is he?" Sonya's voice revealed all the renewed anxiety and fear that the reunion had temporarily pushed aside.

"I am not sure," answered Waylik. "But I was up in the mountains . . ." she hesitated, "looking for Sayeeda. They are together."

"No," Sonya dismissed the notion. "That's not right. Zorena said they weren't together."

"Then it could be a new arrangement." Waylik's voice showed no sign of irritation at being corrected.

"I am sure that two people were held in the cave I found. Who else could they be? And, they were being moved down the mountain. Therefore, I go down."

Barska looked thoughtful and Sonya tried to remember all she'd learned about Mountain Dwellers.

"Down?" Mishwan asked. "Why down? Do they have a fortress we know nothing about?"

"It seems so. We have seen many Mountain Dwellers heading south. They come down the mountain on this side and stay close to it — avoiding Anatawen's long arm. When they near our end of the range, they move into the plain to avoid us. We have not been able to find out why. We simply know that they go.

"Arkola has not deemed it necessary to find out. I . . . am no longer in his service. My capture made it unwise to send me scouting. For a time, at least.

"But I wanted to find Sayeeda, so I left Zukulan. I have, perhaps, more confidence in her resilience." Her eyes twinkled in the firelight.

"Do you think that . . ." Sonya stopped and turned to Barska. "Is it safe to speak openly?"

Barska nodded and Sonya continued.

"Do you think, since you couldn't find the Image, that it's at this other place?"

Waylik nodded. "It is a possibility that I have considered, though no one else seems to share the belief."

"Why would they take Cowis and Sayeeda there?" Sonya asked out loud.

"The bigger question is," put in Barska, "why have they let them live this long?"

Barska stood and paced a few steps. "You are sure there were two people?"

"Yes, and I feel certain that Sayeeda is one of them. Do not ask me how!" She raised her hand palm outward in response to their anxious expressions.

"It is mostly a feeling and not based on hard evidence."

Barska stood by the edge of the firelight facing the night, motionless. They guessed he was contacting Zorena and Sonya whispered an explanation to Waylik. A few short minutes later, he came back to them and sat down.

"I would like to investigate this evidence myself. But if you are correct, we cannot spend the time."

He paused and continued slowly. "Zorena would like to contact you herself."

They all listened carefully, very aware that they were about to be included in a rare event; Sonya suddenly felt afraid for Waylik.

"This contact," he continued, "is not possible unless you are fully open to her and have no objections. Your mind must be devoid of barriers for this kind of . . . incursion. This is no minor mind touch. She will try to see the cave from your eyes, feel what you felt, understand what you understand."

He paused and they all waited. Sonya literally biting her tongue to keep quiet.

"The problem is," he spoke slowly now. "It may not be possible for her to focus immediately on the thing she seeks. Her mind may wander within yours before she finds what she is looking for. You should be prepared for it. It is as though another can see you . . . or be part of you. It is a strange, somewhat frightening experience. You cannot deceive one who has entered directly into your mind."

Waylik's expression changed.

"I do not suggest dishonesty," added Barska quickly. "I simply mean that you cannot hide or even choose to omit the things you would normally keep from others — she will be there, in your mind, among your thoughts.

"It will not take long, will you do it?"

Waylik thought for a moment and nodded. Sonya wondered what went through Waylik's mind, and so quickly. Was there any manipulation going on? Barska and Zorena could do that, couldn't they? She immediately felt ashamed at her distrustful speculations.

"Zorena is, I am sure, a trustworthy enough person to know the secrets of my mind," said Waylik. "What do I do?"

Barska smiled, and his eyes darted around in the familiar way.

"Just relax and think of nothing, not even what she is looking for. Just open your mind and drift, that will remove the barriers. When you feel her presence, try to keep calm. It will startle and even frighten you at first. A sudden move or very strong emotion will force her to break the link. You may feel tired, but that is to be expected."

Waylik nodded and followed his instructions. At first she tried to "remove the barriers," but soon realized that trying wouldn't work. Then she realized she was thinking.

Slowly, she relaxed. She felt her mind go blank, but the feeling didn't register as a real feeling. She heard nothing, saw nothing, and felt nothing.

Then it happened. Zorena reached into her mind — her very consciousness. A terror she'd never known seized Waylik. Neither threat of life, nor pain — emotional or physical — could've caused it: the fear from one's soul, one's total being, as tey lay naked to another, defenseless, uncensored to a single tear.

Barska had tried to warn her, but how could he explain this in words? She tried not to panic, following the alien presence in her mind. She relived parts of her past, things and thoughts that made her happy, sad, or embarrassed. Things that no one else knew, or should know. And she wasn't alone. She tried to trust the great and powerful Zorena. She was, after all, legendary because of her power, wisdom, and trustworthiness. They relived the first meeting of Waylik and Sayeeda. Suddenly Waylik was released.

Waylik slumped a little and blinked her eyes a few times. A far off voice told her to rest, to sleep.

Sonya and Mishwan sat for a few minutes without speaking. Waylik looked like she'd just run a marathon. But the whole thing had only taken a few minutes: Sonya's zukha still steamed in the cup.

Waylik slipped off to sleep, a deep sleep that she normally wouldn't allow. She felt physically exhausted. Could fear alone be such a trying thing on the body, as well as the brain? Was it safe to be so soundly asleep with only these Anatawen to protect her from the wilds? The thoughts turned and tossed as she slept. The sun had climbed beyond the highest peak before she woke.

Waylik jerked to a sitting position and looked around.

Sonya sat by a small fire and the smell of bushytail filled the small cave.

"Welcome back," said Sonya as she poured fresh zukha. Then she threw something into a steaming pot on the fire. The wholesome smell of blueseed pushed through the cave leaving nothing but its fresh scent in the air.

Waylik took the drink gratefully and breathed deeply. She said nothing as the blueseed's virtue shook off her sleep.

After some breakfast she called Longhair, and they all started down the mountain. Sonya noticed that Mishwan spoke little.

"What's the matter, Mish. Thought you'd get to see your honey before our change of plans?"

He nodded and shrugged. "Yes, but love must wait. It is a sore trial, but the way of these things for those such as I who are dedicated to . . ."

"Oh, Mish, put a cork in it, *please!*"

"You do have an odd way with words, Sonya," started Barska. "Have you ever . . ."

"I know, a Tunesmith," interrupted Sonya. "No I have not. And I wish people would stop asking me that."

"Then maybe you should stop talking like that," added Mishwan. He seemed to think he had scored some kind of point.

The next campfire saw a much more relaxed Sonya and Mishwan. Going down the mountain instead of towards the old disasters visibly lifted their spirits.

Only two hang gliders threatened the wilderness here. But they searched the high ground only, allowing the four travelers to make solid progress for two days.

On the third day a breezy plain welcomed them. Their senses filled with an endless horizon of swaying grasses and the sweet smell of over-ripe grain and far-off sagebrush riding the wind to greet them. The thump of the horses on sod sent a safe and warm sound to their ears.

They skirted the mountains and followed the path the Mountain Dwellers had been taking — as far as Waylik could figure.

At their third camp, the second one on the plain, they stopped a little earlier than usual, and spent some time sitting by a low fire beneath a large sky, and in the shadow of the mountains.

Barska smoked his pipe, the tobacco sifting the same

aroma through camp as Tagor's had at Sonya's first waking moment in Anatawen. It seemed a lifetime ago.

"Barska," Waylik's voice sounded thoughtful. "When Zorena entered my mind, how much of her mind was with me? Did her whole consciousness leave her body? Would that not kill her?"

Sonya looked at her friend closely. She'd never heard Waylik ask so many questions so rapidly. Waylik's speech usually inched along, like a snail — slow, guarded, even halting. This stream of questions exploded from her as if a dike had burst.

Barska hesitated, trying to decide which question to answer first.

"Her whole mind did not enter yours. But she would not have died because of that if it had. It was still a mind *touch*, but more extensive."

"Like a mind probe?" Sonya broke in.

"Yes. That is a good way to describe it. You have these things where you come from?"

"No, not really."

They looked puzzled at her non-committal answer. But she obviously would not revise it.

"As I was saying" resumed Barska. "It is possible to use a much more extensive . . . probe. If Zorena had used the full mind probe, she could probably have found the information she wanted quicker, easier, without sending Waylik through random memories. Yet Zorena's mind would also be laid bare to the receiver of the probe.

"It is also extremely dangerous. If, two nights ago something had happened to break the connection suddenly, Zorena would simply have left you. You both would have been released; she was just looking.

"In the case of a total mind probe, it would not be as simple; she would not be just looking, she would be maneuvering through your mind, possibly even manipulating your thoughts. If something happened abruptly to break the link, she would be unable to return to her body.

"It would die — she would die. And you — your mind would be holding two consciousnesses, and you would go insane. It is also possible that she would try to pull back and leave you with your own mind intact, but hers would be lost between here and where her body is, to die slowly without a form, or find another to invade.

"No one has tried a total probe in centuries. The first and last was Ronguin. Ronguin Ruled many centuries ago. She entered the consciousness of another, not heeding the dangers. And she let more of her mind go into the other than was wise.

"Aklon, the sharer of the probe, sat by the sea, across the plain. A wind storm brought Aklon out of his trance suddenly. Ronguin died — the body had no mind to sustain it. But her consciousness lived, in the mind of Aklon. He soon went mad. How could he live with two separate minds? A few days later, he jumped from a high cliff into the raging sea.

"Any sudden movement, touch or loud sound will make the receiver or the sender of the probe aware of tey's physical surroundings. The link breaks instantly, and there is no time to recollect the consciousness. If it is searching, the mind floats. It becomes trapped if it is in the mind of another."

Waylik remembered the terror of Zorena's mind entering hers. Surely she would go insane if it lasted for more than a few minutes. Could it have happened to her?

"But do not worry," Barska assured her. "Zorena is much to wise to over-extend in that manner. She could have instantly returned to herself without any danger to either of you."

Sonya took the first watch, still imagining two minds in one: two entirely different beings, each with its own set of feelings, experiences, expectations and fears. She shuddered. One mind provided enough aggravation for anyone.

Along the Welch-Dickey Loop Trail. White Mountains, NH. May, 2000. © 2003 Beth David

Chapter Twelve

Alone At Last

They traveled pleasantly across the plain for several days. The smell of the grain, the sweeping sound of the wind in the grass, and the largeness of the night sky made the danger of their task a far-off reality. The brown foothills grew larger with each step, bringing the desert closer to them, slowly, deliberately. They camped in the shadow of the hills, taking in the sweet smells of the plain for the last time.

In the early morning, just as the sun's light began to mark their way, they crossed over the foothills and into the desert. The full brightness of morning chased them from behind as they climbed down the other side. Gradually the ground's green growth gave way to sandy patches and ever-growing stretches of desert and dust. The sun ceased to be a welcomed friend.

Sonya would remember it for the rest of her life. They couldn't take the horses; there'd be barely enough food and water for themselves. Her feet hurt. Sand gritted her mouth, and the heat thickened the air till she thought she'd suffocate.

The torn fabric Waylik ripped for their heads gave them all the look of an Arab caravan without the camels. But Sonya doubted her headrag worked as well as the time-tested kafeeya so famous throughout the Arab world.

At night she shivered and shook, listening, looking for, and imagining the sting of scorpions, snakes and spiders — spiders hideously huge in this flat, dusty wasteland.

Sonya would've lost hope without Waylik. She could find water and food no matter how impossible it seemed; though never quite enough to satisfy Sonya.

They spent an eternal week in the drylands before seeing a small mountain range. The weather would be cooler there, and water less scarce. Just the sight of them eased Sonya's aches and helped her mind start working again.

"Waylik, are you sure they came this way? I thought Cowis was in bad shape. Wouldn't this trip be — too much for him?"

"The Mountain Dwellers would be prepared," answered Waylik. "They would be riding in wagons and could carry the water they needed."

Sonya wondered if the Mountain Dwellers would take the time and use the precious water necessary to keep Cowis and Sayeeda alive.

"Cowis is not dead," said Barska as though he'd heard her thoughts. "And his condition is not as bad as it seems. There are unexplainable forces at work interfering with his ability to contact us."

His matter-of-fact tone annoyed her, but she said nothing. She kept her eyes on the rocks ahead, trying to think only of the shade and water hidden in their configurations.

She tried to imagine Barska's thoughts, the plans he

must be devising, and what she would do to help. Even in camp she usually felt useless. Everyone else moved sure-handedly as tey built the fire, prepared the food and drew maps in the ground to discuss their route.

Sonya sat by the fire that Mishwan had started, while Barska and Waylik spoke softly of their direction. Mishwan stood, staring at the stars, as he usually did for a few minutes each night.

Sonya strained to hear Barska and Waylik. But she couldn't understand them. She felt totally inadequate for the task ahead.

But I felt totally inadequate for the last task and we got that Medallion to Arkola.

She faded off to sleep, the sound of the Zukulan coast in her ears and the taste of Zukulan's fresh-grilled fish locked in the memory of her taste buds.

Barska woke them early and announced that Sayeeda and Cowis were together and that they had crossed the desert.

Waylik smiled but said nothing.

Sonya and Mishwan felt more comfortable with their path now.

Waylik sensed their relief but didn't take it personally. To them she was practically a Mountain Dweller, and she was grateful they trusted her at all.

As they reached the foot of the mountains, they found obvious signs of the wagons. They stepped up the pace for a while, full of the new energy these findings brought them. But Sonya soon insisted they stop.

"What good will it be to find them if we're so exhausted we can't do anything about it?" She was whining, and she knew it.

"Correct me if I'm wrong, but heroic rescues are seldom executed by sleepy, footsore, and limp limbs."

"That is not necessarily true!" said Mishwan.

Sonya marveled at his energy.

"I can cite you many a tale from the history of our

great people to support 'limp limbs.' First-"

Waylik abruptly stopped walking, and Mishwan banged into her. He took the hint and they rested in silence near a cold stream with clear, clean-tasting water.

Sonya sat near the bank, listening to the trickle on the rocks and eating her gren. No fire tonight, no real food. She tried to be thankful for the little stream with its unbroken melody. But all her thoughts kept returning to the Mountain Dweller stronghold ahead.

Even in the most rested, ready state of mind and body, Sonya wouldn't know how to rescue Cowis and Sayeeda. And if she found out how to do it, she probably wouldn't be able to. Sonya fell asleep, uneasy dreams invading her tranquility throughout the night.

Long before dawn they started. The sky slowly losing the darkness of the night — ahead of the sun on its journey from the eastern seas. Sonya watched the growing light and remembered Zorena's words: "In a very dark place."

At midday they stopped by a hole in the rocks almost as deep as a cave. Waylik slipped away and soon brought back two small foxes. Barska looked worried.

"We do not know if it is safe Waylik," he said. "I think we should not start a fire."

Waylik started skinning. "You have not felt anything have you? No. And I have not seen anything for miles. This path has not been used in days."

"Smoke carries the eye far, Waylik."

"I know the dangers of an untimely campfire. But the sun hangs high and there is enough dry wood to make a small, smokeless fire. If we are careful, we will have no problem. We all need the strength of meat."

Barska agreed grudgingly. Sonya and Mishwan did what they could do speed up the process. It seemed hours before Waylik let them eat. She tended the fire, the skewered meat, and the herbs, with patience and skill. But she wouldn't let them have their fill. Instead she packed up the meat from one of the foxes and gave a portion to each of them.

"You will thank me the next time we need to eat a cold meal. The gren will not stick so long in the throat if there is something besides water to chase after it."

Both Mishwan and Sonya pouted like children.

"Now, Barska, before we go on, we have a problem to discuss. How do we plan to infiltrate the forces we seek? How do we plan on getting out afterwards. *And* is Cowis in a physical state to help us?"

Barska thought for a moment and looked at each of them as though measuring. When his eyes met Waylik's, a mischievous, knowing grin shot out from her to him. He hid his irritation as best he could. Sonya watched the exchange and waited.

"It was my intention to be captured, of course," he said.

Sonya's surprise was obvious. Mishwan gave no indication of his thoughts. Waylik slapped her knee and shook her head.

"I knew it. That would make sense to a no-sense Anatawen I suppose. But what about us? You were, no doubt going to get yourself separated to be captured. And we would do . . . what?"

"Waylik, please," he pleaded. "Think about it. They want Cowis and Sayeeda alive, Cowis because he is of the Ruling Blood, and Sayeeda because she is the next closest thing. They want the Medallion and we know where it is. I will not only be wanted, but wanted alive; for the same reasons. You will be killed as soon as you are caught."

He made a gesture to rest his case and leaned back against the rock.

Sonya quietly watched them both.

"I will not be caught," Waylik stated matter-of-factly. "Also, I may not be killed so quickly as you think. For the Mountain Dwellers suspect I know something of the Medallion. And you do not know why Cowis and Sayeeda are alive. You are merely speculating.

"And now what? Is it not obvious that we will go with

you, in any case?"

"I am not totally incapable of . . ."

"What a minute," interrupted Sonya. "What *about* us? I just want to make sure I've got this right. We stick right with you, step by miserable step, suffering through the same dangers, disasters, spiders, snakes, *and* scorpions, and then you just wave bye-bye? No way, buddy. I want to know why I was dragged through a desert just to be dumped as soon as we got close."

"The reason you were dragged through a desert is quite simple, Sonya." Barska was definitely exasperated. "You were stubborn, unrealistic, and you would have caused Zorena too much distraction at a time when her concentration is vital to Cowis and Sayeeda."

"So you brought me to the enemy's doorstep for my own protection. So I'd be out of Zorena's hair?" Sonya felt herself losing control. "Well kindly forgive me, sir. Zorena should've just turned me in circles as I walked, I never would've known the difference — such an incompetent nuisance that I am. And what about Waylik? She came in handy, popping in at just the right time like that didn't she? And so, we eat the same dust, fight the same heat, and then get dumped in the mountains. A hell of a group I teamed up with."

"Please, Sonya, still that tongue of yours." The sound of Waylik's voice surprised Sonya.

"And why are you defending him?"

"Because he happens to be correct — partly. You have wondered what would happen when we found them. But did you ever wonder how we would find them? You already had your meeting with Bobby. I am lucky to have escaped mine — and I am still grateful for your quick action in the caves. Surely you do not believe that Bobby will be as careless a second time?"

Sonya shrugged it off. Somehow it seemed silly to believe people plotted her untimely death like an old Robin Hood movie.

"Back off, Waylik, you sound like a cops-and-robbers movie."

Mishwan laughed. Barska did not.

"A minute ago," continued Sonya. "You started this conversation. You change your mind too quickly for someone who's supposed to be so calculated."

Then she turned to Barska. "If you think you can get rid of me, forget it. That has to be the dumbest plan I ever heard: getting yourself stuck in the same situation as the people you're trying to rescue. It's out of the question. Not on your life."

She stomped around the camp and flailed her arms, pointing to one and then the other.

Mishwan watched and then asked. "Who, may I ask abdicated and empowered you with the right of command?"

"Don't tell me you agree with him too!"

"There is a certain logic to his idea. We could be more helpful out here while he is inside. He will be in better physical condition to instruct us than is Cowis. He will be in the same place and therefore able to direct us less blindly."

"A real genius you are, Mishwan. But tell me, oh great general, what happens if they take Barska somewhere else? Please don't tell me no one thought of that? Why would they take him to the same place — where he could give Cowis and Sayeeda emotional support?"

Waylik smiled during the silence that followed.

"Cowis and Sayeeda are together now," answered Barska, "offering support to each other. Why will they separate me from them? And, even if they do, at least we will be within their stronghold."

"No, *you* will be within their stronghold. We will be out here." She shook her head. Why couldn't they see how stupid that was?

"Then what do you suggest?" asked Barska.

Sonya tried to think of something. She looked up the

mountain, then down, and to the sides, but no brilliant idea popped into her mind. They still hadn't even found the so-called stronghold.

"What's wrong with following the signs, slowly, and as secretly as we can, maybe travel by night? And we'll see what we see. At least until we find the place — we don't even know what kind of place it is . . . or anything."

"Wandering around sustained by hope is hardly a solution, Sonya. We cannot waste any more time. This much I know."

Sonya decided then that she didn't like Barska.

"But we should start traveling by night," put in Waylik. "We need not announce our presence before our plan is decided. Especially if we want to keep our number a secret. It is getting dark already. We can walk for another two or three hours, then rest for a while and still have plenty of dark left to travel in this night."

"When do we sleep?"

"There will be time, Sonya," Barska truly sounded irritated now.

"This is not a playful frolic in the woods. Try to push yourself a bit."

Sonya only grunted at him. She thought about the snakes, the heat, the spiders, and the dust in her mouth. Push herself indeed. Suddenly it all hit her at once. She felt restless, tense, filled with the kind of energy that explodes from inside if not properly controlled.

"Let's go, then," she said quickly and started climbing up the hill, throwing on her pack as she went.

Barska and Waylik started after her at their own pace. Mishwan hurried to catch up, buckling his pack as he ran. When he caught up to her, he pulled her to a stop.

"What are you trying to do, Sonya?"

She laughed nervously. "Nothing. I didn't mean to act mad. I'm just so sick and tired of all that talk. If we're going, we might as well git — while the gittin's good."

"Git?"

"Yes, git!"

Mishwan knew when to let a matter drop, and so he did. After a while they stopped to wait for the others. But only the not-so-far-off sounds of swordplay reached their ears. Mishwan and Sonya charged back along the path, swords unsheathed, throwing knives in hand.

Slowly they approached the campfire. The smell of blueseed filled the area and Sonya knew what Waylik had done. Mishwan sensed that Sonya had an idea and so he followed her lead. She followed the scent of the seed, leading Mishwan off the trail and over the rocks they had camped under. Soon they struck another path heading in the same general direction as the one they'd been following. A few yards up Sonya found a tear from Waylik's cloak pointing the way.

A wide and winding path took the best way to avoid rocks and cliffs and other mountain hazards. Neither one of them had any doubt about which way to go. Sonya figured that Barska must be helping them along. The night deepened, but bright stars studded a clear sky and surrounded a bright moon.

Sonya wished she'd had more time to master the art of tracking, especially at night. The hard-packed surface of this often-used trail made it difficult to figure out new tracks from old. An experienced tracker would've known, but Sonya and Mishwan could only hope that Barska or Waylik would find a way to show them any sudden change in direction.

They walked until late and only rested for a short time before continuing. Sonya's eyes started closing on their own, and her legs dragged along the ground. She rubbed her eyes; it seemed that something blocked her vision.

Slowly they made their way to the top of the mountain. The thump of their tired feet filled their ears, and a sickly sweet smell filled their nostrils, its thick taste coating their tongues.

"I've got to rest, Mishwan. It'll be dawn soon, anyway. Over there?"

He nodded, but she didn't look back to see it. She moved off the trail to the left and blinked hard, trying to clear the fog from her eyes. Mishwan couldn't understand why she kept walking. He sat with a thud and Sonya turned midstride toward the noise. Her foot slid on the rocks and she fell on her back.

She cursed loudly and made a great effort to stand, using her arms as much as her legs. She slid backwards and started rolling down the hill. She called out and reached for something, but there was nothing there. She slid and rolled, slowed painfully by the jab of rocks. She stopped abruptly at a small belt of low trees, but started sliding again. She grabbed onto a wide root and called out to Mishwan.

"Mishwan, where are you?"

She heard his answer but couldn't see him. She felt so stupid. Careening out of control down a steep hill was one thing. But sliding slower than a turtle was just plain ridiculous.

She thought of the smell she'd noticed on the trail and wondered if Bobby had discovered some kind of drug. Now that she couldn't smell it anymore, her eyesight cleared, and so did her thinking. *Probably just an adrenaline rush,* she thought.

Mishwan suddenly appeared at the top of the grade, a slowly lightening sky behind him. He looked so far away, and she called out to him several times before he found her. She tried to pull herself up to sit on the tree, but her arms just couldn't manage it.

Mishwan took out his rope. "Sonya, I can find no place to tie the rope. You must trust me to pull you up."

Sonya agreed reluctantly. It actually wasn't a real fall, it was more like a slide. She tied the rope around her waist as the light from the hidden sun slowly surrounded her. Sonya looked down and nearly lost her grip at what she saw. The little belt of trees grew on the last few feet of ground before it curved steeply inward. The bottom looked

Zorena

50 feet away.

Mishwan started to pull, but Sonya held on with frozen muscles. A paralyzing panic took hold of her. She couldn't move; she couldn't let go of the tree.

Her mind raced wildly with thoughts of falling and the feeling she had when she fell in the cave, thoughts of landing with a crack. A different panic struck.

I can't go back now! Not now! She repeated it over and over.

Mishwan called out and told her to let go and climb; his voice far and faint in her mind. Suddenly the pressure on the rope stopped.

She came back to reality and looked for Mishwan. The panic returned with renewed ferocity. She closed her eyes and squelched the tears. Death never seemed so determined as this time. She forced her mind to stop its wild raving, and she looked around her for a solution.

The rope was still tied to her waist. The tree she clung to was sturdy. She pulled with all her energy and locked her right elbow around the tree trunk. With her left, she pulled the rope to her slowly. With great difficulty and concentration, she tied the rope to the tree ... and laughed.

Now what?

If she fell, the rope would hold, hopefully. It would at least break the fall. But it wouldn't do anything to help her up.

She pulled and scrambled and finally managed to climb up onto a branch. Now she could at least relax a little and think. She took off her pack, tears pouring from her eyes as she vowed not to die yet. She found her own rope and tied the two together, leaving one end around her waist. She tied the climbing hook onto one end and tried to throw it over the edge. But her arms had lost all strength and she faced the wrong way.

Where the hell is Mishwan?

She called out to him, but a strong breeze pushed the

scratchy sound of her voice to the bottom of the pit. She tried not to look down, but her eyes refused to listen. She wondered if she'd ever enjoy a roller coaster again. The sun slipped easily over the mountains and revealed a green and full valley below. Way off in the distance she caught a glimmer that must be the ocean.

She tied the rope back to the tree, shorter, and turned herself around to face the hill. She saw no people and was glad the wind had drowned out her voice.

There must be Mountain Dwellers up there. Why else would Mishwan leave her like that? She was much too tired to panic again, but she had to find some way to get up the hill. If her life hadn't been in danger it would have been funny.

She untied the rope and threw the hook again. It landed in something but broke free before she put her weight on it. She rubbed her sore arm, rested it, and tried again. The third time it caught, but far to the right. She tried to pull it free and couldn't.

Sonya steeled herself and started walking up the hill, using the rope and the training she'd thought so stupid at the time; her Batman-and-Robin jokes hardly seemed appropriate anymore.

She swung to the right, lost her balance and froze until she stopped moving, climbed to an upright position and started again. It seemed so much more difficult than it ought to be. Her arms felt like rubber, and each time she opened her fingers it hurt more than the last. She ignored the pain until her muscles went numb. About halfway up she realized she'd never make it.

Sonya wrapped the rope around her arm and leaned backwards against the hill, digging her heels deep into the soft soil. She took up the slack from behind her and wrapped the double rope around her tying it any way she could. She refused to lose even a foot's progress.

Leaning against the rope, she shook her arms back into circulation and caught her breath. She started walking again, watching the taut rope. It suddenly looked very thin.

Where the hell is that damned Ruling Family when you need 'em anyway?

The anger from that thought must've brought her new energy, because finally, she slid over the top and lay on her stomach, trying to breathe.

She remembered that Mishwan was missing and sat up, stood and fell. She slid to a rock and rested. She had to get some sleep. But she couldn't stop now. Mishwan needed her.

Many scuffling feet had been there; Mishwan's knife tossed aside in the fray. Sonya put the knife in her pack and followed the tracks.

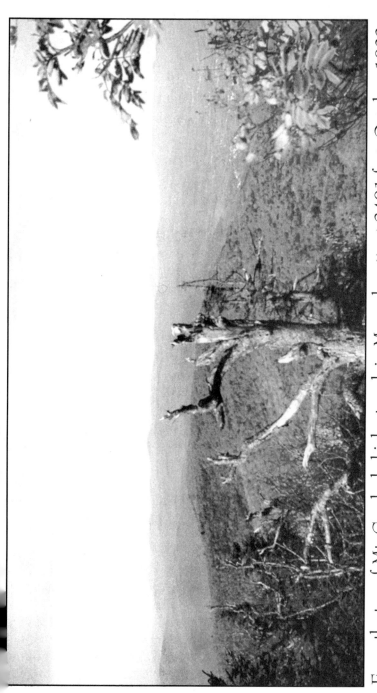

From the top of Mt. Greylock, highest peak in Massachusetts at 3491 feet. October, 1983.

Copyright 2003 Beth David

Chapter Thirteen

Dr. Livingstone, I Presume?

At sunset, Sonya woke with a stiff neck and her pack still strapped to her back. But she felt no lumps or other symptoms of a knock on the head.

She staggered to her feet, took off the pack and stretched her sore muscles. Her quivering legs would not carry her and the pack, so she gulped down the rest of the fox and her last drop of water.

The tracks formed a clear path along the trail — the Mountain Dwellers moved quickly and with no regard for secrecy. Sonya knew she'd need every ounce of her strength and would have to push herself to the limit before each rest.

The trail rounded a high rock face, and Sonya climbed to the highest point to see where the path led. Stunted trees and protruding rocks blocked sight of the winding trail. The view to the left held her eye for a long moment.

The green valley, the blue sky above, the white tipped mountains beyond, and the ocean's sparkle looked back at her with a vastness that made her feel smaller than ever.

In another time and at another place, she would have spent a whole day climbing just to see that greatness. But now, her exhaustion clouded her sight, and an urgency bordering on panic had settled into the pit of her stomach. A hawk dived down below, and Sonya envied him his carefree flight. As he flew out of sight, she climbed down, staying to the right of the wide path.

Sonya hiked steadily and only stopped to sleep when she judged the peak's long end to be two hours away. She woke at midday and started immediately.

Plenty of water flowed along her way, but food never occurred to her until a young fox bounded noisily through the brambles. She took out her large hide skiver. The fox spotted her and darted away. But Sonya had already thrown, and the fox ran directly in front of it. The neck snapped and she winced at the sound but reveled in the thought of fresh meat.

All the details of Bilzite's lectures and his gory show and tell flashed by her as she prepared the meat for cooking. She cooked it carefully, and long — the only protection from disease that she could figure out.

The possibility of getting sick from fresh-killed meat did not concern her Anatawen hosts. Sonya had asked about it, but no one shared her concern. Maybe the meat isn't the problem, she thought, maybe it's the human body that's gotten deformed after generations of noisy, smelly, industrial living. So she cooked her meat all the way through. But these animals of the wild don't lose their taste so easily. Sonya even drank the juice from the little pan. She wrapped the leftovers and started again quickly.

Many different animal tracks suddenly started to appear crossing the path. Sonya followed them carefully — knowing that Mountain Dwellers would follow the same signs. Soon she came to a small pond with a clear, trickling stream at one end.

Sonya drank all she could and washed in the cold, clean stream. She filled her small container and stood up with a groan. "OK, back to the trail," she said out loud.

Sonya stopped at the sound of her voice and tried to chuckle.

Talking to myself so soon? One more reason to find Mishwan fast!

She soon found a peak high enough to command a long view of the next step down. She stood for a long time, watching, looking for a sign, wishing to pierce the rock with her mind. But no sign showed itself; no x-ray vision from the Ruling Family guided her eyes.

Sonya continued in the same direction. If only it hadn't taken so long to get up that damned hill. If only she hadn't fallen in the first place. She remembered the sweet smell and wondered again if Bobby had drugged them.

She headed back to the main path to start the climb down. An inhuman wail froze her to the spot.

Sonya crouched behind a rock and tried to find the noise. The loudness of it filled the air and echoed around her. She moved to the right, and the echo lessened; but the noise actually seemed closer. It started to come in spurts and she slowed down to avoid passing by it. When it screeched through the air again Sonya's heart pounded fiercely.

She crept through a ring of stones into a small clearing. Something scraped against the rock and Sonya turned towards the sound, her throwing knife in hand. Wonder surpassed fear when Sonya's brain translated what her eyes saw.

There stood a brown eagle, not full grown, but large enough to exhibit the majesty expected of it. It tried to flap its brown wings and fly away, but the right side only flopped. A large wolf-like animal circled slowly, its long tongue licking large teeth. The eagle put up a brave defense but clearly had no backup to his threats.

Sonya took out her large hide skiver and loosened her

long hunting knife in its sheath. She threw the skiver and it caught the creature squarely on the shoulder. Sonya heard the crack as she grabbed her throwing knife.

The thing turned, growling and frothing. Sonya's knees weakened but held steady. She knew she'd have to get closer to throw the knife; she'd never completely mastered it. She ran towards the beast — throwing knife in one hand, hunting knife in the other. The throwing knife found its mark in the beast's throat. Sonya followed through by slicing the head from the body with her hunting knife.

The eagle faced her, eyeing her closely. Now what? If she moved within reach of its claws, surely it would attack.

"Not a very pleasant thought," she said out loud.

The eagle eyed the dead beast but didn't move toward it. Sonya unslung her pack, took out some of the fox meat and pushed it toward him. The eagle took a morsel and eyed her again. He didn't seem to be hungry. But what would an eagle be doing there, with a broken wing, and not hungry?

Sonya took out the hunting knife, cut off a slice of the dead beast and threw it gently towards the eagle. He gobbled it down so fast Sonya wondered if he would choke. The claws dug deep into the flesh and Sonya's fascination deepened.

The young eagle ate nearly the whole beast before stopping again to eye Sonya. She cut up small pieces and tried to hand feed it. It took time, but eventually he took food from her. She tried to get a closer look at the injured wing, but he wouldn't let her. Fear and excitement filled her simultaneously. If only she could gain his trust, for just a minute.

She could . . . what, she thought? Tame it? How? *Stupid idea.*

"Too many childhood fantasies interfering with my logic."

The young bird looked right at her when she spoke, and Sonya laughed.

"Great, now I'm talking to a bird."

Sonya watched it closely and noted how young it

looked. She didn't know how to tell that really. But countless movies where large birds are tamed by the gangling young moor resident played out in her mind. She fed it and talked to it and wished she had a harmonica, or something . . . music soothes . . .

Sonya moved closer and closer as she gained courage. The eagle backed away, or flapped his wings, sending clouds of dust billowing through the air. But he didn't yell at her the way he screeched at the beast. And gradually, one small step at a time, he let her get within reach.

Sonya reached out her hand, but stopped short of touching him. He looked at her — as though wondering what her problem was. Even he seemed to know that the whole point was for her to touch the wing.

Slowly, the sun slipped behind the peaks and trees, casting long shadows throughout the little clearing. Finally, she steeled herself and gently caressed the top of the curved part of his wing. Slowly she slid her fingers down along the feathered way. Although Bilzite's lectures fell short of repairing broken eagle's wings, Sonya figured a little logic would uncomplicate the chore.

The bird fluttered and backed away as she found the two breaks and compared the deformed shapes to the others. She made two small splints and the bird watched her intently as she busied herself with the task.

Sonya put her pack high on her shoulders to cover her neck and her head. She approached the bird carefully, with the canvas facing his sharp beak. Sonya tucked the bird's wing under her arm and placed the splints carefully along the breaks. He pushed at her with his head and wailed mournfully, but he didn't use his claws or turn his deadly beak on her.

Sonya examined her hands and felt behind her head for gashes and bruises. She found none and sighed tiredly as she unpacked some cooked meat. She ate leisurely, glad the bird didn't like her food and trying to think of a name for him.

What do you name someone that you've met out in the middle of nowhere expecting, of course, to find no one? Someone that makes you very excited to be where you are? Would he ever answer to the name? The whole idea seemed so presumptuous of her.

"And who would you presume to be?" she asked him. The answer came quite suddenly, and she laughed, "Dr. Livingstone, of course."

She tried it out on him, but he didn't react. He just stared her straight in the eye, occasionally cocking his head to the side for a different view, but only briefly. Sonya tried to recall another beast more prideful or more beautiful, but she couldn't.

Did "Dr. Livingstone" befit such a beast? Sonya didn't know but decided to go with her instincts. It would, at least, be unique — in Anatawen anyway.

She spent two days in the clearing, feeding and talking to Dr. Livingstone. She fed him blueseed as often as he'd take it since Waylik thought it sped up the healing process in humans and animals.

Sonya almost forgot about Mishwan until Dr. Livingstone's whining lessened considerably. The healing process obviously progressed well. Sonya wanted to train him.

Could Zorena Reach the minds of animals? Sonya tried to send her thoughts down the mountain, towards the plains, past the yellow fields and bouncing from the towers to the warmth of the Ruling Family's great hall. Almost, she felt herself gliding over the peaks, her toes pointed toward a sea of swaying amber. Suddenly her stomach tightened and she plummeted toward the great expanse beneath her.

Sonya woke with a start from a sleep she hadn't expected to take.

Dr. Livingstone jumped around the clearing, one wing considerably less agile than the other. Sonya laughed.

"You know I want to get out of here, too, don't you?

Well, it won't be long now. Just don't break 'em again."

Sonya's unease grew to a fever pitch. The dream had stirred an urgency in her that sent her head spinning.

"Whoa, easy, slow down and don't panic," she told herself.

She no longer seemed to hear her own voice. It felt so natural to talk aloud.

"Leave food for the bird, he'll manage. The splints are no match for his wings once they heal — they'll break, fall off, and he'll be on his way."

She stared at him as he tried to fly off.

"You feel it, too, don't you?"

Sonya's weariness and indecision left her in one deep breath. She set off at once to find game for Dr. Livingstone. Soon, she had several small high-country bushytails, a couple of birds, and a fox. Never had she hunted so efficiently. She complimented herself on her skill and left them for the eagle.

"I'm sure I'll find what I need for me," she boasted.

Sonya set the food in the middle of the clearing and strapped on her pack. With one last longing look, she stepped out of the clearing and headed back along the trail.

At first camp she could clearly see that she had moved down the other side. Her bright fire did little to cheer up her sad and lonely camp.

"Lonely," she muttered. "Like you haven't been alone enough to get over a stupid bird? Talk to yourself, probably hate people when you see 'em, like Waylik gets . . ."

She slipped off to sleep, dreaming of bothersome people annoying her with their friendly conversations, invading her thoughts with silly questions and intrusive expectations.

For two days, Sonya followed the trail of the Mountain Dwellers. She saw and heard no signs of them except the trampling of the trail's overgrown vegetation.

As the morning sun of the third day moved overhead, Sonya ate the rest of her meat and started again. She looked up at the chirping birds and stayed that way for a minute or two. She shook her head and went back to the main path.

A loud wail snapped her head back towards the sky. Dr. Livingstone circled in slow, graceful flight. Sonya stood, watching as a child watching the finale of a fireworks show. He landed on a nearby rock and looked at her. Sonya tried to teach him to stand on her arm. She covered it first with her jacket, and when she finally got him to do it, realized she couldn't hold him there for more than a few seconds.

She walked and he flew ahead. Sonya only smiled at her escort.

Her enthusiastic thoughts of how to train him further and what to teach him caused her to be careless. She came face to face with two squat Mountain Dwellers before she knew it.

Her hunting knife was out in a flash. She faced the two and tried not to back up. She held the knife in her right hand, the throwing knife loosened and ready for action. She waited, deciding the defensive would be best.

She felt a sharp pain in her left arm from a quick stab. She pulled back, striking with the knife. She switched hands with the hunting knife and threw the other. The Mountain Dweller on the left fell as he tried to strike a second blow.

She faced the other and tried to ignore the pain in her left arm. This one had his sword drawn. She controlled a strong need to panic. If she couldn't dodge a knife, how could she fight a sword? She looked for a stick, anything to help. The fallen Mountain Dweller's body lay on top of his sword. Sonya couldn't grab it easily. Her remaining opponent smiled and moved closer with a casualness that made Sonya fume.

She held the hunting knife far in front of her and high, exactly as she shouldn't. But the cool mountain air had entered the wide cut and sent her senses reeling. The swordwielder advanced, and Sonya backed up, putting a rock between them — a temporary solution at best; but maybe it would give her time to think.

Suddenly, she saw something behind him. He fell over the rock with a wail, Dr. Livingstone's claws deep in his back. Sonya almost felt the pain herself as he cried out.

She rushed around the rock and pulled Dr. Livingstone away. He flew to a low branch, ruffled his wings, then folded them. The Mountain Dweller was dead. Somewhere in the struggle, he had stabbed himself with his sword.

Sonya remembered that she'd grabbed Dr. Livingstone to pull him away — and he didn't hurt her. She scratched him under the wing and looked at her arm.

The cut was long, but not too deep. She took off her jacket, ripped out the inside lining, and wrapped her arm as tightly as she could.

She went back to where the Mountain Dwellers had first attacked and took the clean sword.

Sonya knew Mishwan must be close by. She searched carefully and thoroughly, systematically fanning out a couple of hundred yards from the point of attack. Four horses, saddled, bridled, and packed with bedrolls, stood tethered near the entrance to a cave.

Very quietly, she approached the horses. Somehow, Dr. Livingstone sensed her need for quiet. He stayed hidden among the trees, preening himself in a smug and self-absorbed manner.

The horses shuffled and muttered when Sonya touched them. But no sound came from the cave. She checked each girth and saddlebag, then slipped back to Dr. Livingstone, where she could keep an eye on things and wait for the gathering dusk.

As the sun fell behind the mountains, sending shadows through the trails, but before the sky began to darken, Sonya approached the entrance to the cave. Dr. Livingstone swooped around her as she walked, giving her a strange confidence that she knew she needed.

A flickering light from a small fire dimly lit the cave. The shadows made it look like an army had gathered there and dropped their belongings in the entrance to move on to some deep place of rest.

She got Dr. Livingstone to stand on her shoulder and then took a deep breath. Why he didn't bolt as soon as they entered the cave, Sonya could never know. She was just glad that he didn't.

Slowly, she heard the sounds of many shuffling feet and loud voices. She followed the sounds. Through a passage she could see a group of people eating, sitting around tables, possibly playing some kind of card game. In a small pocket of the rock before the passage, Mishwan leaned against the wall with a guard watching him closely.

Sonya took out her hunting knife, glad the Mountain Dwellers were preoccupied with meal and play; she had never noticed how loud the knife's unsheathing sounded. She got as close as she dared, hugging the wall and praying that Dr. Livingstone would stay quiet. He stood on her shoulder unmoving.

Slowly she picked up a shield, but Mishwan's guard turned towards it. She burst into the opening and threw a knife to Mishwan. He deftly struck down his guard and moved to her side.

In a moment the Mountain Dwellers near the opening faced them. Sonya and Mishwan stood ready to do battle.

Sonya started counting them and quickly realized how stupid she had been. But Dr. Livingstone took over; he screeched and flew claws first, a deafening echo filling the cave. None of the Mountain Dwellers would face him. Sonya and Mishwan backed slowly out of the passage and ran to the entrance. Dr. Livingstone whooshed past them as they rode off, taking the two extra horses with them.

The Mountain Dwellers charged out of the cave yelling and waving swords, arrows at the ready to take care of Dr. Livingstone. But he already flew well out of range.

Sonya and Mishwan rode off at full speed — not very fast for mountain ponies. Arrows zipped by them both, but mostly too high. It seemed the Mountain Dwellers didn't want to hurt their horses.

Sonya's arm throbbed, and she was glad she didn't have to use it. They rode till nearly dawn, then found a spot shielded by the mountain behind them to the north and a thicket of fir trees to the south.

Sonya took the first watch, even though Dr. Livingstone only left her sight to hunt. And never for long.

Throughout the day, Mishwan slept, and Sonya realized how long it had been since she'd even rested. As the sun took its long turn towards the west, she woke Mishwan and went off to find food. She soon returned with a couple of bushytails and a variety of fragrant leaves.

Soon, their little camp filled with the smell of herbs and tender meat sizzling on the fire. Sonya vowed not to ask too many questions. But she had to find out what Mishwan knew.

"Mishwan," she started cautiously, "Do you think Bobby drugged you?"

"I do not know what drugged means," he answered. "However, if you are suggesting that he used an herb or combination of herbs and plants to make us feel disoriented, yes. I believe he did. I felt as though I had been thrown from a running horse. And I am still not fully recovered, even after my long sleep — for which I thank you.

"I also believe this is how he has kept Cowis and Sayeeda out of the Reach of the Ruling Family without killing them. However, I still do not know why he has not killed them."

"I expect it's for ransom of some kind. But he probably hasn't figured out what's worth the most yet. So he doesn't know what to ask for."

"Ransom," mused Mishwan. "I do not know this word."

"It means that Bobby is holding them to trade for some kind of reward. Where I come from it would be gold or silver. He's probably not sure what he can get for them. So he hasn't asked yet. But he's figured out they're worth something."

"This would explain much. But how does he know

about the Ruling Family's Power?"

"Why do you think he does?" A small tremble rippled through Sonya at the thought of Bobby knowing about Zorena's special talents.

"Why else would he keep them in this state?" asked Mishwan.

Sonya laughed. "Because he's a coward! That's why. He's afraid of what they can do to him without even knowing what they can do to him."

Mishwan didn't argue but changed the subject.

"I heard some things that can help us. It seems that some very important and secret prisoners are a half day's ride down the mountain. There was some concern among my guards that they would not be able to catch up in order to re-capture the two that escaped almost immediately after they were abducted."

They both laughed.

"Barska and Waylik, no doubt," said Sonya.

"No doubt," added Mishwan. "It also seems that they guessed we were all going to rescue Sayeeda and Cowis. That is why most of the Mountain Dwellers headed down the mountain — assuming the rest of us would follow."

"So it's up to us to find our own way, eh Mish?"

"So it would seem," he answered as he tried to pass a piece of meat to Dr. Livingstone.

But the bird played hard to get, burying his beak in his feathers, and looking sideways at Sonya as if to say "who is this guy?"

Eventually, Dr. Livingstone snapped a morsel of meat from Mishwan's shaking hand. Sonya laughed at his reaction — forgetting her own at first.

As soon as the moon rose, they started along the path. They both knew that Mountain Dwellers travelled the same way in front of them and possibly behind them, too. But neither one knew how to bushwack down a mountain. And neither one wanted to give up the horses to try.

So they moved along at a steady pace and continued

until dawn. As the sun started its climb to the right of their forward destination, they could see how far from the top they had traveled. But these mountains could not compare to the grand mountains that separated the Zukulan from the Great Plain.

Sonya found herself looking to the west, wondering if any of Arkola's people knew of Waylik's plight — or cared.

At the next opening of the trees, both Mishwan and Sonya could plainly see a huge dwelling on the flat land below them — much like a castle, built of stone and surrounded by a wall of stone. Sonya couldn't resist the temptation to move towards it.

Mishwan put a restraining hand on her shoulder, but quickly removed it when Dr. Livingstone ruffled his feathers in disapproval.

"We should wait until dark, Sonya," he said.

"I'm sick and tired of waiting till dark." Sonya sighed, but didn't move.

"We will have a much better chance if we do. You cannot walk in and simply announce that we want to rescue their most valuable prisoners."

They waited, Sonya and Dr. Livingstone so restless that Mishwan soon found it difficult to sit still. He left to explore the area and find a plausible way to approach. Sonya stared at the castle from their perch and tried to think of a foolproof way to get in unnoticed and out alive.

Mishwan returned and described the landscape to Sonya. As dusk gathered around them, they made their way slowly and quietly, leaving the horses in a safe place to be picked up later. Dr. Livingstone flew ahead and high above them, but rarely out of sight.

They passed the outlying guards with suspicious ease, but neither acknowledged tey's suspicion to the other. They came to a large clearing before the wall and looked at each other with questioning eyes. Darting to the wall would surely mean discovery. They needed some kind of distraction.

"Fire?" suggested Mishwan.

"And what do we burn?" asked Sonya.

"There is sufficient dry wood around; we will gather it before we split up to make our fires."

Soon, they each crouched at either end of the clearing. Sonya saw the flicker of flames in the distance before she could get her fire going. She'd avoided starting the fires when the others traveled with her and therefore hadn't gotten very "swift with flint" as Waylik would say.

A small group of men rushed out towards Mishwan's fire. When Sonya's blazed they called to the wall. The ensuing commotion sufficed to get Sonya and Mishwan to the gate unnoticed. They ducked into the nearest doorway.

After a reasonable time, but not too long, they jumped from shadow to shadow towards the center of the mini-city.

Dr. Livingstone was nowhere in sight and Sonya hoped he stayed away for awhile; the Mountain Dwellers made a great effort to kill eagles whenever possible. The thought of Dr. Livingstone mounted on some Mountain Dweller's wall infuriated her, sending a bolt of aggressive energy thoroughly through her. She concentrated on where they were going.

Mishwan led the way and Sonya thought briefly of Barska and Waylik as they passed some small huts. They reached the main building in a few minutes.

Getting in posed another problem. They couldn't just walk through the front door. They slipped around to the side and threw a rope over the top. Mishwan climbed first, and Sonya followed him through a window and quietly out into the hallway. Mishwan led the way with a confidence that surprised Sonya; straight to the bottom of the largest staircase — the quiet eerily closing in around them.

Mishwan found two guards and struck them down with a ferocity that scared Sonya. They took a torch and walked down a long, dusty, and moldy smelling passageway. Sonya wanted to turn and run. But the thought of Cowis and Sayeeda drugged, lying on the floor of that wretched place, kept her going.

The faintest noise led Mishwan to them. They had no windows, no fresh air, and a thickly mossed wall separated their chambers. Cowis managed a faint smile as Mishwan fumbled for the keys to unbind him. Sonya felt helpless.

She gave Cowis some water and tried to wake him fully. He drank greedily but couldn't stand. She knew she'd never be able to get him out of there.

"Cowis," tried Sonya, "you've got to try and get Zorena."

He shook his head without saying anything.

"Cowis, listen. I can't carry you out. She'll have to give you the strength."

But he barely had the strength to listen.

Mishwan took water to Sayeeda who was at least more coherent if not much stronger.

In the end, Tagor Reached out to her. Sonya found a new respect (and gratefulness) for the bond of love and the Ruling Power. Sayeeda smiled as they led her out into the hall.

Cowis struggled to his feet and leaned heavily on Sonya's shoulder. He stood up tall, smiled, and laughed.

"Zorena says 'What took you so long?'"

"Well, tell Zorena-"

"No!" said Mishwan in a commanding tone. "We have no time for jokes."

"Yeah, sorry."

As they reached the top of the stairs, a handful of guards found them. Cowis and Sayeeda followed in the path that Mishwan and Sonya made. Her shield arm nearly gave out by the time they reached the passageway. The noise brought the house on them. If only she'd taught Dr. Livingstone to come when she called.

They made the first level, and Mishwan found a way down. But would it be too much for Cowis and Sayeeda?

Sonya chided herself. They should've gotten horses first.

She and Mishwan practically pushed their liberated prisoners down the trellis. Mishwan went first and helped Sayeeda, then he climbed up again to support Cowis on the way down. Sonya stood guard, listening to the stomping and clanging of guards searching and getting closer.

She had half the distance left to climb when she heard the guards coming their way. Sonya jumped to the ground and joined the other three. They ran to the front of the building and stole two horses; Cowis doubled up behind Sonya, and Sayeeda doubled up behind Mishwan.

Mishwan fought well on horseback, but Sonya was in deep trouble. The horse spun in circles while her opponents laughed at her comical swordsmanship — and a frightened Cowis clinging to the saddle.

Sonya knew they were dead when two riders stormed to the support of her foes. Yet, as Sonya watched them approach, a fierce and steely will grew inside of her — she *would* get a few good strikes in first.

But the riders struck down the Mountain Dwellers and sped towards the main gate. She and Mishwan barely had wits enough to follow.

The four horses rode through the gate and out towards the mountains, one mystery rider leading the way, the other pulling up the rear. Dr. Livingstone screeched his welcome from high above.

Ahwatukee Foothills, Tempe, Arizona, Sept., 1978

Chapter Fourteen

If It Ain't One Thing, It's Another

They rode hard until reaching the foot of the mountains. Sonya and Mishwan turned to thank their rescuers and smiled relief to see Waylik and Barska.

"Zorena sent us," was all Waylik said.

"Where were you?" asked Sonya angrily.

Barska answered. "We were within the city, trying to find a more reasonable rescue. However, the two of you blundered in and made it rather difficult for us to adhere to our plan." He paused.

"How did you get them out so quickly?"

Sonya ignored the question. "Doing what we came to do does not seem like a blunder to me."

"It would have been if we had not arrived at precisely the moment we did. We only got through the gates because of the splendid outfits Barska acquired. You would not have made it past the sentries you were battling. *And* we now have the entire nation at our heels." Waylik sighed impatiently.

"A simple 'thank you' would have been sufficient, Sonya."

Sonya laughed and apologized with a flourishing bow.

"But that's what you get for leaving us in the cold," she added.

Dr. Livingstone landed nearby and eyed the two newcomers with caution. Sonya walked over and scratched under his wing.

"This is Dr. Livingstone. Dr. Livingstone, meet Waylik and Barska, friends — even though they left me out in the wilderness to fend for myself against the elements and the enemy."

Neither Barska nor Waylik denied her charges.

"Dr. Livingstone. A unique name, I am sure. How did you come to know him?" asked Barska.

But Mishwan interrupted. "We must keep moving. If you insist on telling stories, do it as we travel. Sonya and I have four horses hidden close by. We must go to them."

They followed Mishwan, and Sonya contemplated the change in him. He had surely proven himself worthy of Zorena's confidence — even if he did seem a bit bossy.

They picked the two fastest horses to ride and packed their gear onto one of the others. They unsaddled and unbridled the fourth and sent it roaming in the mountains.

While the others busied themselves with this task, Sonya gave food to Cowis and Sayeeda.

"Simply leaving that dank place has made much difference," exclaimed Sayeeda.

Cowis nodded but said nothing.

"Now, Barska," demanded Sonya. "I want to know the brilliant plan you and Waylik had contrived."

"We had just learned the routine of the house guards. At the opportune time, we planned to sneak out the prisoners and ride out at night on some pretense of house business. It would have been hours before anyone knew the prisoners were gone and days before anyone realized who took them. This extra time should have been sufficient to find you and Mishwan and travel into the desert undetected. But that is no longer a possibility."

"Well, I don't see how that plan is anything special. What it really means is that you had no plan at all and would've spent days or weeks there before you got them out."

Sonya tried to hide her relief. If they really had devised a brilliant plan, she would have felt foolish.

"But I really want to know why you left us the way you did. Mishwan and I were in some deep trouble there for awhile."

Only the scrape of horse hoofs against mountain rocks and roots disturbed the silence that followed.

"Well?" persisted Sonya.

Barska answered haltingly. "Zorena insisted that we leave when we did. I trusted that she knew more of the situation and would keep you safe."

"Yeah, right. I almost fell off a damned mountain."

But then Sonya fell silent. She had to wonder. What role did Zorena play in the climb up the ridge, and the taming of Dr. Livingstone?

They rode through the night, stopping only for meals. Waylik dug up some lilies of the valley growing at the foot of the mountains on the desert side. She made a salve from the roots and spread it on Sonya's knife wound.

"It will lessen the ugliness of the scar. Although, I fear it will not completely prevent it."

Sonya wondered how she'd explain that scar at home. She'd end up on a psychiatric ward if she told the truth.

I'll probably never make it home alive anyway, she thought, *with the "entire nation" at our heels.*

She began to doubt herself and Mishwan, again.

But Mishwan seemed to have no doubts, even after Barska assured them that Berrot Mure was emptying out in pursuit.

"Well, they have fallen for the bait. Now, to devise the trap," Mishwan smiled a self-satisfied smile.

Sonya felt sick.

Cowis and Sayeeda quickly gained strength as they ate good food, and Bobby's potion wore off.

Barska and Waylik took up the rear to cover their tracks and try to delay their pursuers.

Sayeeda told her story as they moved out of the mountains, heading straight for the desert.

"I encountered this bear-beast once before and so had learned its weakness. Waylik, however, is the one who actually killed the beast."

"This does not change how we felt watching you rush into its arms like a madwoman," Mishwan's anger flared quickly at the memory.

Sayeeda laughed. "I am only now understanding how it must have looked to you. The trick, you see, is to throw the knife directly through the middle of the forehead. The secret of the beast is this: it cannot grasp you if you are close within its reach. Its arms do not bend all the way.

"Unfortunately, the beast and I both stumbled into the waterfall. The descent was less than it looked from above, and the beast somewhat aided in cushioning my landing on a ledge, which threw me into a pool and quickly along a swift current that ran a course different from the main waterfall. The next thing I remember is waking up and being forced to drink some herb mixture that quickly sent me back to oblivion."

"And I," continued Cowis. "Did not dare leave your side. I watched your descent to the pool and tried to follow by land. I believe I was taken by our enemies along that rocky path. I too remember very little except for the herb mixture and a total inability to stay conscious."

"Is that why Zorena couldn't find you?" asked Sonya

"Yes," answered Cowis. "This mixture of Bobby's renders one unconscious, not just asleep. The brain is in a very different state. When you are asleep, it is possible for Zorena to Reach you, wake you, and call for you. But when one is unconscious, this is almost impossible unless standing very nearby. I wonder how Bobby knew this?"

"He probably didn't," ventured Sonya. "He probably just knows that there's some way you all communicate. He's quite the coward, I think. He was afraid you might hurt him even though he didn't really know how."

"Yes, I think you are correct," added Sayeeda. "He questioned me several times but did not seem to know what he was searching for."

"My guess is that he wanted to know if you were worth any kind of ransom. Our Bobby is a greedy little bastard."

"Yes," said Cowis. "This would make sense. He had the Medallion in his possession and yet did not know what to do with it."

"But, he thought it was worth something — he told me so. And the way I grabbed it from him, he's sure to be looking for it again. He knows there's some kind of Power floating around this world, but he doesn't know what exactly it is or how to get it. But he'll be trying to. And he's got those Mountain Dwellers all fired up and ready to do what he tells them to do."

Dr. Livingstone enjoyed the company of the others, rather than being afraid. And he came in handy for awhile. Whenever he saw a Mountain Dweller, he screeched and dove to attack.

Sonya felt proud of her watch-eagle. He learned to come to her whistle and land by her. She just couldn't support the weight of his landing on her arm. But he was often content to sit on her shoulder. And he developed quite the taste for blueseed.

Before they left the cover of the trees, Waylik and Barska made bows. They made some arrows and brought wood for more bows, arrows and various other implements of battle.

They rode into the desert, making as straight a path for Anatawen as they could. They rode the horses this time, and Sonya wondered why. But she had decided to keep quiet about such things. Two members of the Ruling Family were with her, and Waylik.

It somehow seemed perfectly natural for Waylik to ride with them instead of turning for Zukulan.

Sonya watched Dr. Livingstone carefully as they left the mountains and moved farther into the desert, the peaks of Berrot Mure slowly dwindling and fading from sight. She doubted he would be willing, or even able, to leave the mountains. On their second night out he flew off and didn't return.

The harshness of the desert did not lessen with familiarity. If anything, it was worse. Sonya cursed it with every breath. She wondered how the horses could bear it, and she feared they would die. But she said nothing, trusting to the great minds of the Ruling Family.

After the fourth night of desert travel, dawn's growing light revealed a pile of dusty rocks and twisted boulders against a rising landscape. They settled in the nooks of this empty place and unpacked all of the gear they'd brought. Waylik set up a lean-to for some shade.

Sonya's throat ached from lack of water. The horses held their heads low into the rocks, barely shuffling, even to swish the flies away. Mishwan gathered mounds of stones for the trusty slingshot he seldom used. Cowis gave Sonya a stack of sticks and told her to start whittling the bark away to make arrows.

"Wouldn't it be better if we just kept on moving?" Sonya suggested. "I mean, I know we're all tired, and the horses, too. But we can still move, so shouldn't we?"

Barska and Waylik turned towards her but said nothing. Finally, Cowis answered.

"We are wiser to stay here and wait for them."

"Who? How many?" Sonya's anxiety peaked.

Waylik shrugged. Cowis and Barska exchanged knowing glances. Mishwan worked on top of the tallest boulder — stringing bows and fitting arrowheads to the sticks that they'd brought with them.

"Well?" she insisted, looking from one to the other and back again.

"An army," Barska said in monotone.

Sonya never felt her stomach and her hopes drop so low, so fast, and so together.

She scraped the knife against the wood and felt worse for having to depend on it and slingshots. She pulled hers out of the pocket of that ridiculous jacket. She remembered her training with it so long ago, and how she'd nearly hit Tagor, who stood well away from her target.

"Listen guys," Sonya tried to assume her meekest demeanor. "How long do you really think we can hold off an army, and don't you think it would be better if someone got hold of Anatawen and asked them for help?"

"We will do what we can where we are. Continue with your work Sonya," Barska's tone was most condescending.

But Sonya said nothing. After all, the situation was due to her rashness, or at least, worsened by it.

Finally, Cowis could contain himself no longer. He chuckled softly, went to her side, and whispered gently in her ear.

"Zorena has known about the group from Berrot Mure since the beginning. As soon as you and Mishwan decided to enter the palace, she sent a mighty force to meet us. We only need to hold out until they arrive. If we are fortunate, they will reach us before the Mountain Dwellers. They will not attack if there will be a large battle."

"I wouldn't count on that. It'd be a big blow to their egos."

He looked at her blankly. Apparently, Dr. Freud's theories had not reached Anatawen.

She rephrased. "It would make them feel . . . a loss of pride, cause embarrassment to run away from us."

"It never stopped them before."

But it was obviously something they had not seriously considered.

"That's the first thing Bobby did to them, y'know. Got them all fired up about pride and ownership, old wounds, and all that."

"She could be correct," said Sayeeda. "It is the main reason the Mountain Dwellers have not been able to attain equality with, or dominion over, Anatawen."

The Ruling Family didn't like the simplicity of her logic.

"The Zukulan have attained this, through discipline and allegiance — along with a little courtesy," continued Waylik. "These are the only real reasons for the difference between the two peoples."

A silence followed. Sonya concentrated on convincing Cowis.

"If Bobby has managed to attain a position of power, and it is obvious that he has, he'll do what he can to maintain that power. He knows that in order to compete with Anatawen, the Mountain Dwellers must pull together as one unit, not the small groups of sporadic marauders they've been. He just needs to convince them that he's smart enough, or tough enough, or both. That little trick with the hang glider, and his special knack with herbs — probably hallucinogens, too — have probably easily won him loyalty, and a healthy amount of fear."

They agreed but thought her urgency premature.

"You don't understand, our history is filled with situations like this. He'll want every inch of land he can see, then he'll go to the edge of sight and on and on. Zukulan isn't safe either."

No one argued with her. They said nothing at all. Cowis, Waylik and Barska disappeared shortly afterward for a quick conference.

Sonya made her arrows, practiced with her slingshot, and hoped that Bobby hadn't developed any explosives.

Only Cowis nursed her sanity. She hadn't seen him in so long; she enjoyed just being with him more than ever.

And Mishwan started to act like his old self again. Sonya wondered how he managed it under the circumstances.

Waylik slipped into the background, smiling occasionally at her private jokes, although Cowis and Barska made no tactical move without consulting her. She and Sayeeda renewed and solidified their friendship.

Sonya wondered what would happen to them all.

Z Z Z Z Z

The first sounds came in the small light of an approaching dawn. Sonya jumped to wakefulness and turned towards the noises. She pulled her knife and grabbed a bow — useless though it seemed. Then she realized she faced the wrong way. Mountain Dwellers would come from the other direction.

It was Anatawen.

Sonya was never so happy to see a bunch of people she didn't know.

Tagor and Sayeeda had an intense reunion.

The men and women of Anatawen had ridden hard and long to reach them before Bobby's army. Now they prepared to travel quickly, to reach Barsel's Water Hole first and keep the Mountain Dwellers from it. This would force the Mountain Dwellers to turn back.

They left a small group behind to slow down the oncoming attackers. Tagor assumed the role of general. Sayeeda, Barska, Cowis and Waylik rode with him to form an impressive vanguard for the forces of Anatawen.

Fifteen thousand strong they were, with another two thousand protecting Barsel's Water Hole. The whole of Anatawen had answered the call.

They rode long and made little notice of the day or night, stopping for only a few hours at each break. But regular meals and plenty of water made the trip bearable for Sonya. She had the time and the energy to contemplate the Ruling Family.

Tagor was the perfect general. He rode tall and in command, of everything, especially himself. Not the tiniest hint of challenge to his authority entered into anyone's mind.

Close to his side rode Sayeeda, her shoulders falling a full twelve inches below his. Her light colored hair peeked out from beneath her hat, every inch of her white skin covered from the sun's burning rays.

Barska rode off to the side, often falling back to check the rear. The captains reported to him, and he decided what merited Tagor's attention.

Cowis rode close to Tagor, with Sonya, Waylik, and Mishwan close by. No one asked or seemed in any way to question this arrangement.

The little group of travelers had earned each other's trust in a way that would not be separated by structured army organizing.

But what would happen when the fighting started? Sonya's arm healed at a good pace, but not completely, yet. And even in top form, she knew she'd be lost in a real battle. She shuddered at the thought, fear engulfing her as she imagined these men and women fiercely wielding swords, and shooting arrows flying all around her.

In the starlit cold of a desert night, the news reached them. Bobby's army could be seen in pursuit. Thirty thousand as counted by Anatawen's rearguard, which now became the front lines.

The Ruling Family rode to face the danger, leaving Sonya with the food and water wagons. She and Sayeeda would help with the wounded. Tagor had no intentions of letting Sayeeda get any closer to the fighting than absolutely necessary.

Sonya helped where she could, doing what she was told, and managed to avoid any prolonged contact with Sayeeda. A growing guilt bored a hole deep inside Sonya, and only her fear kept her from riding to the battle. Until a wounded Waylik was carried back.

Sonya's guilt overrode her fear and judgement then. She understood, suddenly, that dying would not be the worst thing — only the last thing. She grabbed a shield and sword from an unsuspecting soldier and headed towards the battle.

As she rode toward the shouts, Sonya noticed a vague increase in activity. She rode on, past a patch of open ground. She heard a far off voice calling for her to go back.

Suddenly she was in the midst of the fighting. She looked on the carnage and breathed in an indefinable stench. The horse threw her — the only thing that could've stopped the nausea-induced convulsion that came upon her. She stood as quickly as she could and started to defend herself.

She realized in a moment that she should have stayed in back with the wounded and resting. She would not die a hero, just a fool.

But the hole in her stomach filled with resolve. Adrenaline surged through her, and she heard her own voice as she laughed aloud. Sonya tried not to *think* about what she was doing.

The fighting clashed all around her, it would be impossible to dodge every sword, dart, and spear. She concentrated on her one-on-one sword fight with the enemy facing her. She soon heard Cowis's voice getting closer, calling to the forces of Anatawen to come to his aid, and chiding Sonya for her foolishness.

But the strange feeling inside Sonya did not diminish. She struck down her enemy and turned to find another. But the forces of Anatawen had surrounded her.

A large man carried her off according to Cowis's orders. She collapsed in a state of exhaustion while Sayeeda wrapped a gash in her leg. Sonya faded out of consciousness.

The battled raged fiercely for two days. Anatawen held on to the pile of rocks they'd chosen and gradually the strength of their enemies began to wane. The onslaughts came less often and did not last as long.

Anatawen did not press the enemy. At each setback of the Mountain Dwellers, the Ruling Family expected them to keep going. But still they came back.

Although unable to return to battle, Waylik still took part in the strategy sessions of the captains.

"It seems that Sonya was correct," started Waylik. "Bobby has learned from the past of his people."

"I have waited and hoped that the Mountain Dwellers would someday regain their pride and lose their hatred of us," said a sad Cowis. "Pride and hatred together are dangerous."

Tagor shot him a quick I-told-you-so look.

But Waylik nodded in understanding. She, too, had been waiting for the day when she could roam the whole of the mountains in safety.

"Enough philosophy, Cowis," it was Tagor who spoke. "We cannot parley with shooting arrows. We must fight, or die. Therefore, we will fight. It is not a matter of who will win; it is a matter of how we will win and when. They cannot hold on much longer. With each onslaught, we lessen their numbers."

Two young men brought news then, one from the fighting, one from the guard left at Barsel's Water Hole. The last regroup of the Mountain Dwellers looked more like a retreat. They did not seem to be stopping. The other man reported that Barsel's Water Hole had been poisoned. Most of the two thousand left to guard it were sick, some nearly to their deaths.

"I am one of those who did not drink from the water after its fouling because we had been guarding the outskirts of our camp until your return."

The forces of Anatawen hastened to the Water Hole, now. Sonya woke in a moving wagon with Waylik sitting nearby. Sonya felt foolish.

"I trust you rested well?" asked Waylik.

Sonya only moaned in response. A sharp pain traveled along her leg. Every muscle ached, except her left arm. It was numb. She picked it up and looked at it as though it were foreign to her.

"Do you always do such utterly foolish things, Sonya?"
Sonya nodded and tried to smile.

"You should have known better than to strain the arm before it healed fully, or to join in battle when so inept at swordplay."

Sonya lost all desire to speak. Exhaustion nagged her muscles, her sight blurred, and she wanted to be asleep.

Waylik continued to talk.

"You will feel like that for a short while. It is a combination of your injuries and the healing herbs. You will soon be awake enough to want to know that we won the battle and Cowis is fine. Sleep now, and I will tell you all the details when you are better able to hear them."

Sonya woke again just as the host reached Barsel's Water Hole. Waylik still rode with her.

"Bobby has poisoned the water. Nearly the entire guard is sick. Even heating the water seems to be useless."

"You're probably just not letting it boil long enough," answered Sonya. "We have very few above ground water supplies that are not polluted where I come from. Boiling the water for at least ten minutes — um, the length of that Anatawen song sung twice — should kill pretty much anything that Bobby can dish up."

"I will pass the word to Tagor," Waylik left as she spoke.

Sonya stood up carefully and found a crutch to lighten the load on her leg. As she struggled toward the water, Sayeeda joined her.

"You should not walk on the leg for some time yet, Sonya."

"I know, I know," answered Sonya. But she smiled. Sayeeda's concern was real, and Sonya felt an intense closeness with her.

"Help me along, I want to check out the banks of the river and follow it a bit."

"What are you looking for, Sonya?"

"I'm not sure. I just want to see if I can figure out what Bobby used. I'm hoping he hasn't created any chemical, or found oil, or anything. I'm hoping he just dumped a big pile of manure upstream, and the whole bunch of you just has a bad case of Giardia."

"What is Giardia?"

"It's a parasite that gets into your bloodstream from drinking tainted water. The water gets it from the droppings of deer and bear and other animals."

They walked along the banks of the River. Sonya inspected the edge of the water and the plants. She could find none of the slime she would expect from oil.

"Hey, what's that?" she pointed to a group of plants almost 10 feet high, with long and narrow, notched leaves.

"It is hemp," answered Sayeeda. "Some kind of weed, I think, though useful for making rope and other things."

"Yeah, Cannabis weed. Sayeeda, get someone down here to pull some of those up by the roots."

"Sonya, we have all learned to refrain from doubting you on many of these matters that seem to pertain to your home. However, I would appreciate a hint at what you are planning."

"That's a wonderful weed. A healing hemp. A soothing-to-the-mind plant," she laughed. "It'll stop the nausea. It even kills some bacteria. You can throw it in hot water to make tea, dry it and smoke it, or eat it plain. In any case, get someone down here to pull up some plants by the roots. Let 'em hang upside down for a few hours — days would be better — so the dru . . . ah, medicine seeps down into the leaves."

Sonya supervised the cultivation of the Cannabis and managed to collect a few seeds from some bursting buds.

The strong sun on Anatawen's garden would yield big, healthy, potent plants.

Now every campfire had rapidly boiling water being timed by a dutiful soldier. And many had a steeping pot of marijuana tea to soothe the stomach and ease the mind.

Cowis found Sonya back at her wagon, drinking some of the Soothing Tea — as the soldiers called it.

"I see you are taking your own advice."

"Yes," answered Sonya. "But you'd better not let people overdo it with this stuff. They might not do so hot in battle if they're all high."

"Yes, it puts some people to sleep almost immediately. Others, such as Mishwan, find new energy. It is an interesting discovery, this Cannabis."

"Yeah, I've got some seeds; we can plant some in the garden when we get back. That hot Anatawen sun ought to produce some potent stuff.

"Anyway, tell me what's going on with the Mountain Dwellers. Are they really gone?"

"No, they are not," Cowis sighed. "It seems that Bobby has been very clever and planning this for some time. They have begun to follow us again. I also fear that some will come from the west along the River. We have sent scouts in all directions. We should know something as the sun sets."

They sat for some time by the banks of the river. Slowly, the sun disappeared and Sonya shivered in the night. She returned to the wagons to sleep.

Cowis met with Tagor and the captains to discuss what the scouts had seen.

Sonya woke to the commotion of soldiers getting ready to ride to battle. Bobby's army advanced towards them. And scouts had reported another large host following the River from the west.

The deciding battle would take place before Barsel's Water Hole. Sonya helped Sayeeda and Waylik get ready for the wounded.

It wasn't long before the news reached them along with the hurt and dying. Anatawen was wedged between hatred from the south and now hatred from the west.

But Anatawen did not yield. In a wide half-circle around Barsel's Water Hole they held fast, and beat back the forces of the Mountain Dwellers, foot by foot.

Tagor taxed his mind and body beyond anything he'd ever tried. For the first time since childhood he turned to Zorena for strength. Zorena emptied out the city, but the new forces could not arrive for days.

By dawn, the Mountain Dwellers had broken through the outer defense on the western front and all of the Anatawen were engaged in battle. Tagor's hope dwindled with each drop of the sun towards the horizon. His will alone held his forces to their task.

And so Bobby pushed his army. If he could beat Anatawen, with three of the Ruling Family present, what would stop him from going straight to Anatawen's gate?

Sonya, Sayeeda, and Waylik kept frantically busy. And Anatawen's herb masters found many uses for the hemp plant Sonya had discovered. Even she didn't realize the great healing powers of the Cannabis weed.

A lull in the stream of wounded found Sonya watching Waylik as she stared towards the west, as though trying to see through the desert miles, over the peaks of the western range, to Zukulan.

"Homesick?"

Waylik smiled and shook her head. "Hardly," she answered. "I feel as though a great fate comes from that direction. And the battle wages heavy there, I'm told."

Sayeeda called to them then. "We have a patient that the two of you may be interested in."

Sonya rushed over to find Mishwan among the newest arrivals. He'd managed to save the life of a promising young captain who also was the son of Homak's brother.

"Well, Mish, looks like you made a hero of yourself."

"I think it is not as glorious as the stories may try to make it."

He winced and tried not to moan as Sayeeda washed his torn leg. Sonya fed him Cannabis tea.

"I guess this hero stuff never is."

A horn blast interrupted their conversation, and a cry went out from the western front. With it came surprising news: the Zukulan had arrived.

Following the river from its origin in the mountains, they had kept themselves well-fed and quickly descended upon the Mountain Dwellers from the rear. Soon, Bobby's army became wedged between two unbeatable foes, their only option retreat, the only direction south and back through the desert waste to Berrot Mure.

Waylik joined Tagor and the others as soon as she saw the Zukulan captain ride up.

"It is appropriate that you, Vayorl, are my rescuer."

He grinned fondly and put his arm around her shoulder.

"Even if Arkola could have found someone else to save *you*, I would have come first — I have earned that privilege."

"Yes, you have," Waylik continued. "But it still does not explain how you knew to come at all."

"I am not sure how Arkola knew of this situation. Perhaps the return of the Medallion gives him new sight."

"Perhaps."

But Sonya muttered, "Zorena," and walked away.

That evening Cowis and Barska finally returned from the fighting.

Sonya said little as she and Cowis sat by the River, happy to be alive.

They stayed two more nights at Barsel's Water Hole and then turned towards home in the cool light before dawn.

The Zukulan turned west. Tagor officially extended the Right of Travel to Waylik.

Waylik turned to Sonya but only said, "Fare well."

Sonya smiled. "Thanks, I know you will."

They stood for a moment and said nothing. But Sonya no longer felt uncomfortable at the silence.

Then Waylik mounted her precious Longhair and the Zukulan rode back along the River.

The rest of the ride was pleasant for Sonya. She rode horseback alongside Cowis, enjoying the leisurely pass through the foothills and the fragrance of the plains beyond.

They rode slowly and took long breaks for meals. Still, the grey-white wall of Anatawen, seen between the towers of the outer defenses, was a welcome sight.

Friends Pond, Dartmouth, Mass., Summer, 1981. © 2003 Beth David

Chapter Fifteen

A Sad Farewell

They had, of course, expected Zorena to meet them. If not at the gate, at least at the door. Even Tagor's face showed signs of his surprise.

Sonya shrugged it off at first. Maybe the great and powerful Zorena felt it unnecessary to meet the dusty travelers. But when they walked through the hall and to the stairs, a sick feeling struck her in the pit of her stomach.

She quickly followed Tagor who took three stairs at a stride, though otherwise seemed as calm as always. Sonya bumped into him when he stopped abruptly at Homak's door.

Things of that nature no longer surprised Sonya; she simply followed him.

Sonya couldn't be sure of what happened next. She saw Zorena leaning in the alcove doorway looking very tired — as tired as when she'd made contact with Cowis in the mountains. A deep sadness etched itself in her face, and her whole body drooped with the weight of it.

Sonya wanted to run to her. But an angry Tagor ordered Sonya and Sayeeda out of the room.

A visibly shaken Sonya sat in the kitchen with Sayeeda. The image of Zorena, leaning against the wall, looking almost about to fall, or even cry, had a shattering effect on Sonya.

She and Sayeeda sat staring at each other, the suspense slowly dragging the minutes by.

Finally, Sonya sent someone to find Surriya.

Suddenly, Sayeeda stood up.

"They want me," Sayeeda looked very surprised. "Homak is dying." She rushed out of the kitchen.

Sonya stood for a moment and then sat. She wondered where Mishwan had been taken. The silence in the big house closed in around Sonya as she sipped at her zukha waiting for Surriya.

"What may I do for you, Sonya?" Surriya stood, waiting.

"Sit down, get some zukha."

Surriya poured herself a cup and sat across from Sonya at the little kitchen table. Sonya wondered how to start.

"You pretty much know everything that goes on around here, don't you, Surriya?"

Surriya only smiled and nodded.

"Well, then, ah . . . What's going on?"

Surriya's smile faded. She pulled her chair closer to the table and studied Sonya's face. Sonya became uncomfortable under the scrutiny.

"Homak is dying."

"I know that. But how? And more than that, how could Zorena have kept it from her brothers? I mean, with that mind-" she stopped, suddenly remembering her vow to keep silent, but not remembering which parts were supposed to be secret.

Surriya laughed and held up her hand, palm outward, to show she understood and Sonya need say no more.

"Homak is older than he seems to be to you and many

others. The Ruling Family lives long and stays hale until the end," she looked around for prying ears.

"How Zorena managed to prevent this knowledge from reaching her brothers is another story. I do not know how, or why. But it would explain much."

"What much?" Sonya had little patience for the slow unraveling of Surriya's thoughts.

"Zorena has not been well, either," answered Surriya. "I have been concerned. But all of the Ruling Family members I know best were off at the battle. I had no way of getting word to Tagor. Zorena knew this. She is powerful, Sonya. Powerful enough to communicate with her brothers and still keep this from them. But it is an obvious draw on even her strength. I tried to talk to her, but she would not listen. Even as a child she could be strong and stubborn when all those around her disagreed."

Sonya laughed.

"But still," continued Surriya. "For all her stubborn-ness, it is difficult not to love her."

Sonya nodded, but said nothing for a long moment. "You're leaving something out, aren't you Surriya?"

She smiled, "Yes, I am." And then she called a servant.

"Take Sonya to the houses where the wounded were taken. She will want to find Mishwan and tell him all the news." Surriya left with a bow.

Sonya laughed out loud and followed the servant. They found Mishwan deep in conversation with his father. To Sonya's amazement and embarrassment, Margon bowed and treated her with great honor. He quickly left the two travelers alone.

Mishwan hadn't heard anything concrete, but he knew that things weren't quite right.

Zorena had been neglecting her city.

They talked leisurely for awhile, as word spread through the city that Homak was dying. Suddenly Sonya felt she should go to Homak's rooms.

By now she recognized the signs of being called. She

left quickly for the place she truly wanted to be most but still hesitated at the door. What does one say in Anatawen when the Ruler is dying?

She knocked and entered quietly. Angry faces met her, not sad. She did not see Zorena. Tagor and Barska left the room almost immediately. Sonya faced Cowis but said nothing for a long moment.

"You all look more angry than sad, Cowis. Am I missing something here?"

"Death is not an enemy here, Sonya. At least not for someone like Homak. His life has been long and full of many good things. When it is time to die, those of us with Ruling Blood do not fight it. We simply surrender to the natural way, and those who are left celebrate the life of the one who is gone. Or so we should. But something is wrong here. Zorena needs you."

"Me?"

Cowis laughed. "Yes, you. Zorena is . . . a very private person. She is very powerful. Maybe too powerful. Old legends state that the exact time of the birth of a Ruler's child can add much to the Power already meant for tey. We always knew that Zorena had a special store of strength and power. But I fear it is a detriment to her now. We all had much contact with her, and none of us had any indication of what was happening. They both kept this from us so that we would concentrate on the battle and not rush back. But," he hesitated and looked worried, "she will not let him go now. I am able to understand her sustaining him while we were away. But now it is time to let the natural way follow its course. Yet she continues to give him her strength. It is as though she is . . . afraid . . ." he said the word as though he didn't believe it himself "to inherit his Power. It makes no sense."

"What Power?" asked Sonya.

Cowis raised an eyebrow.

"I *mean*, if she is giving *him* strength, how can he have anything left to give? No! I didn't mean it the way it sounded," she added quickly.

Cowis didn't understand her distress. "You are confusing power with energy. That is a dangerous mistake, and is no matter now. Zorena will not let him go! She must. She will realize this eventually. But she does Homak a great injustice. Her emotion rules her thought. You have won her trust and her heart."

"Are the others angry with you for bringing me here for this?"

"No. They are angry at Zorena, not you."

Sonya moaned. How could she decide this? He was talking about the Anatawen version of pulling the plug. She'd never really thought about it before. How could she make that decision for someone else? Did she have the right to?

Sonya sat and closed her eyes, clenching her teeth till they hurt. She felt so tired she wanted to sleep where she sat.

And for the first time she felt truly angry at the universe. Why was she there? Why was *she* forced to make this decision? Who was she to make it? If Zorena truly could sustain Homak's life, shouldn't she? She was so wrapped up in her own musings that she didn't see Zorena until she sat in the chair by Sonya's side.

"I thought that everyone had left, finally," Zorena poured herself some wine.

Sonya said nothing. She watched Zorena who held the glass up in front of her and turned it.

"Wine is a strange drink. I have seen it cause death, and I have seen it breathe life into the dying. Do you doubt which purpose has more value?"

Sonya remained silent. Zorena looked old. Sonya had never thought of Zorena as any age in particular. She was just . . . Zorena. But now she looked old and tired. That easy, flowing energy had gotten all used up somehow.

Sonya wanted to do something, to say something. But she couldn't.

Zorena looked right through her and Sonya practically stopped breathing. The silence became unbearable, and Sonya got up to stand by the fireplace. Zorena turned from her thoughts.

"Come, Sonya. Sit. Tell me what you feel about this."

Sonya sat and tried to look Zorena in the eye. The old fire had dimmed, but the depth of her gaze had not changed. Sonya looked down at her hands.

"I feel . . . confused, I guess, Zorena. Why are you sustaining him when all the rules say you should not?"

"You are also against me on this?" The weakness in her voice, where there should have been indignation, tore at Sonya and stirred the loyalty she felt.

"I don't know. All I know is that everyone else says you're breaking some big rule. You're defying customs, traditions, and your brothers, and nobody knows why."

"When Homak first became ill, we kept it to ourselves because we did not want my brothers to be distracted in battle. It is not easy to keep this kind of thing from them.

"After the battle I became worried; Homak did not recover, and I feared it would be his last illness. I then planned to call my brothers, to hurry them. It would have been possible at that time to sustain Homak with the Power I possessed, but I could not have hidden it from the others at the same time. Before I made contact something strange happened. I received a surge of Power — from Homak — a Power even I did not know existed. In that surge was the Power to keep the dying alive. I was vaguely aware that this Power existed. But none speak of it. And it is only inherited upon death of the Ruler. It is not a Power that is customarily *given*."

"Can't you see why it isn't?" Sonya asked.

Zorena ignored her. "Why would Homak give me this Power before his death? It is a riddle only he can answer. Yet he refuses to answer it. There is something important to this. I must find out what."

"Zorena," Sonya tried to keep her tone soft, to ease

the bluntness of what she had to say. "The reason it was never given before death was probably to prevent exactly what is happening now." She paused, trying to find a gentle way to speak.

"Can you see that you're violating Homak's wishes? He probably gave you the Power believing that you would be strong enough to resist using it."

Sonya stopped talking. Somehow, she had difficulty believing herself. Why would Homak give Zorena the Power if not for her to use it on him? But would a man of Homak's stature opt for such a frail existence?

"Zorena, you do not have the power to keep the dying living; you have the power to keep the dying dying."

Sonya waited for Zorena's anger. But in its place Sonya saw exhaustion. She forced the next words, wondering when Zorena's anger would surface.

"What is the true reason, Zorena? That you want to know why he gave it to you? I think you would find that out in time. Or is there another reason you want to keep him here? Some reason that makes you . . . afraid to let him go?"

Sonya tried to imagine what she would do in the same situation. But the impossibility of that ever being the case just made her feel relieved she wasn't.

"Sonya," Zorena leaned forward, pleading for total attention. "You are probably right about the reasons for not giving this Power except at death. It is to prevent the heir from doing exactly what I am doing. But why would Homak give it to me if it were not to have me do exactly that? Or for some other reason only he can tell, or both?"

Her eyes filled with the frustration and she walked around the table.

"I don't get it," started Sonya. "What's with the sudden curiosity? What happened to that precious royal patience, nurtured by age? He hasn't told you, he's not going to tell you. Leave it, Zorena. Is it so horrible for you not to know. I'm sure you'll find out soon enough."

"What am I to do if it is, now, as he wants, and I let

him die? I cannot bring life back to the dead."

"And why should he decide that he should not die when it is not within his power to prevent it?"

Zorena whirled on Sonya; the old fire flared.

Sonya jumped up to face her. "Yes, it is not within *his* power to prevent it. The Power is yours. How long do you plan on doing this?"

"I do not know. I need time to think. This decision is not easy."

"But you can't think, Zorena. At least not clearly. You're quite the mess, y'know. You're nervous, uncertain, you're a whole different person. Not the Zorena I used to know. Wouldn't Homak know exactly what would happen to you if you did this? I believe he felt you'd overcome the temptation of this Power. I think it has overcome you, though."

Sonya stood, ready to face the full force of Zorena's anger. But there was horror, not anger, in her eyes. It lasted for only a moment, and Sonya could barely hear Zorena's whisper.

"No, you do not understand," she paused, her eyes staring out the window to the sunlight beyond.

"Sonya, I cannot let him go."

Zorena started walking towards the room in back, but Sonya intercepted with a gentle hand on her arm.

"You have to Zorena, and I think you know that. You can barely walk. You've been neglecting Anatawen and it's beginning to show. The Mountain Dwellers are not completely beaten yet; the Zukulan still need the Image. You are, whether or not you like it, one of the movers of events in this place — you can't ignore all that."

"I will ignore what I choose to ignore and do what I believe is most important," Zorena's eyes flashed in her anger.

"Who are you to question the actions of Anatawen's Ruler? Good bye, Sonya." She pushed past Sonya and through to the other room.

Sonya sighed, looked around, and walked out the

door. She found Cowis in the garden.

Sonya told her story in detail as the sun set towards the mountains, coloring all the world around her with fiery streaks of blazing orange across a darkening sky.

Sonya visited Mishwan after dinner and told him all she dared. They sat outside in the starlit night and talked casually of their times together — the places they'd seen, the people they'd met, the mistakes they'd made, and the lessons they'd learned. But the underlying sadness she felt for Zorena's struggle grew greater in Sonya's mind with each passing hour. She went to her bed early and woke with the rising sun.

Sonya saddled Appy and rode towards the mountains as the sun climbed behind her. She sat beneath the branches of a towering elm that lay along the path of both her journeys. She faced the majestic mountains of the Zukulan.

"You up there, Waylik," she said to the air. "I miss your matter-of-fact handling of things, my friend. Surely you would know what to do."

Sonya walked over to the horse and slipped him a handful of blueseed. A rending screech from above sent Appy running off towards home. Sonya lifted her eyes in anticipation. Never had she experienced a quicker uplifting of spirit as Dr. Livingstone dove towards her in ever-tightening circles.

She stood, waiting impatiently, her childlike excitement barely contained.

Dr. Livingstone landed on her outstretched arm and she held him. He looked at her with inquisitive eyes and she fed him some blueseed.

"Well, I'll be damned," she told him. "How the hell did you get here? Did you follow that mountain range all this way north?"

She put him on her shoulder and started walking back to look for Appy. Before she went far, she could see a rider leading him back towards her. Dr. Livingstone squawked at them but didn't move from Sonya's shoulder.

As they got closer, Sonya recognized Zorena on her shiny chestnut.

"Hello, Sonya," she said as she studied the great bird. "Dr. Livingstone, I presume?"

Sonya laughed so hard at those words, Dr. Livingstone had to fly away. Zorena looked puzzled, but had, by now learned that some of Sonya's private little references were not worth the bother of an explanation.

They sat in silence for awhile, Sonya waiting for Zorena to say what she came to say.

"I believe I must apologize to you, Sonya," the words came out slowly, Zorena forcing every syllable. "I once reprimanded you for becoming angry and leaving the room. Then I did the same to you."

Sonya mumbled something about it being okay. And suddenly she felt uncomfortable.

"You were, I know, trying to force me to see something I could not. You are correct, of course. My reasons for sustaining Homak are self-indulging. I was too busy thinking about my own feelings to realize how unfair this is to Homak, whether he wants it or not — although I am sure he does not. His reasons for giving me this Power are his alone, and I must respect that."

She paused, looked at Sonya and added in a soft voice, "I wanted to kill you yesterday, Sonya."

Fear swept through Sonya, but she kept silent, watching as Zorena raised her arms in hopelessness, the black cape puffing up, then swirling around her as she paced.

"My entire life's energy has been, of late, channeled into sustaining a life. To want, in the midst of that task, to end the life of another, because of words — *words* — nothing truly threatening my life or those under my care; that, Sonya, is a contradiction difficult to live with. I have not acted the way Zorena should act. I have not been thinking the way Zorena should think. I have not been Zorena at all. I have let indecision and emotion rule my every thought and action."

She paused, trying to keep control, each word pushed out of an uncooperative mouth.

"It is difficult for one such as I to admit such a common failing. But I must be weak at the core to give in to a clearly defined forbiddance, and now I nearly give in to . . . to a destructive feeling I am not familiar with." She turned and faced Sonya.

Sonya knew that Zorena held back tears. Sonya stammered through an unconvincing cliche about a good cry making you feel better. And then she jumped onto Appy's back and rode quickly back to the city. Dr. Livingstone flew ahead and high above.

Cowis sat anxiously in the garden when Sonya arrived. She searched for a few last berries, but found none. Cowis followed her around the garden, trying to conceal his impatience.

"You have seen Zorena?"

"Yes, she's fine. You don't have to worry about her anymore."

"You seem to be taking her turmoil rather lightly, Sonya."

"She's over the worst of it now. What's with you guys, anyway? She just needs to feel sorry for herself for a little while longer and she'll be the same old irritating, lovable Zorena once again, I assure you."

He tried to explain the Anatawen philosophy on death and why Zorena's actions were so difficult to accept. The young were mourned for the missed opportunities from a sudden or violent death. But when a person had lived a life like Homak's, no mourning filled the Anatawen heart. Especially if that person was a Ruler — Homak had a right to die.

"We remember a Ruler for the Power and accomplishments of tey's reign," instructed Cowis. "To sully that memory with mourning is expressly forbidden in public. What happens in private is, of course, private."

"Well, maybe. But I still have a lot of questions. And

one big one for Homak. Do you think I can talk to him?"

"You must. He has requested you be brought to him."

Sonya was left alone with Homak who looked sleepy, but otherwise healthy. But she didn't try to second-guess Anatawen's royal healers. He motioned for her to sit by him.

"I am glad you came to say farewell, Sonya." His voice sounded husky but more from lack of use than anything else.

"I am also glad that you convinced Zorena to let me die in peace, as it should be. No, do not interrupt, I have few words to spare."

He smiled weakly, and Sonya tried not to fidget.

"Zorena is strong, Sonya. Too strong, perhaps. So much am I reminded of Sareema. When someone that strong falls to weakness, the descent is long and hard. Tey is stronger in tey's decisions, tey is weaker in tey's indecisions. Tey is more confident in tey's ways, tey is harder on teyself when those ways prove wrong. Tey's beliefs are tey's lives, therefore, confusion is tey's archenemy. You must remember this. For I fear that your importance to Anatawen, and especially to Zorena, has only begun to take root."

"I think I already knew it."

"We often forget the things we know best — often at the least appropriate times. Zorena is alone?"

"Yes. I thought she needed some time to herself. Why did you give her the Power?"

Homak ignored her question, and Sonya asked him again, and then once more.

Homak smiled a wide smile. "Will you badger me until the very end?"

Sonya's stomach took a dive. She almost couldn't take it. She was badgering an old man on his deathbed. She blushed but didn't leave. She had to know.

"Why." It was a command more than a question.

"You and Zorena will have some difficult arguments."

"We already have. I need to know."

He looked her directly in the eye, and Sonya held his

gaze steadily. After a long pause he answered.

"To be sure that she received it."

"But that doesn't make any sense," the exasperation she felt brought a smile to his face.

"I hope that it does not. I fear it was an unfair thing to do, but necessary nonetheless. She must understand that this Power is now hers. You must make her believe that no matter what happens after I am gone, this Power was purposely given and meant only for Zorena."

He said no more and Sonya tried to find a question that would yield answers to untangle her thoughts. But Zorena entered the room and asked Sonya to leave. The brothers waited as she and Sayeeda left.

Homak died shortly after, and Sonya noted affectionately that Sayeeda's reaction did not at all conform to all she'd learned about the "proper" way to deal with death in Anatawen.

But Sayeeda was not Anatawen. She waited with Sonya and Mishwan, the young Todam playing close by at the edge of the pond.

"When Tagor first brought me here, the good people of Anatawen were less than kind. Perhaps if he had not been of the Ruling Family they would have taken it less personally. Or perhaps it would have been impossible to survive at all. It is not necessary, Sonya, for Anatawens to Vow for life in order to build full and long lives together. Especially the Ruling Family.

"On the contrary, Rulers usually do not Vow. This way they are free to change their lives according to what is best for their dominion. So when we Vowed it became more than a bonding between us. It was a sign to the world and beyond. Homak never questioned my motivation or my character. And often he asked my opinion on matters of great importance.

"Zorena and I have not always agreed. Homak was a gentle referee."

"Some people," added Mishwan, "believe that Vowing

is an archaic custom that should be relegated to the past. It is now mostly reserved for the very old, to be sure they will not be alone in the frailty of old age, and for the very greedy, to secure the transfer of property."

Sayeeda laughed. "Well, yes, some men want it relegated to the past because at one time Vowing was used primarily to pass on a family name — the woman's family name. We rarely use family names at all anymore, simply to avoid this foolishness. A child may choose which parent's family suits tey better. Tagor and I decided to Vow to each other so that we will remain bonded to each other for life. You may see a resurgence of this 'archaic' custom, young Mishwan. Do not be surprised."

"And then you'll have to invent divorce," snorted Sonya. "You're better off leaving it stuck in the past."

Z Z Z Z Z

The ritual after Homak's death was long and hot. Sonya stood in the back following the moves of those around her. Mishwan stood with the City Guard at the front. The little garden was filled with all who could fit, and many stood or sat upon the walls.

Homak's body, adorned in deep blues and greens, lay upon a wooden pyre at one corner of the garden. The minstrels played a fast and furious song as the flames crackled and rose to great heights. Slowly as the fire lost its fury and the flames gently turned to dull embers, the row of soldiers dropped their flags to the ground.

A single tunesmith lifted his voice in song — a song of Homak's life and the legacy he left.

Sonya listened to his voice and watched the embers as they cooled in the passing afternoon. Slowly the people of Anatawen left. And Homak's ashes were taken to the highest tower in the city and thrown in every direction, to spread out over Anatawen, to protect it and be remembered by it.

After the service, Sonya and Mishwan sat by the pond. Zorena and her brothers had been closeted in

Zorena's rooms for many hours. Dr. Livingstone flew off for his regular afternoon meat.

"Is it usual for the Ruling Family to have a big meeting like this, Mishwan? Seems kind of strange to me after all they told me about death being so friendly and all."

"I do not know. Homak has been Ruler all of my life and my father's. It may be customary, though I do not think so."

"Well, tell me at least, why you don't think so."

"They did not wear the faces of those performing a routine task. Zorena still does not seem herself."

Sonya nodded at that but tried not to wonder too much. She needed to turn her thoughts to leaving Anatawen, but somehow didn't want to.

What would happen to Dr. Livingstone? She laughed aloud at that thought. He could take care of himself, she knew.

Then why didn't she want to go? But she did want to go. Maybe not completely, though. She felt as though she'd forgotten to do something. But she couldn't remember what. Mishwan guessed her thoughts.

"You are thinking about home, are you not?"

Sonya nodded absently.

"You could stay here, though, could you not?" he asked anxiously.

Sonya grinned at the sincerity in his voice.

"Let's go to the beach!"

Mishwan's surprise put a comical expression on his face.

"It is a two-week journey!"

"So. Why should that stop us? I want to go to the beach. And I want to see Waylik."

Mishwan laughed and shook his head. "I too, have a desire to see Zukulan again. But will a whim be enough to get us there?"

"Sure, and Cowis'll go with us. It'll be fun."

"Fun? Maybe. But I suggest we wait and see what we can find out about this council. And I, being a member of the City Guard, cannot go without permission in any case."

"Boy, you've turned into a sourpuss. What happened —
that uniform sap all your fun energy?"

"Not all of it. I suggest we find a suitable pub, and see
who has the most energy — for merrymaking at least."

"You're on!"

Mount Desert Island, Acadia National Park, Maine,
March, 1984. Copyright 2003 Beth David

Chapter Sixteen

One Last Journey To Home

Sonya slept most of the morning away. Slowly she woke to a foggy head and the bright Anatawen sun shining painfully into the room.

Dr. Livingstone perched himself on the window sill and squawked his disapproval of her all-night rowdiness.

"Shut up, dummy. Can't you see I've got a nasty headache?"

She threw on some clothes and longed for a couple of aspirin.

"Zukha will have to do," she groaned as she headed for the door.

But Zorena swung it open with a bang and set a pot of zukha on the little table.

"Hello, Sonya," she said with a bright smile. "The day promises to be good."

Sonya grunted and poured herself some zukha.

"I welcome your cheerfulness, Zorena. But could you manage it quietly?"

Zorena's laugh rang in her ears and Sonya realized it had been a very long time since she'd heard it. Zorena had recovered.

"So what's with all the secret meetings, Zorena? Is everything okay? I kind of get the impression that I'm missing something important."

Zorena said nothing. She took a cup of zukha to the window and silently scratched Dr. Livingstone's wing.

"Okay, I know I'm not really in the upper echelon of Anatawen government. However, I do need to know what's happening so I can make plans."

"To leave?"

"Yes, to leave. Now what's going on?"

"You are probably correct. You have been here much longer than you expected."

"I didn't expect to be here at all — contrary to popular belief."

They talked for a while and decided Sonya could leave the next day. She took Appy towards the pond looking for Cowis and realized halfway there that Zorena never answered her question.

She laughed when Cowis also refused. But somehow the importance of knowing the answer dwindled with each passing minute.

Sonya spent her day visiting with Tagor, Barska, and especially Sayeeda. She said her goodbyes to Surriya and the household servants she had come to know.

In the morning, she joined Zorena for a long meeting of their minds and hearts. They kept the conversation light and appreciated that they had overcome their difficulties. As the morning wore on, Sonya knew the parting would be difficult. But she also knew she had to go.

Cowis joined them with a special bottle of Anatawen's best wine. They drank heartily amidst the laughter of their stories. When the last drop was gone, they all knew it was time to go.

Sonya embraced Zorena as a rush of memories flooded through her mind: the fire of Zorena's anger, the depth of her gaze, the gentleness of her movements, the arrogant strength of her determination, the heartbreak of her turmoil, the clear, light sound of her laughter.

Sonya pulled away and choked back tears.

The three travelers and Dr. Livingstone left through a gate on the southwestern side of the city. Directly for Zukulan they would go, straight across the Great Plain and to the mountains beyond.

They reached the City By The Sea without mishap and were quickly waved on to the main city.

Waylik's little cottage was empty. But no one had any doubt that she would find them.

They visited quickly with Arkola, as a matter of courtesy. But Sonya was anxious to reach the oceanside. Mishwan went his own way while Cowis and Sonya found a sandy patch of beach as the sun started its slow afternoon descent.

They found a small cove that cornered the last hot rays of light and kept the raging sea at bay. They soaked up the sun and enjoyed the gentle lapping of the waves upon white sand.

"You are thinking about home again, are you not?"

"Yeah," Sonya sighed. "I suddenly feel so anxious. I don't really belong here, y'know."

He smiled. "I know. Our time together has been fun and important to me. However, I knew it would not last forever. Forever is a very long time — especially for those of the Ruling Family. And of course Zorena has been careful to point these things out to me many times. You feel as though you must go back where you *belong*. Do not be surprised if you find you do not belong there anymore."

"Well, if I don't, I guess I'll just have to suffer. Because I'm still not sure how I got here, how to get back, or how I would return. I think we should go to where Tagor found me. That's probably my best bet."

Cowis smiled and drew her close to him.

"No, it is not. You can not go back the same way you came."

"So I've heard. But always look back, especially when hiking, so you're sure to remember where it is you *did* come from.

"You'll take care of Dr. Livingstone for me, won't you?"

Cowis laughed. "No. I think *he* will most likely take care of Mishwan. He seems to like Mishwan more than me. Maybe he's jealous. But Dr. Livingstone needs no one to worry about him."

"Let's go for a swim."

Sonya ran to the water and jumped in without a moment's hesitation. Cowis chased behind her. She was amazed at how agile he was in the water after such a short time. But she still had the advantage.

She swam towards the pond — a tiny bay of calm, tideless water surrounded by a ledge of rocks. She swam to the middle and turned, waiting for Cowis to catch up.

An irresistible force tugged at her feet. She kicked at it and tried to swim away. She struggled in a swirling whirlpool dragging her down deeper, faster, and deeper still. She stopped fighting and tried to hold her breath — maybe Cowis could reach her. She kept going down, surprised at how deep the little pond was. She tried desperately to control herself, but her body wouldn't listen to her. Finally, she could wait no longer and breathed deeply. But Sonya tasted no water.

She woke gasping and grasping at the air.

She lay in a sleeping bag next to a crackling fire, and cold air around her. The sleeping bag was not of Anatawen make and she sat up with a start. An old man smiled at her through the fire.

"Coffee?"

"Coffee?" she asked surprised.

"Yes," he said calmly. "You have returned."

Sonya stared suspiciously at him, and he smiled again. "You have been on Loraden, no?"

"Yes. But how do you know?"

"Do you think you're the only one that ever went there?"

Sonya studied her left arm and found the long scar from her knife wound so long ago.

"Yes," he answered gently. "It is real. You are not crazy. And no one will believe you."

They both laughed then. And Sonya took a sip of coffee. She preferred zukha.

"Why not zukha, then? It certainly tastes better."

"We do not have the plant here. I have searched endlessly."

Sonya wondered if Cowis would think she drowned.

"When were you in Anatawen?"

"Twenty years ago? Something like that. Zorena is Ruler now?"

"Yes, Homak died a few weeks . . . how does time work?"

"I don't know. I lost track of the days while I was gone. It seems to be somewhat comparable, though. Your family has probably stopped looking for you. I've been waiting for you."

"How did you know I'd be here," Sonya smiled — that "how" word again!

"Someone must be here to receive those that return, or they could die. You must keep your mind open to the call. You will find them naked to the world and cold. You must build a fire, clothe and warm them."

"How will I know I'm supposed to go, and how will I know where to go?" Sonya didn't want to trust to the Ruling Family's little tricks while so far away from them.

"You will know if you keep your mind open to them. Now, tell me of your trip. Tell me of that simple place where right and wrong are so easily defined and the enemy so clear in one's sight."

Sonya shook her head remembering the turmoil that Zorena felt.

"I'm not sure how simple it is."

But she told him her story. They talked for a long while. Sonya learned a little from the man, but he learned every detail of her trip.

"You will go back," he said when she had finished.

"I doubt it."

"You will. They will need you again. There is more to this Power transfer than meets the eye. When you see Zorena, remind her of the story of Fayén."

"Who's Fayén?"

"She is a legend in the lore of the Zukulan. She was cheated out of her birthright and turned to the magicians of Wizards Lair. Zorena will tell you all the details."

Sonya fell asleep as he spoke. The next day, all that was left of the man was a piece of paper with an address written on it, clipped to five ten-dollar bills. Sonya put the money and the address in her pocket, followed the trail down the mountain, out of the woods, and onto a noisy highway.

White Mountains, New Hampshire, June, 2001
Copyright 2003 Beth David